TROUBADOR PUBLISHING LTD

Tony Edwards is regarded as one of London's most original and creative PR consultants and the brains behind the annual celebrity 'Rear of the Year' competition. A former journalist and comedy script writer, he was the publicist who helped turn world attention on 'Swinging London' and Carnaby Street in the 1960's and 1970's.

TONY EDWARDS

DARK GLASSES

Copyright © 2008 Tony Edwards

The moral right of the author has been asserted.

Apart from any fair dealing for the purposes of research or private study, or criticism or review, as permitted under the Copyright, Designs and Patents Act 1988, this publication may only be reproduced, stored or transmitted, in any form or by any means, with the prior permission in writing of the publishers, or in the case of reprographic reproduction in accordance with the terms of licences issued by the Copyright Licensing Agency. Enquiries concerning reproduction outside those terms should be sent to the publishers.

Troubador Publishing Ltd
9 De Montfort Mews
Leicester LE1 7FW, UK
Tel: (+44) 116 255 9311 / 9312
Email: books@troubador.co.uk
Web: www.troubador.co.uk/matador

ISBN 978-1906510 466

Typeset in 11pt Book Antiqua by Troubador Publishing Ltd, Leicester, UK

t² is an imprint of Troubador Publishing Ltd

Printed by Cromwell Press, Trowbridge

*To the memory of Charlie & Win
who were never entirely sure
what their son did for a living*

A celebrity is a person who works hard to become well known, then wears dark glasses to avoid being recognised.

Comedian Fred Alllen

CHAPTER 1

Life had stubbornly refused to make Lizzie Beckman a star so a warm, spring day, at the start of a new millennium, seemed as good a time as any to give death a try. But it's a sorry fact that show business wasn't in the blood. A single strand of her long blonde hair would have testified to a DNA deficiency in the talent to entertain and any star qualities which might have hi-jacked her chromosomes during a childhood chock-a-block with ballet classes, piano lessons and a spell at a north London acting school, were now floating, face down, in Lizzie Beckman's genes pool.

Genetically speaking she had about as much chance of seeing her name up in lights as the taxi driver who'd dropped her off near the boating lake in Hyde Park; perhaps less. Even this laid-back London cabbie delivered a string of mildly entertaining one-liners, about who was to blame for the weather and what should be done with illegal immigrants, with the timing of a seasoned pro.

The good news was that Lizzie, recently 20, had more than her fair share of chutzpah, the shameless impudence and brazen bluff which can by-pass talent and transform monosyllabic shop girls into minor celebrities. She craved fame like a junkie, hooked on the dream of stardom, and had convinced herself that a mild flirtation with death would provide just the fix she was looking for.

Dressed for her untimely passing in flimsy white taffeta, a small bottle of tablets and sufficient vodka to numb the senses, neatly packed into a Louis Vitton handbag, Lizzie chose The Serpentine as the tranquil but theatrical setting for a very public suicide; the honey varnished hull of a small row boat her carriage to eternity on a cloudless, May afternoon. Four neatly-typed pink pages, tied with matching ribbon, told an ungrateful world how she should be remembered; more of an obituary than a suicide note and a ready-made press statement for any newspaper reporters who might cover the sad story. With any luck today would transform the London lake into a shrine to lost talent.

But even as she plumped-up the cushion for her head and carefully displayed the goodbye message in the folds of her dress, close to her heart, Lizzie couldn't help wondering if her suicide might appear to lack a certain spontaneity, perhaps even seem a trifle contrived. And vodka, swigged straight from the bottle while the sun was still high in the four o'clock sky might not, for some, personify the spirit of parting's sweet sorrow. Without a dash of Coca Cola, which she'd forgotten to bring, it was also a bit harsh on the throat.

Too late. The scene was set and the star was ready, centre stage, for the final curtain in the sad but brief performance that was Lizzie Beckman's life.

She gazed towards heaven, now somehow nearer than before, felt her fingers lightly touch the chill water, and wondered how this momentous day, Tuesday, May 2nd, could have started so well, so full of hope, with suicide the very last thing on her mind.

2

Just five short hours earlier the morning rain had stopped, as if in deference to an aspiring celebrity, at the precise moment she stepped out of Harrods and turned into Beauchamp Place to an impromptu fanfare of oafish whistles and smutty innuendo caterwauling from the tangle of scaffolding and planks clinging to the building opposite. She'd stuck two fingers in the air with a resolute sweep of her right arm and masterly flick of the wrist, as a wheelbarrow load of rubble cascaded down a chute and crashed, noisily, into the skip below, sending a cloud of dust across the narrow street in the general direction of the extravagantly white Armani suit.

At times like that she often wished she'd kept up the kick boxing classes and ignored her mother's scare mongering about stray punches and what they might do to her boobs, and how all that aggressively physical, macho stuff could play havoc with the hormones and upset the oestrogen balance. She glanced up at the three grinning schmucks cavorting, like apes, around the bars near the top of the building and decided that today was not a day for confrontation. Today was about her future life as a celebrity and her ten o'clock meeting with the top notch PR guy, one floor up from the lingerie shop, was more important than reprisals for a light coating of brick dust.

Lizzie's dad, a ferret of a man with anxious eyes that searched for treachery in other people's faces, boasted he could write a passable PhD thesis on PR people, if only he could find the time. When all was said and done, hadn't he hired and fired some of the best and a few of the worst to publicise nearly two decades of changing teenage fashions from The Beckman Clothing Company Ltd? And, press cutting for cutting, hard-earned pound for pound, didn't he always get more newspaper coverage than the rest of Margaret Street's 'rag' trade put together? Yes on both counts. Samuel Beckman prided himself on understanding PRs and their devious ways but he also recognised talent when he saw it; and Toby Stone was, without the shadow of a doubt, the very best in the business. Why else would he pay him a £60,000 a year retainer? Besides, Toby Stone had finally agreed to launch a publicity campaign for Lizzie by 'special arrangement' with the Beckman organisation. And the all-important F-word was used – Free.

A discreet brass plaque pointed the way to the first floor offices of Toby Stone Associates; the shiny black door on the landing, portal to a parallel universe where a chosen few would transmute into alien beings, destined to exist only in the fake and fragile world of press publicity, their lives measured in column inches and a tally of chat show appearances.

Toby Stone, smart but casual in tailored denim, sat at a wide oak desk with his back to a magnificent arched window, the morning sunshine in a spiritual glow about the closely cropped, flaxen hair. He looked up, smiled weakly, but said nothing, examining the youthful face before him from all angles. The nose was good, almost perfect and there was definitely something about the mouth and the half smile but, taken as a whole, there was no more than a passing resemblance to Princess Diana. The look-alike option, always a last resort as a pathway to publicity, melted from his mind in an instant.

'You're not what I'd call a beauty,' he confided before she'd quite settled herself in the chair opposite. 'Pretty, perhaps, but that's about it.' He stared at her, unblinking. 'Would you say you were amusing?'

'Amusing? In what way amusing?'

'In a way that might make me smile, for example. Are you humorous, able to make people laugh?'

Lizzie glared back at the chiselled features and ski-slopes sun tan, gathering her thoughts protectively around her. 'I don't tell jokes, if that's what you mean.'

'No, that's not what I mean.' He rose slowly from the chair and turned to face the window, fiddling casually with his shirt cuffs. His attention strayed across the road to the window of the fashion shop opposite where a young girl wrestled with the lifeless limbs and rigid torso of a display dummy, in a futile struggle to create a natural pose. He could sympathise. 'Tell me about your hopes and ambitions,' he mumbled through a stifled yawn. 'Intrigue me, excite me, fill me with admiration for your talent. Talk to me about your career plans.'

She rearranged herself on the chair, left profile turned, instinctively, towards the question. 'I'm going to be an A-list celebrity,' she said. 'An international star.'

'Highly commendable, if a trifle unoriginal.' He wondered how many times he'd heard the same sad story from a string of deluded wannabes. 'I wonder if you could oblige me with a bit more detail,' he sighed. 'How, exactly, do you plan to ascend to such dizzy heights?'

The door slammed closed with a crash that shook the room and rattled the framed photographs of vaguely familiar aliens on the wall opposite. Lizzie hurried down the narrow staircase to the street below.

Mobile phone clasped to her ear with one hand, the other gesticulating wildly, prosecuting council in the case against Toby Stone presented her damning evidence to Judge Samuel Beckman in the time it took to cross the road and hail a taxi. Justice was equally swift; guilty as charged.

Toby watched her speed away and turn right towards the West End before the irritating warble from a telephone summoned him away from the window and back to his desk. He slumped into the red leather chair and leaned back, legs outstretched, handset resting casually in the angle between his neck and shoulder.

The eloquent female voice from reception was quiet and seemingly unfazed. 'Miss Beckman asked me to give you a message before she left.' There was a brief but telling pause while she checked her notes. 'I'm to tell you, and here I quote, "The man's a complete arsehole".'

He shook his head, slowly, in quiet resignation. 'Did she manage to say anything more constructive before leaving? Anything at all?'

'I'm afraid not. That was all from Miss Beckman.' She hesitated again, just for a moment. 'But I have Mr Beckman on the line; says he'd like a quick word.'

Samuel Beckman was unhappy, very unhappy. And why was he so unhappy? Because his daughter had been insulted, that's why he was so unhappy. His voice trembled with clipped, jerky words which tripped and tumbled into incoherent piles at the end of each disjointed sentence.

Toby recognised a defining moment in his life; a split second when finely balanced scales, deep in the subconscious, weigh pride against profit and, thankfully, profit usually wins. But not today. Words charged across his tongue like troops from the trenches, bayonets fixed, banner held high, PRIDE written all over it in big red letters – £60,000 worth of them.

The onslaught was brief but deadly. A spoilt, petulant child, he called her; arrogant, rude and, above all, impulsive. How could he hope to pinpoint her USP if she refused to answer questions and stormed out of meetings in a huff? And if they were going to talk about insults, try arsehole; that was an insult. The quiet of the room surged softly back when he was done. Then a moment of complete silence before Beckman spoke, the voice unusually subdued.

'Tell me something. This USP you're trying to pinpoint; what exactly would that be?'

Toby sensed a partial truce and the possibility of maybe hanging on to a £60,000 a year PR fee with pride still in tact. 'A Unique Selling Proposition,' he began cautiously. 'It's the special, all-important something which will help to separate Lizzie from the crowd. Something unique to her and her alone.'

Beckman paused to think about it. 'And are you sure she's got one of these USP things?' he asked, with more than a hint of uncertainty in his voice.

'If she hasn't, we'll invent one,' said Toby, bringing the conversation to a diplomatic close. 'We'll put our heads together here, see what we can come up with.'

But Toby Stone was not one for meetings. Great ideas, like falling in love, were meant to strike like a bolt of lightning when you least expected them. And nobody ever got struck by lightning sitting round a boardroom table in the comparative safety of first floor offices in Knightsbridge. Some of the greatest ideas were born while taking a shower, waiting for a train, or trying to find a parking space. One of his best turned-up while he was dead to the world, fast asleep. He dreamt about a girl in a skimpy dress and traffic chaos in Sloane Street as beguiled drivers shunted into each other.

The dream took a giant stride towards reality the very next morning. A call to one of the motoring organisations confirmed that sexy clothing was a common distraction and posed a real and present danger to motorists; more likely to cause a collision than thick fog.

At least one national newspaper gave front page prominence to Toby Stone's tongue-in-cheek press statement.

'Beckman fashions are a serious road hazard – and that's official,' he proclaimed, awarding the new Spring collection a 'Bent Bumper Risk Rating' of over 90% and sending a clear PR message to impressionable young girls that these were the sexiest styles in town. A new catch phrase, 'Designed to turn men's heads', sparkled in gold from black swing-tickets and garment labels and continued to dominate Beckman's PR and advertising campaigns more than a year later.

People were simply products with attitude; they, too, needed impressive labels if they expected the world to recognise them. So before there was Toby Stone, PR consultant, there was Tobias Strauss, journalist, who had been Thomas Smith, schoolboy. And anyone with half a mind can work out that plain Tom Smith is not a label for success in the competitive world of PR; not like Toby Stone, solid as a rock, sparkling like a gem. It followed that Lizzie Beckman's celebrity swing-ticket might be 'Lizzie B', a girl with 'buzz', something like that, anyway.

It would do for now, at least until the former Tobias Strauss, a man whose words once waltzed across the pages of a well-known national newspapers, could decide how to make her newsworthy and appealing to cynical journalists. He'd sit back and wait for the bolt of lightening to strike. And, besides, there was a parrot waiting for him in reception, come to collect a cheque for £250.

Not just any parrot, an African Grey who squawked and cackled with a slight hint of the Irish and lived-up to the name Salome with slow but rhythmic plucking of small feathers, baring her breast for all to see. Mrs Flynn, who gently tapped the cage, said it was just nerves; it happened sometimes when Salome was slightly tense or agitated and the past week had been quite an ordeal for her, what with all the lights, cameras and everything.

There had been only three replies to Toby's advertisement for a parrot with a wide vocabulary, a month earlier, but the deal was clinched when Salome demonstrated her unique way with words by reciting a few lines from Treasure Island over the telephone.

Bird fm, a new radio station, duly handed over the breakfast show to Salome for an hour a few days later when, in a subtle but necessary mix of live banter and carefully pre-recorded phrases, the world's first parrot presenter took to the airwaves in a blaze of publicity for the station. But this was no bolt of lightening publicity stunt, no sudden inspiration from the gods. This was an idea just waiting to happen, the obvious, staring you in the face. Bird fm... talking parrot presenter... perfect branding... highly newsworthy.... maximum press interest... loads of publicity... a perfect concept for a radio station called Bird fm. Five TV news programmes had scrambled for interviews with Salome who then happily posed, wide-eyed, for a bevy of press photographers before finally stepping back into her cage for the journey back home to Portsmouth.

News of Salome's radio debut was flashed around the country and reached the offices of the Portsmouth Evening

News half an hour before Mrs Flynn and her protégée had even boarded the train at Waterloo.

Urgent questions from reporters bombarded Toby's 'phone for the rest of that memorable day. Could Salome sing? Was Salome planning to record an album? How old was she? Would she be doing TV chat shows? Was she in a relationship? And the big one; did she know what she was saying or did she simply repeat things – well, parrot fashion?

Salome was in the spotlight, headline news for a day. But now, less than a week later, she was just another parrot in a cage and Mrs Flynn, precious press cuttings in a beige folder under her arm, was taking her to see an agent who booked animals for TV commercials. The faithless, fickle finger of fame was pointing elsewhere.

And it would be the same for 'Lizzie B' unless her publicity campaign had 'legs' and could go the distance without fizzling out. Toby decided against another face-to-face meeting with Samuel Beckman's petulant offspring; not for a while anyway. Instead, he called her mobile 'phone.

'Sorree …. can't take your call right now….. please leave a message and I'll get back to you. Byee.' The cold shoulder of 21st century communications stopped him firmly in his tracks.

He didn't bother to leave a message. High on Toby's list of unwritten rules; never talk to somebody who isn't there and will probably misinterpret or delete what you've said when and if they ever return. Waste of time and money, and totally demeaning for someone in the communications business. It ranked alongside never telephone anyone after ten in the evening, when words you might later regret often seemed to find an unwelcome voice, particularly after a glass or two of wine.

Lizzie's call, a few minutes later, was curt. 'You rang my mobile?' she snapped accusingly, as if he'd just stolen a fiver from her purse or tweaked her bum while her back was turned. More of a scolding than a question.

'I simply wondered why you stormed out of our meeting,' he explained apologetically.

'Because you don't like me.'

'And what gave you that idea?'

'That sick little doodle on your blotter, for starters.'

Toby glanced down at the pool of ball-point blood, the dagger, wedged firmly in the potato-shaped head, half a dozen arrows porcupined into a female torso, swinging from a gallows. Not his usual creative triangles, cubes and squares, perhaps, but a harmless desk blotter scribble all the same.

'I might ask why you were looking at my doodle in the first place,' he said, cursing the choice of words even before the 'oodle' had left his lips. 'Besides, it has nothing to do with you. I did it weeks ago.'

'Wha-ever.' The word struggled to her lips wrapped in well-chewed gum, the letter T totally deleted in the process.

Toby cringed. 'I think we should get together as soon as possible; start again at the beginning, so to speak, work out a publicity campaign to get you into the headlines.'

'You needn't bother yourself,' she muttered dispassionately, 'I've got an idea of my own.'

And it was just a handful of sleeping tablets and four miniatures of vodka later that the idea became a reality. Lizzie Beckman, celebrity newcomer, starring in her very own publicity stunt, the soon-to-be centre of attention, slap bang in the centre of The Serpentine.

She guessed her hour on the lake was up and they'd soon be calling her in. Then someone would quickly realise something was wrong, row out to get her, whisk her off in an ambulance in the nick of time, cheat death by seconds. Save her, just as she'd planned it.

For this was a superficial suicide, a cosmetic gesture

without injury or pain and, above all, without death. This was the kind of suicide which was meant to send a wake-up call to an unappreciative world; a harmless but timely warning for everyone to sit-up and take notice of Lizzie Beckman before it was too late and a virtuoso talent was lost for all time.

But, as her head sank deeper into the cushion and her thoughts slowly drifted to somewhere beyond the lake, there were flashbacks; twenty short years of her young, uneventful life from start to finish, fast-forward from earliest childhood memories, re-played in a few short moments and then gone. It crossed her mind that she might inadvertently become the first of the Beckman family to kill themselves, and that wasn't the plan; not a bit of it.

Hers was a suicide which, with the help of some heroic, quick-thinking somebody-or-another, would neatly side-step death in the nick of time. If she'd wanted it any other way she'd have jumped in front of a train or blown her brains out with a shotgun. But an uncompromising, no-way-back pact with death kind of suicide was never on the agenda and it was about time her would-be rescuers, over at the boat hire jetty, started to pay attention.

At the point when her hands became numb and the dazzling white rays of the sun blinded her to the man who said his name was Michael and not to worry, it would be OK, Lizzie Beckman had already taken her first faltering step on a silvery stairway to heaven. Just the one step up and then, in an instant, back down to earth with a jolt that shocked the senses.

A minor boating accident warranted five lines in the next day's evening paper which mentioned The Serpentine but not the name of the teenage "binge drinker" who'd spent the night in hospital before being released. They hadn't even got her age right so it wasn't surprising they'd forgotten to mention her long, blonde hair and deep blue eyes or the fact that she was a talented newcomer, set for stardom.

Lizzie thought about it for a few days; where she'd gone wrong, and why her suicide stunt hadn't grabbed the headlines. By the end of the week she'd decided it might be best to leave press publicity to the professionals and concentrate, instead, on preparing for stardom; practising the celebrity walk, getting the smile and the casual wave just right, all the important elements for her future life in the spotlight. Perhaps she'd give Toby Stone just one more chance.

Lunch the next day at the Italian restaurant, a few doors down from Toby Stone's office, was a disappointment. The pasta was fine but the clientele was distinctly average on a rare celebrity-free day at San Lorenzo; nobody who was anybody worthy of note was anywhere to be seen, although the waiter confided that Madonna had been in the previous evening and Valentino was expected later.

Lizzie wasn't sure she'd recognise Valentino, if and when he ever showed-up, but she was certain this was the right place to be and be seen, breathing the same air as super stars, pondering the same menu, drinking from wine glasses which had touched celebrity lips. The extravagant scent of show business lingered on long after the beautiful people had been whisked away in their expensive cars; impregnated into the very fabric of the walls, as much a part of the place as the décor itself. And she too felt part of it. This was where she belonged.

Her failed DIY attempt at press publicity wasn't something she'd planned to talk about but it just slipped out; probably the wine, she wasn't sure.

Toby peered across the rim of his coffee cup listening, expressionless, apparently unmoved, but said nothing. When she'd finished he gestured to the waiter for some more coffee then sat back, arms folded, eyes narrowed in a quizzical expression which seemed to question her sanity.

'So where did I go wrong?' she asked, casually sweeping breadcrumbs into a neat pile with a crumpled napkin. 'Why no headlines?'

He turned away, the suspicion of a smile on his lips. 'Attempted suicides are strictly for celebrities,' he said quietly. 'Nobody cares when a Miss Nobody tries to kill herself. Dead or alive, she's neither newsworthy nor important.'

'But your Miss Nobody would bloody soon become newsworthy and important if she slept with a Mr Somebody, wouldn't she? Then someone like you would sell her story to a magazine and she'd be all over the papers. That's how it works, isn't it?'

Toby's arms fell limply to his side, the blow to his integrity like an arrow to the heart. 'Now let's get one thing clear,' he said wearily. 'I'm a Publicity Consultant not a Porn Broker like some so-called PRs I won't mention. I don't sell seedy kiss-and-tell stories to the tabloids.'

They starred at each other in silence for a moment before Lizzie took a mirror from her handbag and busied herself with a lipstick and brush, shielding herself from the wounded ego on the other side of the table.

'Where do we go from here then?' she muttered, barely audible through stretched lips, freshly painted scarlet.

Toby swirled his cognac round the glass in quiet contemplation, wishing he was somewhere else; anywhere else. 'We go back to where we left off,' he half whispered. 'Only this time I want to hear about your talents and aspirations without all the tantrums.'

'I already told you. I want to be an A-list celebrity; famous. That's it.'

'Famous for doing what?'

Lizzie's eyes rolled. 'I don't particularly want to *do* anything,' she sighed, searching the ceiling for help. 'Why do you have to bloody well *do* something to be a celebrity?'

Lightning struck in Knightsbridge at that precise moment; a big, bright, thunderous bolt of the stuff which flared down Beauchamp Place, through the front door of the San Lorenzo, and crashed across Toby Stone's table in a blaze of possibilities, unseen by mere mortals. Inspiration,

the priceless essence of a great ideas, served up on a plate; a gourmet dish from the gods, sautéed in originality and garnished with a liberal sprinkling of humour.
'But of course. You're absolutely right,' he said, downing the cognac in one to fuel a modest surge of enthusiasm. 'Why should you have to *do* anything when you could make a virtue of doing nothing.'
Lizzie flopped back in the chair as if her spine had suddenly turned to jelly. A disapproving frown wrinkled her nose. 'And what's that supposed to mean?'
'It means, Lizzie, that I have a brilliant idea.'
She waited patiently for him to pay the bill, carefully slip the receipt into his wallet, and place a ten pound note under the coffee cup, before she spoke. 'So, what's your brill idea then?' she said, trying not to sound too interested.
He stood up and gently eased the table to one side to let her out. 'Unfortunately ideas are cheap,' he said with a smug smile. 'Making them work is the clever bit. I'll tell you about it when it's all clear in my own mind. Promise.'
But even as the taxi driver asked her "where to luv?" and she told him "London Palladium, stage door", rather than "top end of Carnaby Street" and her favourite shoe shop on the opposite side of the road, Toby began to wonder if his deluded client was up to the challenge and whether the gods had, maybe, dished up a duff idea.
The burning question, during a slow walk back to the office, was could Nothing, the direct antithesis of Anything and Everything, be the unique Something to turn the media spotlight on Lizzie Beckman? Doing nothing, nothing whatsoever, and turning that ultimate zero into an art form, was a highly original but difficult stunt to pull off.
He considered some of the variations on the Nothing theme on his way up the stairs and decided that doing nothing for charity had the right feel to it; sponsored inactivity on behalf of a worthy cause; a pound-a-minute for sitting perfectly still, unblinking, motionless. While the nameless made charitable jam for England's crumbling

spires and the famous fed the entire third world with a suitable song from their latest album, Lizzie Beckman would do absolutely nothing, zilch, sod all, for her chosen cause. And such supreme sloth in the cause of righteousness was the ultimate contradiction, the stuff of headlines, the beginnings of celebrity. It was a bloody good story.

But Toby was not one for wasting time, especially time which couldn't be invoiced at his usual £250 an hour. It was, therefore, with a certain sense of achievement that he declared Lizzie Beckman's publicity problems solved before he sat down at his desk to deal with the more rewarding business of the day. The phrase Good-for-Nothing dawdled across his mind and loitered there for the rest of the day.

CHAPTER 2

Thank you: Two small words, generally accepted as a simple expression of gratitude for help *given*. But, in the fuzzy world of Lizzie Beckman logic, it's also an admission that help had been *needed*. And that's a sign of weakness and imperfection; undignified, demeaning, humiliating even. Above all, it's highly embarrassing and the main reason why the words very rarely passed Lizzie's lips.

Yet she heard herself repeat them, distinctly, sincerely, as if she really meant it.

'Thank you,' she said tearfully. 'I owe you my life.'

And this wasn't the no-hoper-needing-help-from-some-smart-arse kind of 'thank you'. This was different; an unbridled appreciation of kindness and compassion; a way of acknowledging the love of a fellow human being.

But Lizzie knew how to wake herself from dreams when they got out of hand and this dream was beginning to irritate. It turned up on cue every night, like a commercial break in the middle of an otherwise peaceful sleep. Always the same; she was back on The Serpentine, the chap called Michael gazing into her eyes, assuring her that all was well. Then a blinding light and a warm, tingling sensation like a power surge through the body. And, finally, her heartfelt 'thank you', which seemed to echo, embarrassingly, across the lake, loud enough for the rest of the world to hear.

At the point when she began to feel like a gold-plated loser, Lizzie usually pressed the stop-button in her slumbering sub-conscious and brought the dream to a premature halt, waking to a pink chintz bedroom and the welcome reality of the first floor Bayswater flat. And it would have been the same this night too, but something kept her finger off the button.

In the cold light of morning, eyes open, fully awake, completely compos mentis, the dream made no more sense than the night before; probably less. 'You have a power,' he'd said. 'Use it well, use it wisely.'

Lizzie examined her face in the bathroom mirror and searched for the presence of power through tired eyes. She certainly didn't feel powerful. The hot water tap was as stiff and stubborn as ever and a few token morning exercises left her feeling like a vampire's mistress; more pooped than powerful. If it hadn't been for Porky's ten o'clock touch down from New York she'd probably have gone back to bed for another hour or so.

Porky, who wasn't fat but, with a name like Barry Gammon, more or less asked for it, waited until he was nearly thirty to fall in love for the very first time. And it was love at first sight the moment Lizzie Beckman stepped unsteadily into his life by way of a wonky wooden gangplank which bridged the gap between dry land in Chelsea and a bijou house boat on the Thames where Porky had been lured for a surprise twenty eighth birthday party the previous October.

Porky was a late Libran, born on the twenty second of the month but, true to his star sign, a great mediator and a natural balance between opposites. He even resembled a set of scales; tall, slim and upright with hands that often seemed to be weighing up the odds while his head wobbled from side to side with indecision.

And it's an unhappy truth that chartered accountants are doomed to exist in the recent past, their lives spent a whole financial year behind the rest of us, calculating the worth of a previous twelve months' period, tabulating success or failure in columns of debit and credit, profit and loss, sub totals and bottom lines. But would-be celebrities are a very different species. They live somewhere in the future, craving fame before fortune, recognition before riches, looking well beyond today to a magical time when day dreams become reality.

So Lizzie and Porky were alien beings from different worlds but that didn't stop him proposing to her, regularly, round about the thirtieth of the month when the invoices went out. His words always hung heavily in the air like second-hand cigar smoke, waiting for her to take a deep breath and cough-up some sort of an answer. A simple and decisive 'Sorry, but I'm afraid I don't love you' would have brought the monthly ritual to a close but she wasn't sure it was true.

Porky was practical, reliable and secure, like double glazing only more economical and nearly as transparent. The airport was a case in point.

'Be an angel and pick me up from Terminal four on Tuesday at around ten,' he'd cooed three days earlier when she dropped him off at Heathrow, as if the inconvenience of it all brought her somehow closer to God. A taxi would have cost him no more than twenty five pounds but he preferred to drag her out of bed and half way across London to save a few lousy quid.

And anyway, Lizzie didn't like airports; all that scurrying to and fro. It reminded her of ants around an anthill but at least ants were probably doing something constructive. Airports were just giant waiting rooms where airlines conspired to put people's lives on hold with muffled apologies for not sticking to their side of the bargain, broadcast, inaudibly, from somewhere in the ceiling.

But Porky's flight was on time. He marched purposefully from the arrivals gate, a case in each hand, yesterday's Wall Street Journal under his arm, eyes searching the crowd, the beginnings of an expectant smile on his face.

Lizzie sent an urgent signal to her face not to smile back and waited, tight-lipped, arms folded, feet firmly glued to the floor, until he'd kissed her on both cheeks. The muscles in her neck tightened into a yawn. Tired or bored? Probably a bit of both, she wasn't sure. But she wanted him to know that this highly inconvenient airport pick-up was reluctantly brought about by a budding celebrity with better things to do and was not, as he seemed to think, the work of a bloody "angel".

'Good flight?' she asked, turning away to check her watch with the flashing computer clock on the wall.

Porky's head wobbled from side to side for a moment, weighing-up the airline's performance. 'So so,' he said eventually. 'Could have been better. No complaints.'

Lizzie frowned. 'Why do you do that?' she snapped.

'Do what?'

'Say things that mean nothing. So so, no complaints, things that make no sense whatsoever to the average Earthling.'

Porky shrugged as best he could with a suit case tugging at each arm, and headed for the car park.

At the exit barrier he made his apologies and slipped effortlessly into a jet-lagged sleep in the back of the car before they'd left the Heathrow tunnel and joined the motorway; head back, mouth open, hands slumped limply in his lap.

Lizzie glanced at him through the rear view mirror. The red silk tie was new, probably Fifth Avenue, but the black chalk stripe suit was solid Savile Row, less than a year old and one of his favourites. She remembered all the fuss over four fittings; how the jacket needed to be slightly more waisted and the trousers tighter around the rear. Snug, they called it at Gieves and Hawkes.

And the back seat of a Renault Clio was also a bit snug for a tall man with big feet. Porky looked cramped and uncomfortable but, in the circumstances, reasonably dignified, apart from the rebellious black curly hair which steadfastly refused to comply with the picture of elegant respectability he tried to achieve; more Romany gypsy than reputable city gent.

But beneath the carefree hair lurked the number-crunching, mathematical mind of a chartered accountant who had somehow acquired a controlling interest in Porky's body. The well-toned, six foot frame was designed for a more swash buckling, devil-may-care life somewhere in the sun, unencumbered by books, ledgers and the latest set of PAYE tax tables from the Shipley office of the Inland Revenue; except Porky's surrogate brain didn't see it that way at all. His alien intellect seemed content to allow the tennis star torso to vegetate at a desk in the second floor offices of Golding Gammon & Lee, just off Hanover Square.

The brighter news was that GGL, as they liked to be known, numbered two theatrical agents and a film production company among their clients so, while Porky had nothing to do with the 'show' of show business, he was inextricably linked to the 'business' by way of audited annual accounts.

Porky's knees twisted painfully to a slightly more comfortable position in the back of the car as he slowly opened his eyes to damp, mid-morning Hammersmith and three lines of traffic wedged firmly below the flyover. 'We made good time then?' he said, attempting to rub some life back into his hands. 'Less than thirty minutes by my watch.'

Lizzie half turned towards him, wondering why he always felt it necessary to say 'by my watch', as if his prized Rolex kept a different intergalactic time to other watches.

'It always takes half an hour.... by anyone's watch,' she announced with a dismissive sigh. 'And, looking at the traffic, it'll take another half an hour to get from here to Bayswater.'

Porky leaned forward and gently stroked the nape of her neck. 'You seem a bit tense this morning Lizzie,' he whispered softly. 'Everything OK?'

She wriggled free and quickly turned on the radio, bringing the conversation to an abrupt close for the remainder of the journey.

The coffee percolator had fizzed into life and was calming down on the kitchen table before either of them spoke.

'The man's bloody mad,' she squealed, giving a backhander to the letter from Toby Stone Associates which had turned-up in the morning post. 'He wants me to sit down and do nothing for half an hour at some hotel or another.'

Porky seemed slightly bewildered. 'Who wants you to do nothing, and why?' he asked calmly, opening a packet of biscuits.

'Here,' she said, tossing the letter across the table. 'Read it for yourself.'

His face softened into a smile, recognising the opening sequence to a familiar and well-rehearsed performance. 'Sounds like fun,' he murmured, then quickly folded the letter and handed it back without further comment, neatly side-stepping any potential involvement or responsibility. He poured the coffee, slowly and precisely, avoiding eye contact with the hostile forces gathering on the other side of the table, and prepared himself for the inevitable broadside.

'You just don't give a damn, do you?' Lizzie's voice, surprisingly muted for her usual style of unarmed verbal combat, soared to a higher, more aggressive pitch with the second volley. 'Aren't you even slightly interested in my future career,' she yelled. 'Don't you want to know what I'm doing with my life?'

'Of course I do,' Porky answered wearily. 'I want to know everything but could it wait until I've had a bit of sleep? I'm completely shattered.'

She starred at him across the table, unblinking, while he finished his coffee, daring him to retaliate, exact some kind of retribution for her wholly unwarranted outburst, avenge himself, get bloody even for Christ's sake. But she knew he wouldn't. Tit-for-tat squabbles simply weren't Porky's Libran style and, as always, he seemed happy for her to have the last word.

At the point in the performance where she breathed a deep sigh of indignation, her usual cue to storm out of the room, head shaking in solemn disbelief, leaving Porky to ponder his many imperfections and shortcomings, he reached out for her hand and gripped it tightly.

'That's enough Lizzie,' he said quietly but firmly and with uncharacteristic authority. 'The show's over.'

'You're hurting my hand,' she snarled, eyelashes fluttering with rage.

Porky slowly relaxed his grip and settled back in the chair, perfectly still, quite suddenly aware that this was the pivotal moment he'd been dreading since he stepped off the plane at Heathrow. Here and now, the precise point in time to talk about fate, destiny and the things life throws at you when you're busy making other plans. He'd intended to break the news, calmly, quietly, later that evening with a lightly warmed brandy to soothe the senses; lovers facing adversity together. But maybe this was better; Lizzie defiant, spoiling for a fight, a well-armed opponent.

'Sorry, but I can't have children,' he announced blandly as if he might be talking about a peanut allergy or something.

The smug smile on her face hardened. 'You're not supposed to. That's what women do.'

'No jokes Lizzie. I'm sterile.'

She starred at him blankly for a moment. 'Who says so?'

'The top men in the field. It's one of the reasons why I went to New York.'

'But everything's OK with us in bed.'

Porky nodded. 'I can fire the shots but I'm afraid the

gun's not loaded. Never has been, they reckon.'

She shrugged her shoulders. 'Oh well. If that's the way it is, that's the way it is.'

At this juncture in Porky's unhappy tale they were meant to hold each other close and perhaps shed a tear for the children who would never call them mum and dad. But life rarely lives up to expectations.

Instead, Lizzie quickly spotted the upside to the problem and embraced it with open arms; no need for the pill and no point in getting married; a double plus. She emptied the remains of the coffee pot into her cup and returned to Toby Stone's letter.

'Do you think I should do it then?' she asked through a mouthful of biscuit. 'Sounds a bit weird, sitting around doing nothing to get my face in the papers.'

Porky rose slowly from the table, fists kneading the small of his aching back, and made towards the door. 'I'm afraid my mind's still lingering somewhere at Kennedy Airport,' he whispered. 'Think I'll just nip off to bed and wait for it to catch-up with the rest of me.'

She waited until she heard the bedroom door close before making the call to Toby Stone.

Two days later, dressed in denim jeans and a white T-shirt with the words "I'm Doing Nothing for Charity" printed across the front in red letters, Lizzie Beckman sat on a bar stool, expressionless, unmoving, while half a dozen press photographers struggled to capture the essence of self-induced immobility in one perfect picture.

Twenty sponsors had each pledged ten pounds a minute, according to Toby Stone's press release, raising a cool six thousand pounds for charity if 'Lizzie B' could stay perfectly still for the full half hour and become the first person in history to do nothing whatsoever for the benefit of a worthy cause.

'Lizzie Will Be Bizzie Doing Nothing at The Ritz', it said on the gilt edged invitation to the legendary hotel which had opened its private gardens to the mid-morning press reception. The focus of everyone's attention sat, motionless, in the centre of the courtyard; above her on the terrace, animated and in full flow, Toby Stone holding court with a bevy of reporters.

Yes, she would be permitted to blink her eyes. No, scratching an itch was definitely not allowed. Yes, Lizzie had undergone a strict training regime for the inactivity now in progress; an hour a day for well over a week. Yes, there were other plans for Lizzie to do nothing. Details later. And, sorry, but everyone would have to wait until she'd completed her full half hour before interviews could begin.

But this was more of a challenge for Lizzie than anyone could have possibly imagined. The idea of doing and saying nothing for more than a few minutes was a complete anathema and from where she was sitting, uncomfortably on a wooden stool, worth every penny of the six thousand pounds in sponsorship money.

And then it was over. Toby counted down from ten to zero, encouraging everyone to join in, a loud buzzer sounded from somewhere beyond the cameras, and Lizzie happily stopped doing nothing, accompanied by a round of applause.

A willowy girl from the radio news service raised a philosophical question about whether it was possible to stop doing nothing when, if you were doing nothing, there was nothing to stop? She pointed a bulbous red latex microphone head in Lizzie's general direction, self-consciously flicking the fringe from her eyes while she waited for the answer.

The mole on her pale, slender neck was unremarkable; barely visible above the collar of a silk blouse and no more than a minor blemish on otherwise flawless skin. But it positively dared Lizzie to reach out and touch it. She at once sensed the confrontation, recognised the challenge as she stepped towards the question.

'I guess you stop doing nothing when you start doing something else,' Lizzie replied, moving closer, eyes now firmly fixed on the small brown mark. The tips of her fingers brushed lightly across the other woman's neck and felt the malignant energy loitering just below the surface of the skin. She paused, unsure for only a moment, and then stepped back. 'It's done,' she said.

'What do you mean?' The girl smiled nervously and adjusted the neck of her blouse. 'What's done?'

Lizzie shook her head. 'Not sure. Never done it before.'

She felt woozy, cotton wool for a brain, and was grateful for Toby's timely interruption. He took her by the hand, made his apologies to the radio reporter, promising to return, and led her towards a TV camera in the far corner of the terrace where a flame red bougainvillea was to provide the colourful backdrop for an interview.

'Television's more important than radio and time is short,' Toby insisted while he quickly arranged her, like a bouquet of flowers, in front of the camera. 'And remember to look at the interviewer, not at the camera lens,' he whispered.

But Lizzie's attention had already strayed from the TV camera, back across the courtyard to where the girl with the red microphone now leaned casually against a wall, talking with some of the other reporters. They glanced in her direction as the laughter grew steadily louder then stopped abruptly after a call for quiet from the TV crew on the terrace. Lizzie felt suddenly vulnerable and slightly silly, as if a close friend had just betrayed a confidence and turned it into a huge joke.

She remembered the schoolgirl secret entrusted to Amy Pollard and how the rest of the class knew all the intimate details by home time; even the boys, but especially Mark Hopper who stopped writing his beautiful letters and tried to pretend they'd never been deeply in love. Amy Pollard was a cow; she knew exactly what she was doing. But this young reporter could probably be forgiven for wondering what the hell was going on. Lizzie wasn't totally sure herself.

'When you're ready Lizzie.' The TV presenter stood to her right and quietly talked her through his plans for the interview. They'd try to keep things light-hearted and fun, starting off with her standing, motionless, expressionless, doing nothing and refusing to answer any of his questions. He'd then explain to the viewers how she'd spent the past thirty minutes doing nothing to raise six thousand pounds for charity; cue for her to relax, smile and tell her story. And, not to worry, they could always start again if she fluffed any part of it.

But she didn't; she was faultless and full of confidence. Toby said she was a natural.

Lizzie quickly checked her lipstick, pinched some colour into her cheeks and presented her best profile to half a dozen photographers who'd huddled together in a group just a few feet away.

They starred back blankly, cameras hanging heavily about their necks, uninspired, trying to decide what to do next. After a brief conflab one of them stepped forward, carefully positioned a garden chair to her left and gestured to her to sit. He moved closer for a moment, checked the light level, then quickly turned and rejoined the others who'd become considerably more animated and were shouting instructions to the bewildered object of their attention.

'Lean well back Lizzie. Hands behind yer head.'
'Stretch yer legs out Lizzie. Keep 'em straight.'
'Feet crossed please Lizzie.'

Lizzie obligingly took up the pose but it wasn't quite the picture they wanted and the demands continued.

'Bit more relaxed please Lizzie.'
'Check the T-shirt Lizzie. Can't see the words.'

'Eyes wide Lizzie. Big smile.'
'Straight to camera Lizzie. Over 'ere.'
'Try looking bored Lizzie? A yawn would be good.'
At some point during the contortions she must have got it right because cameras flashed and shutters clicked in harmony for a full minute. And then, weighed down with cameras and computers, they were gone; off to the launch of a luxury sports car and the promise of a former page three girl at the wheel with the new whiz kid racing ace.

But the morning press reception had shown Lizzie a new and exciting landscape, like the first fleeting glimpse of the sea beyond the downs at the start of a childhood summer holiday and with the same promise of good times to come.

Her brief appearance on the six o'clock news that evening was less encouraging and raised serious doubts about stardom.

Lizzie, head comfortably cushioned at one end of the couch, feet on Porky's lap at the other, cringed. 'Do I really look like that?'

Porky glanced first at the face, screwed-up in shock and denial, at the other end of the couch and then back at the TV screen. 'Pretty well identical,' he said with a solemn nod of the head.

'But my face looks so fat.'

Porky shrugged. 'I wouldn't say that. Not really.'

'Not really? What does that mean?'

Porky's eyes were already beginning to glaze over when he closed them tight to a potential row about whether Lizzie's cheeks were slightly chubby or her entire face had suffered a sudden attack of gross obesity. And, anyway, somewhere in the back of his mind there was something about TV making people look fatter than in real life.

Lizzie stared into a magnifying mirror over the bathroom sink, looking for signs of cellulite. 'Do you think mouth exercises would help?' she called out.

The notion that Lizzie's mouth might possibly need

more exercise sent a smile across Porkie's face. He pulled himself wearily from the couch and tossed a coin in his mind. Heads, a weak, sweet tea; tails a large Scotch and soda. Tails it was.

'Can I get you a drink?' he asked, quickly changing the subject from podgy faces and potential remedies for the aforesaid affliction to more pleasant things.

Lizzie's hand mirror entered the room slowly, a straight arm's length ahead of her, and made towards the last of the fading light at the front window which overlooked the tube station. 'My face isn't as fat as it looked on TV, is it?'

'Certainly not,' Porky reassured her. 'And besides, you were only on for a split second so there was absolutely no chance to study your face.'

Lizzie frowned. 'It was a bit bloody brief wasn't it? I'm not sure they even mentioned my name.'

'They mentioned the name of the charity,' said Porky wrestling with a plastic ice cube tray. 'Now how about that drink?'

'Just a mineral water thanks; alcohol's fattening.' She sat down on the edge of the couch and played back the recording. Less than a minute, and only the briefest mention of her name. But the face was definitely podgy and, on second viewing, the rest of her appeared substantially wider too; dress size twelve at least, up two sizes from her usual eight in one brief TV interview.

Lizzie's tumbler of mineral water, two ice cubes and a thin slice of lemon, ceremoniously delivered to the coffee table on a silver tray, lacked the aesthetic appeal of Porky's single malt whisky which stood next to it, amber and sparkling in lead crystal.

'I think I've changed my mind,' she announced, reaching for the whisky. 'Something stronger would hit the spot.'

Porky grabbed his glass in a modest but effective gesture of defiance. 'Sorry my darling, yours is the non alcoholic, less fattening one.'

'But I've changed my mind,' she repeated indignantly, the lips already beginning to quiver into a well defined pout.

He closed his eyes and shrank back in the cushions, savouring the first sweet sip of his favourite Glenfiddich; two fingers with just a dash of soda and no ice. But he knew the exquisite moment would be short-lived. In a matter of seconds the rebellion would be quashed and he'd be summoned, like a genie from a bottle, to grant her latest wish. As always, he'd oblige, without argument, to avoid an emotional scene.

The brittle voice from the kitchen was barely audible above the sound of cupboard doors slamming. 'That's right,' it said. 'You just lounge about like deposed royalty while I fix my own drink.'

The crash of breaking glass brought Porky to his feet. He appeared, silent, expressionless, in the doorway to the kitchen, handed her what remained of his drink then poured another, slightly larger, for himself and returned to his original position on the couch, leaving her to clear up the shards of glass from the broken tumbler.

Hostilities were temporarily suspended with the unexpected arrival of Toby Stone who, with hurried assurances that this was a fleeting visit, en route to somewhere else, quickly introduced himself to Porky and produced a copy of the London evening newspaper from his briefcase in the time it took to cross the narrow hallway into the lounge.

'Page six,' he announced proudly, spreading the paper across the coffee table. 'Not a bad picture and quite a positive story.'

'Doing Nothing For £6,000', it said over a close-up picture of Lizzie yawning. The caption said she was a model with a bright idea to raise money for charity.

'Why model?' Lizzie asked indignantly. 'I'm not a model, never have been a model and have no plans to be a model.'

'If you're a young, attractive female and not an actress, singer or TV presenter, you must be a model. It's simple newspaper logic,' said Toby. 'Besides, model is a major improvement on teenage binge drinker don't you think?'

Blushing wasn't in Lizzie Beckman's repertoire and the crimson flush now rising, involuntarily, in her face, was a new experience. Porky stared at the two ripe tomatoes which had been Lizzie's cheeks a few moments earlier and permitted himself a superior smile.

'Teenage binge drinker?' he repeated, slowly shaking his head. 'Not you, Lizzie? Surely not you?'

She turned her back on Porky's snigger and looked to Toby for help.

'Just a misunderstanding,' Toby explained. He clicked shut his briefcase and prepared to leave. 'Lizzie will tell you all about it.'

But Lizzie had no intention of telling anyone all about anything. Mistakes and errors of judgement were automatically consigned to a file marked Private & Confidential somewhere in the back of her mind where they would remain, unopened, until somebody else was prepared to take responsibility for them.

'There's nothing to tell,' she mumbled with a shrug of her shoulders. 'Just an idiot reporter who got his facts wrong that's all.'

Toby nodded his support. 'Happens all the time I'm afraid.'

The brief charade to cover Lizzie's blushes told Porky that he was probably in the way; a barrier to constructive debate between PR and client. 'If you don't mind, I'll say goodnight,' he said, reaching out to shake Toby's hand. 'Got a few things to catch up on in the other room.'

'Please don't go on my account,' Toby interrupted. 'I've got to be off now anyway.'

'It's not a problem old chum.' Porky topped-up his half empty glass before retreating to a tiny bedroom which moonlighted as a makeshift study on the other side of the hall. 'You stay and finish your chat,' he called out without looking back. The door slammed closed behind him.

Toby felt uneasy. 'I really think I'd best be off Lizzie,' he whispered. 'Perhaps I could call you first thing in the morning with an up-date on press coverage?'

She nodded and followed him to the front door. 'Thanks for today,' she said. 'Doing nothing in front of all those cameras wasn't as boring or daft as I'd imagined. In fact it was quite an experience.'

'How do you feel about introducing a bit of action next time? Perhaps make it a touch more daring?'

She hesitated for a moment, brushed some barely perceptible specks from the lapels of his jacket, searching his face for clues. But the boyish smile gave nothing away. 'Why not?' she said after a long pause. 'Sounds like fun.'

'That's settled then. I'll run it past you tomorrow.' He quickly checked his pockets for car keys then glanced at his watch.

At exactly 6-37pm, Toby Stone kissed Lizzie Beckman lightly on the cheek and took an executive decision to delete one of his cardinal rules with immediate effect; the one about never sleeping with clients.

CHAPTER 3

Somewhere in a remote, uncharted region of Toby Stone's bustling imagination, where mundane reality was routinely abandoned to spectacular illusion, Lizzie Beckman stood naked and perfectly still.

But she was not alone. Wearing nothing for charity, the next logical step from doing nothing, but with better picture potential, was just one of a gang of wild ideas which regularly rampaged through Toby's mind in a frantic search for the exit sign.

The notorious car thief who waited anxiously in the shadows for his call to glory, was a living, breathing example of a great Toby Stone idea which had found the exit. This self-confessed king of car crime, a dubious title endorsed by the police, had agreed to spill the beans on the tricks of his former trade. In return he was handed a consultancy fee and a non-executive seat on the board of a top auto security company, giving Toby's crime-busting client the inside track on ways to keep even top criminals out of other people's cars.

The press interest which inevitably pursues controversial ideas, like paying convicted villains to help beat crime, hit a snag at the first TV interview. Toby's poacher-turned-gamekeeper clammed up, unable to speak; the inevitable result of a criminal life-time spent refusing to answer incriminating questions from the police. But two weeks at a TV training school finally produced a star publicity performer and a unique new media personality.

And, next in line, Toby's fleet of specially imported rickshaws, scheduled to ferry tourists from luxury London hotels to a swanky new Chinese restaurant? It was a novel idea which was to become all the more newsworthy thanks to some antique by-laws which threatened to stop the entire project in its tracks. The battle for the right to run rickshaws down Baker Street raged for less than a week before an embarrassing climb-down by the local authority handed a publicity coup to Toby Stone's wealthy Hong Kong client.

But, in the whimsical world of press publicity, a single word can spawn a great idea. Like the word 'house' which jumped out from the property developer's brochure and danced across Toby's brain, daring him to ignore the usual protocol of selling houses and try something completely new.

'Visit our Show House', it said on the first of five pages of blurb about the luxury living on offer from Bliss Homes Ltd. And you don't need to be an estate agent to realise that houses are empty buildings which become homes only when someone settles down, pours themselves a drink and turns on the telly.

So simple logic demands that a Show House needs a couple of residents if it has serious ambitions to become a Show Home. The lucky couple who were paid £500 a week each to live in the Bliss Homes Ltd Show Home for a month focussed world attention on that modest but newsworthy hypothesis. But it was the enviable job description that captured the media imagination. Receiving a salary to sit with your feet up, read the newspaper, watch TV and generally lounge about with a cup of coffee in a rent free home, was not generally on offer in the Sits Vac columns or down at the Job Centre.

But that's the skill of it all. The red 'Sold' sign appeared on the windows of twenty brand new houses in less than a week because the show house was turned into a home; the smell of damp plaster camouflaged by the aroma of coffee, fresh-cut flowers to replace the lifeless plastic tulips, and a live-in couple to show potential buyers around, instead of a sales executive with an eye on the sales graph.

Yet nothing is ever that simple. The sudden Bliss Homes sales boom convinced an irate client that Toby had been negligent in allowing the houses to be sold too cheaply. Why else, he argued, were they all snapped up so quickly? The muddle-minded thinking conveniently ignored the fact that no houses had been sold in the two months prior to Toby's appointment and the PR campaign was a desperate last resort after weeks of expensive advertising had failed miserably.

And so to the vision of Lizzie Beckman, naked as the day she was born in a worthy cause; a good idea waiting patiently at the forefront of Toby Stone's imagination, the very nub of 'Lizzie B's' publicity drive. Fate, on the other hand, was already making alternative plans, and fate usually gets what it wants; it's one of life's little constants, as certain as day following night or Lizzie Beckman changing her mind, without warning, at the very last moment.

It had been agreed and confirmed; Lizzie would be at Toby's office sometime between ten and eleven. She couldn't be more specific because she was going to the hairdresser first thing and they'd vaguely talked about a change of style; nothing definite, but a strong possibility.

But it's a matter of fact and fate that Lizzie Beckman never reached the Bond Street salon. Instead, she turned off the Bayswater Road opposite Lancaster Gate tube station and into Hyde Park, headed directly for the The Serpentine. Yet, even as she stepped out of the car and walked confidently towards the boat hire sign, she felt the growing unease in the centre of her stomach and knew that this was a meeting she'd been trying to avoid.

A young man, no more than twenty five, looked up from his newspaper and smiled. 'You look a bit perkier than the last time I saw you love,' he said, eying her up and down. 'How goes it?'

'You recognised me then?'

'How could I forget someone who almost topped 'emselves in one of our boats?'

Lizzie looked past the man to the ticket kiosk, then across to the row boats by the water's edge. 'Is the other man here?' she asked. 'I think his name was Michael.'

He shook his head. 'Nobody called Michael love. Not here.'

'But it was Michael who came out to me. Told me not to worry.'

'That was Ted love. Oldish chap, bald head, grey beard? Not here today but I'll tell him you were asking after him if you like'.

She stared out across the lake with only hazy recollections of the kind, sensitive face. 'Perhaps Michael was one of the ambulance men?' she suggested after a moment.

He shook his head again. 'Doubt it love. They were women; both of 'em. And, anyway, it was Ted who went out and got you, nobody else.'

Lizzie smiled weakly. 'And your name?' she asked.

'Dave love.'

'Well thank you Dave. And please thank Ted for me when you see him. I really am very grateful for what he did,' she said, turning to go.

'He'll be sorry he missed you,' the young man called after her. 'But he'd be dead chuffed if you'd sign his picture?' He pointed to a newspaper cutting on the wall of the tiny kiosk. 'Good for Nothing'. said the headline above her picture. 'He recognised you at once.'

It was with a sudden and unexpected sense of self-importance that Lizzie Beckman caught her first real glimpse of fame and carefully signed her autograph on a picture torn from the Daily Star, pinned to the wall of a

35

ticket kiosk on The Serpentine. She returned to the car with a new spring in her step.

But by noon, when she arrived, late, at Toby Stone's office, the world took on a slightly different hue.

It would all be in the very best possible taste; doing nothing but with the added media attraction of wearing nothing. This was the absolute nothing; nought but not naughty, sensual but in no way seedy, erotic but far from explicit. A twenty first century Lady Godiva, but instead of riding, naked, through Coventry to lower taxes, Lizzie would pose naked and unmoving in London, to raise money. All in a good cause and in the best possible taste.

Toby explained the details.

It would all take place at the Savoy Hotel. A fanfare of trumpets would announce Lizzie's theatrical entrance from the wings of a small stage in the private Beaufort reception room, wearing one of Beckman Fashions' latest spring styles. Centre stage in the spotlight, she'd allow the dress to fall gracefully from her shoulders at the very moment she sat down, body only half turned to the waiting photographers. And that's how she'd remain for fifteen minutes, doing absolutely nothing, revealing next to nothing, before the curtains would close and she'd replace the dress. Then she'd step from the stage to well-earned applause for the usual interviews.

Lizzie fidgeted uncomfortably on a red leather Chesterfield couch strategically placed near the window of Toby Stone's office, overlooking Beauchamp Place. 'No knickers, no bra then?' she asked as coolly as she could manage.

'No bra, no pants, no nothing. That's the whole point,' said Toby. 'But nobody will actually see anything because of your discreet angle to the audience.'

She glanced across at the workmen on the building opposite and pictured their moronic faces gawping at her, naked, in the paper. OK, she'd only be half turned to the camera, but naked all the same.

'It was bad enough last time,' she said icily, still ruffled at being called a "model" by the evening paper. 'Next time I suppose it'll be "nude model" or worse, maybe a…..'

'And that's where you'd be one hundred per cent wrong,' Toby interrupted with a decisive clap of the hands. 'Next time they'll be more reverent. They'll say you're one of the special celebrity guests who've been invited to stay at The Manor.'

'The Manor?' she repeated as if he might be talking in a foreign language. 'What does that mean – The Manor?'

'To be honest it's more of a mansion.' Toby leaned across to his computer screen and re-read the beginning of the e-mail from the TV company. 'It's in Sussex. Penfold Manor, the stately setting for a new reality TV show, it says here.'

Lizzie frowned. 'What, exactly, am I expected to do in this stately setting?'

'Absolutely nothing; which is probably why they chose you.'

'And the others?' she asked, busying herself with the clasp of a gold bracelet, pretending the names were unimportant to her. 'Anyone I might perhaps recognise?'

Toby turned again to the computer. 'Sorry, can't help you. They're not giving anything away on that score. But they do say it'll be equal numbers; three boys, three girls, and all of them celebrities.'

Lizzie frowned. 'It sounds like Big Brother meets Lord Snooty. Not my style. Not my style at all.'

Toby cleared his throat, took a deep breath, carefully folded his arms in front of him and prepared to deliver some overdue home truths to his thankless, thoughtless client.

'Now let's get one thing clear,' he began, the words clipped and precise, the voice more hushed than usual but with an unexpected hint of retribution. 'It's the best opportunity you'll get this side of your state pension. And if you don't take it or, worse, if you mess it up, you'd better start looking for another publicity agent.' He fixed her with an angry stare and settled back in his chair.

Lizzie rose slowly from the couch, expressionless, apparently unconcerned, and sauntered across to the window. She stood quietly for a moment, cuddling her arms, considering the options, before turning slowly to face him.

'Six celebrities rattling around in a bloody great stately home doesn't sound like much of a TV show to me,' she declared with a dismissive shrug. 'Who'd tune-in to that?'

Toby shook his head in disbelief. 'Only an estimated ten million people, that's all for Christ's sake,' he snapped, then stopped short to regain his composure. 'Look, this show is going to be compulsive viewing. Cameras on you every hour of the day and night, recording your conversations, generally snooping around, looking for angles to titillate the viewers and provoke or embarrass the guests.'

He paused for the inevitable howls of outrage but there were none. Instead she stared straight ahead, unblinking, humming quietly but defiantly to herself, waiting for him to finish.

'And now the really good news,' he went on. 'It's a £50,000 fee, half in advance, and a further £100,000 if you win.'

The humming stopped abruptly. 'Win?' she sniggered. 'You mean if you're the last one to get voted out by a numskull TV audience.'

Toby hunched forward, elbows on the desk, chin in his hands. 'Actually, no, that's not what I meant. This time the TV viewers won't decide who goes or who stays.'

'So how do you win?'

'You make damn sure you're the last person to leave Penfold Manor.'

'You've lost me,' she sighed. 'We'll all be there forever and a day at that rate.'

Toby laughed. 'I very much doubt that my love,' he said flatly. 'Nothing's ever that simple.'

She stared back at him, eyes narrowed, but remained silent.

'The Lady of the Manor may persuade you all to leave rather sooner than you think,' he continued, with a quick glance at the computer screen. 'Elizabeth Penfold, 1861 to 1886. They say she haunts Penfold Manor.'

Lizzie flopped down on the red leather couch. 'So it's Big Brother Meets Dracula's Daughter then,' she said with the first, faint flicker of a smile. 'That sounds like much more fun.'

'Do you know what?' Toby said after a moment. 'That's the first time you've shown even a vague hint of enthusiasm for anything I've said since we met.'

Her smile broadened. 'That's probably because it's the first time you've said anything to get enthusiastic about.'

'I hope you feel the same way when you settle in to Penfold Manor.'

'You needn't be concerned about me,' she answered. 'I don't believe in ghosts.'

'Then it's settled.' He hesitated for a second, self-consciously shuffled some papers around the desk for no good reason. 'I was wondering if you'd like to have dinner with me this evening. We could discuss the PR programme in a bit more detail?'

'Do we *need* to discuss the PR programme in more detail?' Lizzie asked. She checked her watch and stood up to leave.

'No,' he said at once. 'Not really.'

'Good then we can have dinner just because we want to.' She strutted confidently towards the door, turned and glanced around at the celebrity photographs on the wall. 'I hope you realise I'm going to be a bigger star than any of this lot,' she announced with a casual sweep of her arm. 'Much, much bigger'.

'Possibly,' Toby said, rising slowly rising to his feet. 'All things are possible.'

She ran her tongue provocatively across her lips. 'The

word you're looking for is inevitable. Like us going to bed together; it's inevitable.'

Toby Stone stepped from behind his desk and stood perfectly still, staring at the slim figure in the doorway. 'Do you know, I think you could be right,' he said coolly. 'Don't forget to bring a toothbrush.'

❖

It isn't the clatter of cutlery or the animated conversation that have earned the Sale e Pepe its reputation as one of the noisiest restaurants in London; it's more to do with the amateur operatics of three Italian waiters who sing, loudly, in their top register, as they slip effortlessly between the tightly-packed tables.

Never more than a bar or two at a time, always in Italian, often unrecognisable but somehow familiar, and rarely repeated during the course of the evening, the impromptu performances flavour the atmosphere of the small but popular Knightsbridge rendezvous, accompanied by the steady hum of orders shouted to an unseen chef somewhere beyond two heavy, swing doors. He'd made the first of his brief, twice nightly appearances to the enthusiastic applause of half a dozen regular diners at the precise moment Toby and Lizzie took their seats at a corner table on the far side of the restaurant. Menus appeared, magically, like rabbits from a hat, as the evening's specials were recited, between arias, like a passage from Shakespeare.

'I think,' said Toby, reaching for a breadstick, 'this must be the noisiest, most cramped yet totally amazing restaurant in London. It breaks all the rules but it seems to somehow work.'

Lizzie put her menu to one side and quickly surveyed the long, narrow room. 'Do many celebrities eat here?'

'From time to time.'

'I don't see any.'

Toby nodded towards the bar. 'Chap from Eastenders. Black leather jacket, white polo sweater. Talking to the frizzy-haired blonde with the bee-sting lips.'

'I don't watch Eastenders.'

'Then he's just another bloke at the bar,' said Toby. 'Celebrities don't exist unless and until you bother to recognise them.'

Lizzie adjusted the front of a low-cut, black, silk blouse and stared blankly into space, head up, lips slightly apart, eyes barely blinking. 'You mean if somebody recognises me, I'm a celebrity?'

Toby shrugged. 'The difference between being a familiar face and a celebrity is the *number* of people who recognise you. By the time you've done your doing-nothing-wearing-nothing photo-call you'll almost certainly be a familiar face but a few days at Penfold Manor will definitely turn you into a celebrity.'

She turned to face him, her expression suddenly more intense. 'I don't just *want* to be a celebrity, I've *got* to be,' she announced as if she might be swearing an oath of allegiance. 'It's imperative.'

Toby smiled uncertainly. 'That's a mighty big responsibility you've handed me,' he said quietly. 'You must understand that fame is an elusive commodity, hard to find and even more difficult to keep.'

'I understand; of course I do.' She hesitated for a moment. 'But failure simply isn't an option.'

'I think it's probably time for a glass of Champagne,' said Toby, cupping imaginary breasts with his hands as he nodded to a passing waiter.

The waiter flashed a knowing grin and quickly returned with a bottle of Dom Perignon in an ice bucket, and two Champagne glasses.

'What was the miming all about?' Lizzie sighed. 'It looked like some kind of smutty schoolboy joke about ladies' knockers.'

'Not quite,' said Toby, handing her an empty

Champagne glass. 'Legend has it that the Champagne coupe, or saucer-shaped glass you see before you, was modelled from the bosom of none other than Marie-Antoinette.'
'What pervert came up with that idea?' she asked blandly.
'Her husband, Louis the sixteenth actually.' Toby ran his finger around the rim of the glass with a satisfied smile. 'He thought the shape of the queen's boobs would be more interesting than the long flute glasses. Sort of a romantic royal compliment really.'
'Did Marie Antoinette return the romantic royal compliment, I wonder? Long flute Champagne glasses modelled from her husband's Willy perhaps, or was that how the thimble came into being?'
The waiter burst intrusively into song, popped the Champagne cork and filled two glasses with a flourish, bringing the conversation to an abrupt halt before Toby could begin a doubtful story about Napoleon Bonaparte's private parts.
'I can never understand how they justify the cost of this stuff,' Lizzie declared, emptying her glass in a single gulp, as if it might be mineral water.
Toby quietly sipped his drink then placed the glass ceremoniously back on the table. 'Time is money,' he said. 'And Champagne needs a lot of time to reach maturity; a bit like some people really.'
'I hope you're not saying I'm immature?'
'Not at all. I'm simply suggesting that some things shouldn't be rushed. Slow sips inevitably taste better than quick swigs, and the glass will be just as empty when you're done.'
Lizzie fidgeted uncomfortably on her chair. 'I suppose that's meant to convey some kind of deep psychological message, right?'
'I'd say it has a certain ring of truth about it.'
'That sounds like the sort of meaningless nonsense Porky might come out with.'

Toby settled back in his chair, resting his thumbs in the pockets of a black velvet waistcoat. 'Do you love him?' he asked casually.

'Pass.'

'Meaning either you don't love him or you don't *know* if you love him.'

'Meaning I love him but I'm not in love with him. Will that do?' She sipped her Dom Perignon, slowly and deliberately then paused for a moment. 'I think I prefer drinking Champagne my way,' she said. 'It's much more fun.'

Toby's glass was topped-up and then quickly emptied with one swallow. 'Sorry, can't agree,' he breathed through a stifled burp. 'Gets right up your nose.'

'A bit like some people,' she whispered with a hint of sarcasm.

'Meaning me?'

She nodded. 'You and a few other people I could mention.'

It crossed Toby's mind that bickering was probably fundamental to Lizzie Beckman's personality; the need to argue over petty and trivial matters a spontaneous conversational reflex in much the same way that other people might tell unfunny jokes or bore you with a detailed account of the quickest route from A to B, cleverly avoiding roadworks on the A27. Lizzie was, he decided, a natural antagonist, a living, breathing contradiction to almost any proposition.

'What do you fancy?' he asked. Running his finger down the list of starters. 'I can recommend the grilled tiger prawns.'

'Right now, if I'm totally honest, I fancy you Toby,' she answered, without looking up. 'But first I'll have a spaghetti vongole, followed by the seabass. And I may even manage a tiny portion of tiramisu after.'

'Pity,' he said, draping a napkin across her lap. 'The prawns are to die for; absolutely enormous.'

'And I probably would die,' she sighed. 'I'm allergic to prawns.'

'Funny thing, allergies,' said Toby. 'I read somewhere that people are sometimes allergic to each other.'
She lightly touched her lips with the tip of her finger.
'Only one way to find out.'
Less that an hour later, seabass barely touched and tiramisu deleted altogether, the taxi turned into Oakley Street and came to a halt outside Toby Stone's Chelsea flat.
Lizzie stared at the number 13 on the front door. 'Isn't that tempting fate just a little bit?'
'It's my lucky number,' said Toby. 'Has been since I fell in love with Penny Williams on my thirteenth birthday.'
'Did she bring you luck?'
'In a way. Her father worked on the Daily Express and was a great mentor and support when I left school and decided to have a go at journalism.'
Toby's flat was tidy, very tidy by Lizzie Beckman standards. It made her feel slightly uneasy; magazines, neatly stacked on a sparkling, glass-topped coffee table, regiments of leather-bound books standing to attention, covering an entire wall, the fireplace, opposite, with ornate carved oak surround, filled with creamy-pink lilies in a delicate porcelain vase and, on the far side of the room, by a tall sash window, a rich chestnut desk, a solitary file carefully positioned on a green leather blotter. Altogether too neat, too perfect for Lizzie's taste.
'Do you live here or just stand quietly in a corner and admire it all?' she asked, flopping down in one of three cream leather couches in front of the fireplace, ruffling-up two cushions and tossing them, carelessly, to one side in an act of token vandalism.
'I enjoy order, symmetry, balance, harmony,' said Toby, his arms outstretched as if he were embracing the room. 'It pleases me, relaxes me. I need it to keep chaos and disorder locked out of my life.'
Lizzie slipped off her shoes and swung her legs onto the couch. 'You're not gay, are you?'
Toby poured two brandies and sat down beside her.

'The answer to that question, of course, is Yes.... I'm not gay. But I've never quite understood why it's assumed that heterosexual males prefer to live in chaos.'

She stared at him for a moment, ran her hands down her thighs and settled back into the comfort of the couch.

'Are you an early riser?' she asked with a slow, suggestive and altogether laboured wink.

'Something in your eye?' he said with a look of genuine concern.

'That, for your information, was one of my most seductive and alluring looks, designed to inflame the passions of the neatest and tidiest of heterosexual men.'

'OK. Consider my passions suitably inflamed.' He reached for the brandy decanter and re-filled their glasses.

'Black silk sheets,' she announced suddenly, as if she'd just received a psychic message. 'Black sheets and a king size bed, covered in goose down pillows. Am I right?'

'Wrong. Try scarlet satin with coordinating cushions and a mink bedspread.'

'Wow. Now that sounds exotic.'

'But I'm afraid you'd be wrong again,' said Toby. 'It's a large bed, not king size by any means, with rather ordinary navy blue sheets and a couple of pale blue cushions. Sorry if that's a let down.'

She raised her right arm, casually jangled half a dozen gold bracelets then let them fall back to her wrist. 'I'm sure it won't be a let down,' she whispered. 'Blue's one of my favourite colours.'

Toby got up, unsteadily, from the couch and made towards the door. 'I think that last brandy went straight to my knees,' he announced with a quick shake of the head.

'You don't think it may have something to do with having Champagne, red wine and brandy all in the space of a few hours?'

He paused in the doorway then turned, one hand on the door handle the other gently rubbing his forehead. 'Highly unlikely,' he said. 'And besides, you feel OK don't you?'

'I feel fine. But then I haven't drunk as much as you,' she called out as he disappeared into the bathroom.

Toby returned after a couple of minutes, white-faced, a small, amber bottle of pills in his hand. 'I forgot about the antibiotics. Alcohol not recommended while you're taking them. See for yourself.' He tossed the bottle into her lap.

She stared at the label for a moment. 'It says here, quite clearly, to avoid alcohol.'

Toby nodded. 'And so I have, honestly, for over a week. But a few drinks at the end of the course shouldn't make too much difference.'

'What are they for?' she asked, examining the red and black capsule she'd shaken into the palm of her hand. 'They look like the ones I took for pneumonia a few years back.'

'Nothing so serious; just a bit of bronchial trouble.' He slapped his chest with a flat hand, coughed a few times to verify the symptoms, then drained the remains of his brandy in a token gesture of defiance. 'Always been a bit dodgy in the lungs department, ever since I was a kid.'

Lizzie Beckman had been blissfully unaware that she had a maternal instinct until that precise moment. It embraced her quite suddenly her like a warm breeze, filling her with tenderness, compassion and a new and urgent compulsion to pamper and protect the man now leaning uncertainly against the fireplace.

'Let me get you to bed,' she said taking hold of his left hand and confiscating the empty brandy glass from the other.

Toby looked embarrassed. 'I'm not altogether sure I'm up to it,' he mumbled by way of an apology.

'I'm quite certain you're not up to anything. What you need is a good night's uninterrupted sleep.' She led him shakily towards the door.

But Toby Stone was not a man to be fussed and, in a display of stubborn independence, took himself to the bathroom, abandoned his clothes and wrapped himself in a scarlet bath towel before crashing into bed with muffled assurances that he'd be right as rain after a five minute nap. He dragged the duvet awkwardly across his legs, sunk his head into the pillows and lay, motionless, in a deep sleep.

Lizzie gently stroked his cheek, traced the contours of his face with the tip of her finger. 'Goodnight Mr Stone,' she whispered, 'sleep tight,' then draped her clothes across a corner chair and slipped, quietly, into bed beside him. She stared up at the high Georgian ceiling with its ornate cornices and delicate pastel blues; Toby's personal, private ceiling which she would share with him tonight.

The persistent hum of traffic had begun to fade when she finally switched off the bedside light and drifted off to sleep.

Bright, early morning sun found a gap in the curtains and woke her soon after seven, a vivid dream about Michael still clear in her mind, her fingers strangely hot and tingling and Toby gone, nowhere to be seen.

'What's happening?' she called out anxiously. 'Where are you?'

Toby appeared at the bedroom door in blue denims and a T-shirt.

'I'm preparing breakfast in the kitchen,' he announced cheerfully, wiping his hands on a tea towel. 'How do you fancy scrambled eggs on toast with a couple of grilled tomatoes?' He'd gone before she could answer.

She caught a glimpse of herself, naked, in the mirrored wardrobe as she threw back the duvet, swung her feet to the thick blue carpet and opened the bedroom curtains to a sunny Chelsea morning. Toby's black velvet dressing gown, soft, comfy and far too big, was quickly hijacked from the back of the door and wrapped snugly about her before she stepped resolutely into the hall towards the smell of burnt toast and coffee.

'How's the head?' she asked casually, the sudden chill of terracotta kitchen tiles on her bare feet sending her quickly back to the relative comfort of the hall carpet.

Toby turned away from the cooker, a saucepan of

scrambled eggs in one hand, a wooden spoon in the other. 'My head is just fine, thank you. But my lungs……….' He paused in mid sentence, thrust out his chest, took a deep breath then slowly exhaled. 'It's as if they've had a ten thousand mile service.'

She glanced down at her hands, palms still pinkish red, fingers faintly tingling, Michael's words beginning to percolate into her conscious mind.

'I think I may have done it,' she announced, sounding like a schoolgirl owning-up to a childish prank.

His eyes narrowed, a smile creeping across his face. 'Sorry, you've lost me.' He quickly served the scrambled eggs on to willow-patterned plates and pulled two chairs back from the kitchen table. 'You've done what exactly?' he asked, gesturing to her to sit.

Lizzie tightened the dressing gown protectively around her waist and sat down opposite him. 'Your lungs,' she said quietly, the voice hesitant and uncertain. 'I think I may have helped to heal them.'

He looked up, blankly. 'And how did you do that?'

She shrugged. 'I'm not sure I can answer that, not precisely or exactly anyway. All I know is that Michael helps me to heal people.'

'Michael? Remind me, who is Michael.' Toby rocked back on his chair and waited, hands clasped casually behind his head.

Lizzie ruffled her hair impatiently, trying to focus her thoughts. 'OK. Here it is,' she said eventually. 'Take it or leave it.'

He waited, silent, unmoving, until she had quite finished, brushed aside a natural cynicism for matters of a spiritual nature, and decided he'd prefer to take it rather than leave it.

'But promise me,' he said with a solemnity Lizzie had not seen before, 'you won't talk about this, whatever it is, to anyone else. Not for a while, anyway.'

She nodded uncertainly. 'OK. I promise. But I don't

understand why. Didn't you say your lungs felt as if they'd been in for a ten thousand mile service?'
'It really doesn't matter what I think or feel,' he sighed. 'What matters is how the rest of the world sees things.'
'Surely they'd be totally amazed?'
Toby shook his head. 'Some people might be vaguely amused but they'd see it as a cheap trick.'
'But it's not a cheap trick.' She turned quickly away with a look of indignation. 'Michael helps me to heal people; really he does.'
'And that, I'm very much afraid, is all a bit too heavy and serious for this frivolous world,' said Toby. 'Only one celebrity healer's really made the big time in the past two thousand years......... and they crucified him.'

Soon after breakfast, Lizzie Beckman temporarily consigned all thoughts of Michael and the business of healing to the farthest corner of her mind and, at 11-30am on the dot the following day, discreetly but with a dazzling smile, removed all her clothes for charity at London's Savoy Hotel. Nowhere in the many pages of press publicity which followed the doing-nothing-wearing-nothing celebrity stunt were there any mentions of cheap tricks.

CHAPTER 4

Blatantly sexy styles, hanging immodestly from the dress rails at Beckman Clothing's West End showroom, backed up the bawdy but highly plausible claim on the company swing tickets; 'Designed to turn men's heads', they proclaimed in shiny gold letters. But the burning question was whether or not such slinky, diaphanous creations were a suitable wardrobe for an indefinite stay in a haunted house.

Toby Stone was in no doubt. A stroke of genius he called it; Samuel Beckman's latest fashions, effectively modelled on national television by his wannabe celebrity daughter who might, from time to time, casually mention the Beckman brand name in conversation with her fellow house guests at Penfold Manor; the ideal PR two-for-the-price-of-one deal, and all perfectly reasonable and above board.

The look of suspicion on Samuel Beckman's face softened into a gentle smile as he quickly totted up the wholesale cost of sixteen chosen dresses, added a modest fifty five per cent retail mark-up, and then checked the sum total against TV advertising rates. Three thousand pounds worth of garments which might give him a quarter of a million in television exposure for the new collection; a bargain.

'But tell me,' he said, 'will the TV people mind if Lizzie keeps mentioning the Beckman Clothing Company Limited of Margaret Street, London, West One, fashion designed to turn men's heads?'

Toby forced a reluctant grin. 'Let me explain,' he began hesitantly, 'it doesn't quite work like that. We need to be slightly more subtle.'

'Subtle? I don't do subtle. How can you do subtle when you want to tell everyone about your product?'

'Well, Lizzie might, for example, say she's wearing her favourite Beckman dress, or she adores the femininity of Beckman styles.'

Samuel Beckman sucked his teeth and thought for a moment. 'What about the address? Can't she say it's her favourite dress from Beckman Clothing of Margaret Street, London, W1, maybe?'

'Not really,' said Toby. 'But she might perhaps mention how she likes to buy clothes from top London fashion houses like Beckman.'

Lizzie Beckman appeared from the changing room and swished the hem of a flimsy, georgette dress. 'This one is definitely me,' she announced with growing enthusiasm. 'And I could turn to camera saying something subtle like my father had this Beckman dress designed with me in mind.'

'Hmm, something like that,' Toby said, trying to bring the conversation to a close. 'You'll just have to play it by ear.'

Samuel Beckman shrugged his shoulders and sighed. 'Just remember please, for three thousand pounds worth of garments, we don't want too much of the subtle.' He made off towards a small office at the far end of the showroom but turned with a final thought before he'd reached the door. 'Maybe Lizzie could wear a T-shirt with our telephone number printed on the front.'

Toby took a deep breath, shut his eyes tight and counted to ten. 'And that man's about as subtle a Get-Well-Soon card from an undertaker,' he mumbled quietly to himself.

'He might not be subtle but he's successful,' Lizzie snapped back defensively. 'And that, surely, is what it's all about.' She twisted her hair back into a pony tail, pushed the sleeves of her sweater up to her elbows and set to work packing sixteen dresses and a mountain of tissue into Beckman Clothing Company carrier bags.

After a twenty minute wait on the corner of Regent Street, four bags in each hand, they finally abandoned all hope of ever finding a London taxi and took the underground from Oxford Circus to Queensway station, then walked the short distance to Lizzie's Bayswater flat.

The heavy scent of roses which permeated the hallway offered only a hint of the floral spectacular waiting in the lounge. Long stem, red roses, eighty four of them Lizzie guessed, reaching upwards and outwards from a round, fat porcelain pot in the middle of the coffee table. And a cream envelope, Lizzie's name in red ink, propped up against a single red candle.

'It can't be the twenty ninth already,' she said without bothering to read the message.

'It better be or we'll arrive at Penfold Manor on the wrong day.' Toby stood back to admire the flowers. 'Anniversary of some kind?' he asked casually, not wanting to appear too inquisitive.

'Seven months since Porky and I met. A dozen roses for each of them.'

Toby felt uncomfortable and decided to wait in the hall while she packed her favourite jeans and tops, enough shoes to keep Amelda Markos well-heeled and happy for a life-time, and her usual make-up.

'Am I allowed to take a hair dryer?' she called out from the bedroom.

'No idea. Pack it anyway.' Toby hesitated for a

moment, unsure of the best way to phrase the next question. 'Porky knows you might be away for a while I suppose?' He paused again. 'I mean, you *have* told him about Penfold Manor?'

'More or less,' she said, dragging two suitcases into the hall. 'More about the TV show and less about not being here for the twenty ninth. To be brutally honest, I'd quite forgotten all about it.'

'Shouldn't you leave him a note or something?'

'I'm not big on writing letters.' She shrugged, gave an impatient sigh. 'Besides, I'll call him later, when he gets in from the office.'

'No 'phone calls allowed once you check-in at the manor, as I recall.'

Lizzie tut-tutted, scribbled a few words on a sheet of paper torn from a notepad by the 'phone, and placed it in front of the roses.

'May I know what you said?' Toby asked.

She slowly shook her head and looked away. 'Probably best if I wait here while you pick up your car eh?' she said quietly.

'Makes sense. See you in half and hour.'

Lizzie's luggage filled the boot of the Mercedes and overflowed into the back seat of the car for the drive to Penfold Manor; ninety valuable minutes for a final briefing on Toby's plans to grab the newspaper headlines.

'I've dug up some details on Elizabeth Penfold,' he said, taking a buff envelope from the glove compartment. 'It's all in here, the old girl's life and times.'

'Old girl? I thought you said she was only twenty five when she died?'

'She was. But that was a hundred and twenty years ago, which makes her an old girl.'

Lizzie glanced at the notes. 'Suicide?'

'She drowned in the lake at Penfold Manor while husband Wilfred was playing-away with a local lass, or so the story goes.'

'Perhaps she was just trying to draw attention to herself but it all went terribly wrong.'

'Read on,' Toby said with a schoolboy grin. 'They say she's been seen looking out over the lake, her long, black hair matted with weed. At other times she's said to appear at one of the bedroom windows in the east wing of the house.'

Lizzie looked out across the Sussex countryside through the fading light of evening. 'Load of old rubbish,' she yawned. 'Sounds to me like one of your publicity stunts.'

'I'd have said that too if it weren't for the number of people who've corroborated the story over the years, some of them so-called experts on the paranormal.'

Lizzie hugged herself protectively with slender arms. 'Surely you don't believe in ghosts, do you?' she asked in a hushed voice.

'Me? Not a chance. You're either dead or you're alive and anything in the middle is pure make-believe.' Toby slowed the car at the road sign to Charlton and took a sharp left down a narrow country lane.

'Bit of an out-of-the-way place, this Penfold Manor, isn't it?'

'But of course,' said Toby checking the map. 'People who build manor houses usually try to avoid having next door neighbours.'

The crowd gathered at the haughty iron gates, a short distance ahead, was unexpected; perhaps thirty people, including three or four photographers and a TV crew.

'It begins,' said Toby, quickly lowering the front windows of the car. 'Check your lipstick, if you please, clip on your broadest smile and if anyone asks, you definitely don't believe in ghosts.'

Lizzie leaned uncertainly towards the sea of blank faces which peered, expressionless, through the open window into the car and felt suddenly vulnerable. 'Do you suppose any of them even vaguely recognise me?' she whispered.

'I very much doubt it,' said Toby. 'But they'll assume you must be somebody moderately well-known or you wouldn't be here, now would you?'

Lizzie smiled, cameras flashed, and a man in a faded and ill-fitting red commissionaire's uniform, waved the car through the gates with instructions for checking-in at the house, just visible beyond the trees at the end of a gravel drive which snaked imposingly across acres of velvet lawn and mature woodland.

'Why are you so anxious for me to tell everyone I don't believe in ghosts?' she asked, checking her make up in the visor mirror.

'Because you will be the first to come face-to-face with the sad, tormented spirit of Elizabeth Penfold,' Toby announced as if it had been preordained. 'Not immediately, you understand, but on day two or three when you've all settled in and your imaginations have had time to play a few tricks.'

'You mean I should fake it, make something up.'

Toby reached for her hand and squeezed it reassuringly. 'This ghost story was made-up a long time ago. All you have to do is go along with it.'

'But I don't get it; why would I do that?'

'Because a self-proclaimed sceptic who eventually says she's seen a ghost has a certain ring of truth about it. And that, dear Lizzie, could hand us some valuable press publicity.'

Toby slowed the car as the house loomed into view just ahead of them, a sprawling silhouette against the dying embers of a warm, summer sky. 'It might also persuade some of your fellow guests to pack-up and leave,' he added with a grin. 'And that would be a result.'

Lizzie stepped confidently from the car, head held high, and crossed the drive to wide granite steps which swept grandly up to two broad oak doors on the terrace above; two eagles, one either side, carved wings spread wide, eyes fixed in a stony, silent scrutiny. She turned to

Toby and took a deep breath.

'This is it then,' she said wistfully. 'Three boys, three girls, and the ghost of Elizabeth Penfold. Wish me luck.'

'You won't need luck,' Toby called after her. 'It'll be a doddle. Just think of it as 'The Two Lizzies' show and forget about everyone else.'

She stood for a moment, stock-still and silent, watching the car disappear into the darkness before she climbed the well-worn steps and entered the flimsy, counterfeit world of reality television.

'Welcome to Penfold Manor.' The voice, resonant, cultured and totally English, came from the far side of the entrance hall, where a tall, slim man with silver hair stepped forward and offered his hand in greeting. 'My name is Bennington,' he announced with a subtle nod of the head, back straight, hands firmly at his side.

He reminded her of an uncle she'd adored as a child; perhaps it was his military manners and well-scrubbed smell, tinged with lemons, as much as the immaculately-tailored black suit and crisp white shirt. She warmed to him at once.

Lizzie Beckman,' she said, looking back towards the drive, wondering what had become of her luggage.

'I took the liberty of having your cases sent up to your room madam,' Bennington assured her with a polite smile. 'Please allow me to show you the way.'

She followed him across the panelled hallway then paused at the foot of the staircase; the blackest oak, richly carved, rising and turning to a galleried landing immediately above and then beyond to a second floor.

'Jacobean and completely original,' said Bennington, running the tips of his fingers lovingly across the smooth contours of the banister. 'A silent witness to the entire history of the house.'

A suit of dull, grey armour stood guard over the first floor landing, lifeless and empty, the discarded chrysalis of former glory, hollow gauntlet hands grasping a phantom sword.

'He must have been a bit of a titch,' said Lizzie. 'No more than five feet or so.'

Bennington straightened up to his full six feet and spoke to the chandelier above. 'Undoubtedly he'd be considered short by today's standard. But five feet was a manly size in the sixteenth century.'

'Ello, ello, ello. Anyone at 'ome?' The coarse, cockney accent from the entrance hall echoed across the landing.

Bennington closed his eyes and inhaled deeply, lightly touching the side of his forehead in quiet contemplation, then turned with a bogus, painful smile. 'One of your fellow guests,' he announced through tight lips. 'A comedian, I believe.'

Lizzie crouched down and peered through the banisters at the diminutive but vaguely familiar figure standing in the hall. 'Isn't that Harry Hale?' she whispered.

Bennington nodded. 'Happy Harry Hale, I believe he's called.'

'But he's so much shorter and fatter than on telly. And, anyway, isn't he supposed to be dead?'

'He's very much alive and, at five feet, one inch exactly, a fine figure of sixteenth century manhood,' said Bennington. 'Unfortunately his jokes date back to the same era so he's not only short on height but also on humour.'

But Happy Harry Hale was in fine form. 'I went to see the psychiatrist yesterday wearing clingfilm shorts,' he told the smartly-dressed woman who'd greeted him the hall. 'And the shrink says to me, I can clearly see your nuts.'

Harry Hale laughed, loudly, nudged his passive audience with a bony elbow to ensure her full attention and launched, seamlessly, into a story about an Irishman and a fruitless search for a pair of camouflage trousers.

Bennington winced. 'My wife can't stand him either,' he said, opening the door to a sunny yellow bedroom overlooking a small but well-stocked rose garden, framed by a mellow brick wall.

Lizzie glanced back to the hall. 'That lady is your wife?'

'Molly,' said Bennington proudly. 'She's the housekeeper here at Penfold Manor.'

Lizzie settled herself comfortably into a deep settee near the bedroom window and gazed up at rows of blonde oak beams, set like ancient sentinels in the vaulted ceiling, dutifully watching over a king size bed; a rich mulberry bedspread scattered with faded tapestry cushions. And on the wall opposite, two gilt framed portraits; men without smiles, peering through darkened canvas at the faded remnants of another time.

'This isn't the east wing of the house is it?' she asked hesitantly.

'Definitely not; this is the west wing, madam,' said Bennington. 'Nobody stays in the East wing.' He took a creamy white envelope from his inside pocket, placed it on the bedside table, without explanation, and turned to go.

Lizzie stood up as he reached the door. 'When do I get to meet my fellow guests then?'

'Dinner, at eight, in the dining hall,' he said, then quietly closed the door behind him.

She stared at the envelope for a moment; 'For the Personal Attention of Ms Beckman', it said, the words Private & Confidential, scrawled across one corner. But opening it right away would be un-cool and definitely not the way a celebrity should behave. Instead, she casually set about arranging her clothes in a tall, carved amoire wardrobe, which smelled faintly musty with a trace of old lavender, and told herself the envelope could wait. And, besides, perhaps there was a TV camera hidden somewhere in the bedroom, monitoring her every move. She'd have to ask about that sort of thing over dinner.

At eight o'clock Lizzie Beckman stood in front of a full-length mirror, zipped up the back of a black sequined dress and reached across for the envelope. Inside was a single sheet of paper, neatly folded and, in the centre, scripted lettering from an artistic hand. She read the words twice, the second time out loud.

'In the shadow of the willow, undisturbed, the soul which has no rest, waits for you by moonlight, her honoured, welcome quest.'

A wry grin dimpled her cheeks as she slipped the note into her handbag. 'Childish nonsense,' she whispered to herself, then set off in search of the dining hall and her five fellow guests.

The sound of laughter echoed across the hall; a steady ripple of girlish giggles punctuated by short bursts of raucous, baritone cackle. Harry Hale in full flow, legs astride in front of a stone hearth which dominated the oak panelled room; a crystal tumbler of whisky in one hand, the other firmly clamped to the plump, bejewelled wrist of a mature redhead with a generous but frozen smile.

'Health freaks are going to feel really stupid one day,' Harry Hale squawked into her ear. 'They'll all be lying in hospital, dying of nothing.' He patted her bottom in a brief round of self-applause.

The name came to Lizzie almost at once; Maggie Keen, a singer with a rich, husky voice which dominated London's West End theatres just a few years earlier. But not lately, not since the incident in the nightclub; drugs, a stabbing, Lizzie couldn't remember the details.

Already seated at the long, oak table, their backs to the fireside performance, Donny Jackson, DJ and TV presenter, seventies pony tail still deceitfully black for its years. And next to him, a pale and fragile figure with bloodless lips and pastel blue eyes, hanging on his every word; Yvette Duncan, star of a string of highly forgettable historical dramas; the archetypal damsel in distress both on and off the screen or, as an eminent film critic had once cruelly described her, a truly distressing damsel who was beyond rescue.

Lizzie stood for a moment in the open doorway, handbag on her arm, hands loosely clasped in front of her, waiting to be introduced.

Harry Hale stopped abruptly in mid joke, rattled his

finger nails on the rim of his glass for attention. 'And then there were five,' he spluttered unpleasantly through a mouthful of salted peanuts.

'Six actually.' Lizzie turned towards the public school accent and the less than familiar figure of a man in his late fifties, crossing the hall.

'The name's Hartley, Rupert Hartley.' He smiled, gently took her hand and led her to the centre of the room. 'And this lovely lady,' he announced proudly to the others, 'is Miss Elizabeth Beckman.'

'You know who I am?' she whispered.

He nodded. 'Bennington was most obliging.'

Lizzie glanced down at the brown suede shoes and cavalry twills. 'Aren't you that politician?' she asked hesitantly, searching for his name.

'Very probably,' he sighed, before she could go on. 'But, for the avoidance of doubt, I'm the one who had a brief, extra-marital fling with a Chinese girl and not the other one who did three months for fraud. People sometimes get the two of us confused.'

Harry Hale pinged the rim of his glass impatiently. 'Two MPs walked into the House of Commons the other day.' He paused for a moment, scanned the room to satisfy himself that his audience was suitably attentive, then started again, voice slightly louder than before. 'Two MPs walked into the House of Commons the other day,' he repeated, barely able to control his own giggles. 'You'd have thought one of them would have looked where they were going.'

The MP managed a weak smile. 'I wonder, Harry, if we might come to some kind of arrangement,' he said, playfully prodding the comedian's belly with a rigid finger. 'I promise not to talk politics over dinner if you could spare us the comedy routine for an hour or two.'

Harry Hale shrugged. 'Politics, comedy; what's the difference? They're both a bit of a joke.'

'And I totally agree with you,' Hartley replied with a dismissive flick of the wrist. 'Politicians *are* sometimes very amusing. On the other hand,' he continued, 'some comedians are frequently neither amusing, entertaining or the least bit funny.'

Lizzie turned her back on the bickering and reached for a glass of Champagne from a large, round silver tray which had been placed in the centre of an ornate sideboard to one side of the room. She stared into the gilt-framed mirror above, flicked her fingers through her hair, adjusted the neckline of her dress and quickly checked her lipstick. From behind her left shoulder, and only for a moment, a woman peered back at her; expressionless, black hair, long and lank, framing pallid cheeks. Lizzie moved politely to one side and turned to introduce herself but the other woman had gone.

A cheap trick, she told herself at once. Probably nothing more than a black and white image reflected from somewhere on the wall opposite. All done by mirrors; wasn't that what they used to say? Something like that.

The gong which rang out in the hall brought a sudden silence to the room.

'Dinner is served,' Bennington announced from a narrow doorway which had just appeared, as if my magic, in the panelled oak wall. He quickly laid photographs of each of the six guests on place mats around the table; small colour portraits of each of them, glued to the backs of playing cards, and then asked them to be seated.

Rupert Hartley and Maggie Keen, the King and Queen of diamonds, were positioned at each end of the table. Lizzie and Yvette Duncan, the Aces of spades and clubs, either side of the MP, with Donny Jackson and Harry Hale, both Jokers, to the right and left of the singer.

'We seem to have a promising poker hand here if nothing else,' Hartley observed, glancing around the table.

'Are they meant to be somehow significant?' Donny Jackson asked, casually flicking his card across the table to the comedian. 'You're the only professional joker here so you might as well have my card too. I don't tell jokes.'

A small camera, high in the corner of the room, caught Lizzie's eye. 'I suppose we're all being filmed,' she said to nobody in particular.

'But of course,' Bennington assured her, pointing to cameras at either end of the room. 'That is, after all, why you are here, isn't it?'

Lizzie draped her napkin across her lap. 'I suppose it is,' she said pensively. 'But surely some rooms are off-limits to the cameras.....like the bathroom, for example.'

'You may prefer to think that,' said Bennington quietly. 'I couldn't possibly comment.'

'Filming me doing a wee wouldn't be very entertaining,' Harry Hale quipped. 'If I see a camera in my loo I'll throw my Y-fronts at it.'

Maggie Keen began to look embarrassed. 'Would you mind terribly if we changed the subject?' she asked timidly, staring at the bowl of thick, green soup which Mrs Bennington had just placed before her. 'Men's underwear isn't a very pleasant subject for dinner-time conversation.'

'This bloody soup isn't very pleasant either,' Hale snorted. 'Looks more like cream of caterpillar and cabbage leaves and tastes like wet sawdust with a dash of salt.'

'Actually it's watercress soup,' Mrs Bennington enlightened him with a frown. 'Prepared especially for the vegetarians among us.'

'You mean I'm not the only vegetarian here?' said Donny Jackson, looking round the table for signs of a kindred spirit.

Lizzie shook her head. 'Not me, I'm a committed carnivore.'

'I suppose I am,' Yvette Duncan cooed. 'I don't eat meat but I still eat seafood so I don't yet have the full vegetarian halo.'

'I went to a seafood disco the other night and pulled a mussel,' Harry Hale screamed on cue, slapping the table with the palm of his hand. My health freak friend drowned in a bowl of muesli,' he went on, without pausing for breath. 'A strong current pulled him in.'

Rupert Hartley frowned. 'I thought we had an arrangement Harry old chap. No politics from me in return for no jokes from you.'

'That was before I was handed the Joker's card. Anyway, why did the MP *stand* for Parliament?'

'Could it have been because he lost his *seat* at the last election,' Hartley sighed. 'And now I've got one for you. Why did the comedian suddenly shut up?'

Harry Hale thought for a moment. 'Was it because he had a terrific gag on the tip of his tongue?'

'An excellent try but quite wrong,' said Hartley. 'The comedian shut up because, if he hadn't, the MP would have got up, dragged him from his chair and punched him, very hard indeed, in the face….possibly as many as three or four times.'

The two men stared at each other, silent, unsmiling, while the others finished their soup.

Lizzie was the first to speak. 'Did anyone else see the woman in the mirror?' she asked casually.

'Did anyone see *what* woman in what mirror darling?' Yvette Duncan's words, soft and reassuring, belied the narrow-lipped, fragile smile. 'You're surely not saying you've encountered the notorious Elizabeth Penfold already?' she sneered.

'Correct.' Lizzie snapped back. 'I'm not saying any such thing.'

The actress leaned forward, elbows on the table, head delicately framed in her hands. 'What exactly are you saying then darling?'

Toby Stone's words echoed in Lizzie's ears. If anyone asked her, she definitely didn't believe in ghosts; he'd made the point a couple of times on the way there. A self-proclaimed sceptic who eventually says she's seen the ghost of Elizabeth Penfold would have a ring of truth about it, she remembered, even if it was a pack of lies. But not just yet. This was too soon; she was supposed to wait a few days, allow a bit of time for everyone's imaginations to start playing tricks.

'I'm saying it was some kind of childish trickery sweetie.' Lizzie stared confidently into the other woman's eyes. 'Something that might frighten feeble-minded people who believe in ghosts.'

'And do you? Believe in ghosts, I mean?'

Lizzie shook her head. 'Definitely not sweetie,' she said firmly. 'How about you?'

'I'm not totally sure.' Yvette Duncan dabbed her mouth with her napkin and settled back in the chair. 'I like to think I have a very open mind on most subjects.'

'But it's so easy to confuse an open mind with an empty one, sweetie?' Lizzie whispered coyly. 'A simple yes or no will do.'

'Well darling, if someone like you thinks the answer's no, then I'd have to say yes.'

A lead crystal wine glass rang out twice as Harry Hale's soup spoon crashed against the fragile rim. 'End of round one, I think girls. Back to your corners.'

Lizzie looked away. 'And do the King and Queen of diamonds believe in ghosts?' she asked, turning first towards Maggie Keen and then to Hartley at the other end of the table.

'I think I probably do,' said the singer. 'Why not?'

The MP carefully tweaked starched, white shirt cuffs to a full inch or so beyond the sleeves of his jacket and pondered the floor for inspiration before he spoke. 'In the light of available evidence at the current time,' he pronounced solemnly, 'I believe it would be impossible to support the proposition…….. as it stands.'

'Should we take that as a no then from the honourable gentleman?' Harry Hale scoffed. 'Only most of us don't speak Emm Pee, that strange foreign language where you say exactly the opposite to what you really mean.'

'I said no and I meant no,' Hartley sighed dismissively. 'So that's Rupert and myself who think no and Yvette and Maggie who think yes,' said Lizzie. 'Which leaves our two Jokers.' She looked across the table to Donny Jackson. 'Do TV presenters believe in ghosts?'

'I'd prefer to call them spirits,' said Donny. 'But, yes, I believe in them.'

Lizzie turned to the comedian. 'That just leaves you.'

'I prefer to call them spirits too,' he cackled. 'But I only believe in the bottled ones with forty per cent proof on the label.'

'Then we have an even split,' said Lizzie. 'Three believers and three non-believers.'

Bennington stepped forward from the corner of the room to remove the soup plates. 'If I may interject,' he said with a polite nod. 'There are two other believers in the house. Both my wife and I support the proposition, as Mr Hartley would put it, so it's five votes to three.'

Lizzie's eyes narrowed. 'Do you believe in one particular ghost or ghosts in general?' she asked, hoping to fuel the growing unease she was beginning to sense in the other two women.

'You can't believe in one particular ghost without accepting the existence of others,' said Bennington.

Lizzie reached into her handbag for the cryptic message he'd left on her bedside table. 'And the soul which has no rest?' she asked, handing him the note. 'Does that refer to a specific ghost?'

'Make of it what you will,' he said quietly. 'Each of you had the same message and you must each must decide what it means.'

Harry Hale tapped the rim of his glass, stood up and bowed to the camera, on his right. 'I know what it means,' he giggled, picking up the note and reading it out loud. 'In the shadow of the willow, undisturbed, the soul which has no rest, waits for you by moonlight, her honoured, welcome guest'. He glanced round the table. 'You'll probably all have spotted the spelling mistake. It's actually a call for help from a fish, a lost sole, asking us to go down to the lake, fish her out, and take her back to Dover, where she belongs.'

Nobody laughed, not even Happy Harry Hale who, quite suddenly and totally unexpectedly, slumped back into his chair, hands gripping his throat as if he might have been poisoned.

Yvette Duncan let out a deep sigh and slowly clapped her hands. 'Very theatrical darling. But please don't call us, we'll call you.'

Harry Hale remained perfectly still and silent, eyes open wide, staring blankly at the wall opposite, hands now resting limply in his lap.

'I think, for once, the old bugger's not actually joking,' Rupert Hartley called out.

Bennington quickly checked the comedian's pulse. 'Could be a heart attack,' he said, signalling to his wife to call an ambulance.

'Could be anything,' said Hartley. 'Perhaps he chocked on something; possibly the soup.'

Harry Hales jaw dropped open and a dark green watercress tinted tongue slipped out from the side of his mouth. A gurgling sound bubbled up from somewhere in the back of his throat.

'Sounds to me as if he's having a fit of some kind,' Yvette Duncan volunteered. 'I think you're supposed to put something in their mouths so they don't bite their tongues.'

Donny Jackson shook his head. He thought it might be a stroke having seen an elderly aunt collapse in a very similar way a few months earlier. But the two paramedics, who turned-up within minutes of Mrs Bennington's call, weren't at all convinced. While they couldn't rule out a heart attack or a stroke, the patient's heart beat, body temperature, breathing and the pupils of his eyes, suggested there was nothing seriously wrong.

Harry Hale was lifted from his chair, carefully laid on a

stretcher and was half-way across the hall, en route to the front door, when he raised himself up on one arm, waved first to the camera, then to the others, and declared that he was glad to be the first to leave Penfold Manor and escape such boring people.

'You lot are about as much fun as a triple by-pass,' he yelled with a croaky voice. 'No sense of humour whatsoever.'

The ambulance left Penfold Manor, siren sounding, shortly before nine, followed by a small group of photographers. Less than fifteen minutes later, after an official warning about false alarms and wasting NHS funds, Happy Harry Hale posed for pictures on the hospital steps and told waiting reporters that his five fellow celebrities should get on well with the ghost of Penfold Manor as they were, he quipped, already half dead themselves. Then he headed happily for home in a taxi.

But Yvette Duncan wasn't amused; in fact she was furious. It was beyond belief that a third rate comic, who laughed at his own jokes, should have the nerve to call *her* boring…….. or anyone else for that matter, she quickly added, not wanting to offend the others.

'I really couldn't care less,' said Lizzie. 'To be called boring by someone like Happeee Harreee is really something of a compliment.' She stretched her arms high above her head and yawned, then slowly rose to her feet, smoothing the front of her dress with her hand. 'My father, who incidentally owns Beckman fashions and who designed this dress, always says names can never hurt you.'

Maggie Keen laughed gently. 'Was that a quick commercial break?' she asked. 'Because, if it was, I'd like to announce my forthcoming singing tour, with appearances at leading venues throughout the UK from September, beginning at the Nottingham Arena and culminating in December at the Hammersmith Apollo.'

Lizzie picked up her almost empty glass of wine and

drained it then turned back towards to the mirror over the sideboard. She spread her fingers wide and ran them through her hair, staring back at her reflection, hoping to catch a glimpse of the insipid, expressionless features of the mystery woman. But, this time, there was nothing.

'Why don't we all take up our invitations,' she said, twirling daintily around to face the others. 'She waits for us in the shadow of the willow, by moonlight. Isn't that how it goes?'

Maggie Keen gently massaged her brow and sighed deeply. 'I think I shall have to pass on that invitation,' she huffed. 'I've a bit of a headache.'

'Bit of fresh air will do you good,' said Hartley, reaching for the decanter. 'Let's all have a large brandy before we venture out.'

Half an hour and a few brandies later, at ten minutes to twelve, five celebrity guests dawdled across the lawn towards the tall willow at the edge of the lake.

Lizzie's stiletto heels sank deep into the soft turf, already damp with dew and cold to her feet as she slipped out of her sling backs and continued, barefoot, shoes dangling from her left hand.

'Careful you don't tread in something nasty darling,' Yvette said in a hushed but carelessly mocking voice. 'The moon's not very bright this evening.'

'That makes two of you then sweetie,' Lizzie snapped back. 'You can always wash your feet but you can't do much about scuffed heels.'

The actress ignored the gibe and edged closer to Rupert Hartley, taking hold of his arm and wrapping it tightly around her waist. 'It's getting a bit nippy, don't you think?' she purred, gazing up into his face.

Hartley slipped off his jacket and draped it around her shoulders. 'Can't have you catching a chill, now can we?' he said, placing his arm back around her waist and drawing her closer as they stepped carefully between the gnarled and twisted roots of the willow which reached out like tentacles across the edge of the lake.

'Now what?' Donny Jackson asked, leaning, hands in pockets, against the tree, looking back towards the house. 'Now nothing,' said Lizzie. 'This is all a big spoof.' Maggie cuddled herself against the night chill with sun-tanned arms. 'Less than forty eight hours ago I was in sunny Marrakech so this is a bit of a climate shock for me. But, spoof or not, I'm for going back to the house and getting a good night's sleep.'

An owl hooted from the other side of the lake. Yvette wriggled closer to the MP and rested her head on his shoulder. 'Perhaps we should give it ten minutes or so,' she said, checking a Cartier wrist watch. 'It's only just gone midnight.'

Lizzie stood uncertainly, staring up into the canopy of willow fronds which cascaded down to the water, wondering if Elizabeth Penfold might have stood under the very same tree more than a century earlier.

'How old do you suppose this tree is?' she called out to the others. 'I mean could it have been here, say, a hundred years ago?'

'Search me,' said Donny. 'All I know about willows is that you make cricket bats out of them.'

'And the music boxes of harps,' Maggie interjected.

'This tree's probably well over a century old, looking at the size of the trunk,' said Hartley. 'Why do you ask?'

Lizzie looked out across the lake. 'Oh, I just wondered if the so-called ghost of Elizabeth Penfold would have meant this willow tree or, perhaps, another one.'

'Good point,' said Donny. 'We could all be at the wrong place.'

'Well this is definitely the wrong place for me right now,' Maggie groaned, slapping a mosquito from the side of her neck as she walked away. 'I'm off to bed.'

Donny took a half empty packet of Rothmans from his jacket pocket and lit up with cupped hands. 'A quick ciggie before turning in,' he said with the relish of an inveterate smoker, sending the spent match spinning towards the lake.

'I'll say goodnight too.' Lizzie glanced down at the unlikely couple snuggled together like lost children under the tree. 'See you two in the morning then.'

Hartley waved a lethargic hand in acknowledgement but said nothing.

'Ill mannered bastards,' Lizzie muttered under her breath as she turned back towards the house. 'Hope you both freeze to dea…..' The words dried in her mouth as she gazed into lifeless, hollow eyes; the woman in the mirror, motionless, close enough to touch and then, in an instant, gone.

She heard herself cry out; a stifled, involuntary sound which seemed to rise up from the centre of her body and then evaporate into the quiet of the night as her sense of reason surged back with a rational explanation. Just another cheap trick.

A short distance ahead of her, Donny Jackson silhouetted in the light from the terrace, totally unaware, unconcerned. And at the edge of the lake, behind her, Yvette and Rupert, blissfully entwined, oblivious to the rest of the universe.

Lizzie reminded herself that the whole silly charade was probably being filmed and, more importantly, that she was not really looking her best for a TV appearance. She took a deep breath, checked her hemline and swaggered back across the lawn, shoes swinging freely from a hooked finger pointing lazily towards the heavens in a pose borrowed from Vogue magazine.

Bennington appeared at the terrace doors, a white towel draped across his left arm. 'Perhaps you would like to dry your feet madam?' he said, more as an instruction than a suggestion. 'And I've taken the liberty of running you a hot bath.'

He looked down the length of the lawn to the lake and the huddled figures under the willow. 'Do you think the others will be long?' he asked quietly.

Lizzie shrugged. 'Unlikely. I think they'll be tucked up

in bed shortly,' she said, leaning back against the low terrace wall to dry her feet. 'Probably in the same bed.'

A look of mild irritation replaced Bennington's practised smile as the house telephone rang out twice and then stopped. He hesitated for a moment, checked his watch, and turned to leave. 'May I wish you goodnight?' he said, picking up the towel and making towards the door. 'Breakfast is served here, on the terrace, from eight.'

The light from Lizzie's bedroom filtered through the balcony's ornate balusters, sending shadows out across the rose garden and over to the mellow brick wall below. She tightened a white satin dressing gown around her and stared into the night sky, wondering what Toby would make of her first evening's performance at Penfold Manor and whether Porky had been upset by her curt little note, for which she'd already decided to apologise when she got home. And then the big question; would she be able to sleep in what looked like a particularly uncomfortable, antiquated, king size bed?

Somebody had already turned back the covers and plumped up the pillows, making it slightly more inviting but the mattress was hard, lumpy and unforgiving. She stretched out, legs and arms spread wide, and gazed through tired eyes at the vaulted ceiling. A moth fluttered obstinately around her bedside lamp before finally settling on a beam directly above, and from somewhere in the distance, like a desperate cry for help, the anxious, chilling screech of peacocks echoed through the trees.

Lizzie slid between the sheets then reached across and turned out the light before drifting off into a deep sleep.

A noise outside on the landing woke her just after three. For a moment she lay perfectly still, listening, wondering if it might have been a creaking floorboard or the groan of an old beam. But then she heard it again; two resolute knocks on her bedroom door followed by complete silence.

'Who is it?' she called out in a half whisper but nobody answered.

She switched on the lamp and called out again, this time louder and with more urgency. 'Is somebody there?'

'Sorry, it's only me.' Donny Jackson peered cautiously around the half open door with an impish smile. 'Mind if I come in?'

'As a matter of fact, I do,' Lizzie yawned. 'What the hell do you want at this time of night?'

'I couldn't sleep. Thought you might fancy a chat.'

'Well think again. I'm tired.'

'Just five minutes,' he said, closing the door quietly behind him. 'Then I'll go. Promise.'

Lizzie sat bolt upright, bedclothes wrapped tight around her, cuddling her knees. She stared at the thigh-length kimono dressing gown; black with gold dragons on the sleeves, and below, like freshly kneaded dough, two pale, plump legs, firm but shapeless, bulbous feet, strapped tight in leather sandals.

'I'll give you exactly one minute,' she said wearily. 'Now what is it you want?'

Donny ran a hand over the front of his hair, gave the pony tail an arrogant swish and flexed his shoulders and arms like a prize fighter limbering up for the main event. 'I've decided we should spend the night together,' he said calmly, edging closer to the bed and beginning to loosen the sash around the kimono.

'You've had your sixty seconds,' Lizzie sighed. 'Now do us both a favour and bugger off back to your own bed.'

'Chill out babe. You're missing a trick here.'

'Out,' she said firmly, pointing towards the door.

He shook his head in quiet disbelief, took a step backwards and leaned casually against the bedroom wall, arms folded. 'Look, if they think we've got it together, we'll get some easy publicity,' he explained. 'You don't have to fancy me or any of that stuff.'

'Why don't you put the idea to Maggie, she's more your age?'

'I have and she will,' he said with a shrug. 'But it'll be

more interesting for the papers if I make out with both of you.'

Lizzie's face hardened. 'I only did two grades in kick boxing but I think I've probably learned enough to knock a few of your teeth out and rearrange your pompous nose.'

'Up to you babe. But I honestly think you're throwing away a great opportunity here.'

She stared at him, unblinking, totally silent, while he backed slowly out of the room and, with a childish wink, made off down the corridor. Lizzie locked the door behind him and went back to sleep.

The terrace overlooking the lake seemed more welcoming the next day. Early morning sun speckled through a wisteria covered pergola, casting dappled patterns across the white table cloth, already laid for breakfast; five place settings each with a single white rose, resplendent in a narrow crystal vase. And Maggie Keen in a white caftan, hiding behind big, round sunglasses, under a straw hat, sitting alone at the far end of the table, reading a book.

Lizzie poured a cup of coffee and settled herself opposite. 'Sleep well?' she asked more by way of polite conversation than any real sense of interest.

Maggie peered over her glasses. 'Not really, no,' she said. 'Strange bed, strange sounds. How about you?'

Lizzie rolled her eyes. 'Tell me about it.' She paused to reach across to a basket of croissant in the centre of the table. 'Perhaps we both had the same late night visitor?'

'Almost certainly,' Maggie said at once, slapping her book firmly closed. 'But I sent him packing.'

'No plans to have sex with him then?'

The singer took off her hat and ruffled up the wild red hair with the tips of her fingers. 'I've never liked pony tails,' she said in a hushed voice. 'But I positively detest them on men of a certain age who really should know better.'

'So how do you feel about Karate Kid kimonos?' Lizzie sniggered through a mouthful of croissant.

The two women looked at each other for a moment, lips quivering, then finally gave way to screams of laughter at the precise moment Donny Jackson appeared at the edge of the terrace.

'Wanna share the joke?' he asked, folding back the cuffs of a blue denim shirt which very nearly matched the shabby chic, faded jeans with badly frayed bottoms.

'Sounds like it was a good one.'

Maggie's laughter slowly faded to a withering smile. 'I was just telling Lizzie how we used to take LSD to make the world weird but now the world is full of weirdoes and people take Prozac to make it seem normal.'

Donny looked directly at her, eyes narrowed. 'Unlike a lot of people in show business, I don't do drugs,' he said pointedly. 'Never felt the need.'

'And you're a vegetarian too,' Maggie sneered. 'So, apart from the chain smoking and a drink problem, you're pretty well perfect eh?'

'Some would say irresistible even,' Lizzie added, straight faced.

He took an apple from a large crystal bowl of fruit and bit into it before he sat down at the table, staring out across the lawn towards the fountain. 'Shall we get real here?' he said after a moment. 'My idea of sex with you two was all about getting ourselves some publicity while we wait for the Phantom of the Opera, or whatever her name is, to liven things up.' He paused to take another bite from the apple, eyes fixed on each of them in turn. 'Don't flatter yourselves it's love girls; I'm just being professional,' he huffed. 'Geddit?'

'What you're being is totally pathetic,' Maggie yelled across the table. 'It's pretty bloody sad that tiny minds like yours can't come up with anything more original than screwing someone to get themselves in the papers.'

'Get off your high horse luv. It's what the public wants that matters. And what they undoubtedly want is sex.'

'I think you'll find that the Right Honourable

gentleman has already been at it with the movie industry's queen of the turkeys,' Lizzie announced with a gentle laugh and a nod towards the willow where the actress and the MP stood, hand in hand, in front of a TV camera.

Donny Jackson tossed the remains of his apple across the lawn. 'What the bloody hell do they think they're doing?' he raged. 'Nobody mentioned close-up TV interviews to me. Just fly-on-the-wall filming, they said, impromptu coverage of the daily goings on, not the Yvette & Rupert breakfast show.'

'Well they seem to have changed their minds,' said Maggie. 'Perhaps our two love birds were rather more than just a one-night-stand. Looks like their making an official announcement.'

Lizzie cringed. 'Christ, that sounds a bit desperate,' she said topping up her coffee. 'And, anyway, isn't he supposed to be married already?'

'He *was* married,' said Maggie. 'Has been quite a few times. But, as far as I know, he's free as a bird right now.'

Donny rocked back on his chair, hands clasped together, muttering quietly to himself. 'The good news,' he said eventually, 'is they'll probably leave Penfold Manor today, maybe right away.'

Lizzie gave him a sour smile. 'And what makes you think they'll quit?'

'Bloody obvious, innit?' said Donny. 'Kindred spirits find love in a haunted house, and all that stuff. They'll get more publicity on the outside than stuck in here with us.'

Maggie smoothed the brim on her straw hat, set it elegantly across one eye and rose to her feet, hands resting flat on the table. 'I'm off down to the lake to see what's going on,' she declared slightly stiffly, looking as if she might be opening a church fete. 'Too much supposition can be very boring you know.'

She'd swept gracefully past the fountain and was half way across the lawn before Lizzie noticed the figure on the far side of the lake; a woman alone, standing at the water's edge, motionless, looking out towards the willow. She was dressed entirely in black; a long black dress with a shawl perhaps, or it might have been a hooded cloak; too far away for Lizzie to be certain

'Do you see her?' she called out to Maggie. 'The woman on the other side of the lake.'

Maggie stopped abruptly in her tracks, took off her sunglasses and looked back towards the house. 'Sorry darling,' she shouted, with an emphatic shrug of the shoulders. 'Where do you mean?'

'Across the lake; the woman in black. You can't miss her.' Lizzie swung round quickly to face Donny. 'You can see her, can't you?'

He stood up, hand shielding his eyes against the bright morning sun, and quickly glanced around the perimeter of the lake. 'Nice try Lizzie,' he said after a minute. 'But I don't think anybody's buying this Penfold ghost story nonsense.'

Lizzie wasn't listening and had already started towards the water's edge; slow deliberate steps, eyes fixed on the solitary figure waiting in the reeds on the opposite side of the lake.

A warm breeze rustled through the birch trees, set in a silver cluster around the wooden jetty, as she stepped down into the small rowboat with only a fleeting glance along the bank towards the willow where Maggie was now in deep conversation with the other two.

Short, stubby oars, too thick and heavy for Lizzie's slender hands, churned up a dark, mouldering sediment from the shallows, swirling rotting leaves across the surface of the lake and with them the putrid smell of decay. She pulled hard to deeper, clearer water and relaxed for a moment, allowing the boat to drift slowly towards the opposite bank.

The hazy recall of a senseless afternoon on The Serpentine flickered through her mind as the bow of the boat turned towards the sun. She remembered the dazzling white rays that had momentarily blinded her to the man who'd said it would all be OK. And here she was once again, unsure, drifting towards the unknown.

A dull thud brought the row boat to a halt as it bumped gently into the grassy bank, sending a family of coots scurrying along the edge of the lake to the safety of the reeds where the woman had stood, motionless, only moments earlier. But now she was gone.

Lizzie swivelled the oars awkwardly into the boat and scrambled up the bank in time to see the figure in black hasten through the long grass towards a rich thicket of trees beyond.

'Please wait,' Lizzie cried out, but was at once gripped by a sense of fear and foreboding as the woman stopped and turned slowly towards her, the face almost entirely obscured by a lace shawl, a small drawstring bag, hanging loosely from her wrist.

The morning breeze, which had earlier seemed so warm and reassuring, now breathed an icy sigh across Lizzie's skin, whispering of other places which are not for the living and sending a shiver through her bones. She watched, transfixed, while pale, porcelain hands reached slowly and carefully into the drawstring bag, followed by a second of hesitation before three playing cards were allowed to fall gently to the ground. And then a strange, lingering silence as the women turned away and hurried off into the thicket.

Lizzie took a deep breath, rubbed her arms against the chill of the moment, and stepped warily towards the cards, face up in the long grass; the king of diamonds and a joker, each with inky punctures where the eyes had been spitefully obliterated by a childlike scribble. And a second joker with a red line drawn from corner to corner.

She rowed quickly back to the jetty from where she could see the TV crew scattering the best part of a loaf of bread, in bite size pieces, across the shallows of the lake, luring two swans majestically into frame; a symbolic picture to round off the news item about Rupert and Yvette's whirlwind romance, destined for the six o'clock slot on national television.

A second bottle of Champagne popped its cork as Lizzie reached the terrace where the others had already gathered together in a little huddle under the canopy of wisteria. Bennington handed her a long flute glass, filled it to overflowing then dropped in a strawberry for good measure.

'To the happy couple,' Maggie gushed effusively from the shade of her straw hat. 'A match made in heaven.'

'Absolutely,' said Lizzie, raising her glass and forcing a weak smile. 'Congratulations to both of you.'

Yvette shook her head. 'Actually darling it's not really done to congratulate the lady when two people get together; just the man.'

'So sorry,' said Lizzie. 'Consider my congratulations withdrawn.'

'But perhaps we should congratulate you?' Yvette asked staring directly into Lizzie's eyes. 'Did you find your lady in black after all that shouting and screaming?'

'As a matter of fact I did,' Lizzie muttered.

Yvette drew closer. 'And what did she have to say, darling?'

'She said nothing but she left these.' Lizzie fanned out the three cards. 'This is your card, isn't it?' she asked, handing the king of diamonds to Rupert. 'And one of these jokers must be yours,' she said, turning quickly to Donny, a card in each hand. 'Take your pick.'

'I think you'll find the one with the red line through it belongs to Harry Hale,' Bennington joined in. 'It means he's no longer in the game.'

Donny Jackson stared at his card. 'But someone's poked the joker's eyes out. What kind of bloody game's that?'

'Poker, obviously,' Hartley chuckled.

'I think you'll find it's symbolic,' said Bennington,

popping open a third bottle of Champagne and topping-up each of the glasses in turn. 'Tradition has it that unseeing eyes usually indicate death.'

Donny quickly drained his glass and sat down. 'Are you saying that Lizzie's phantom lady in black wants to kill me?'

'I think not,' Bennington said with a reassuring smile. 'The spirit of a departed soul is incapable of murder.' He paused for a moment, smoothed down the neatly parted silver hair with the flat of his hand. 'Of course,' he continued solemnly, 'that wouldn't preclude them from *wishing* you dead.'

'Why little old me?' Donny chuckled, trying hard not to appear ruffled 'What have I bloody well done?'

'Not a thing,' said Bennington. He glanced across the lawn to the lake. 'The story goes that the late Mrs Penfold blames *all* men for her untimely death but, apart from the fishing incident, there's never been any suggestion of foul play.'

'The fishing incident?' Donny leaned forward and reached for a cigarette. 'What was that all about?'

Bennington placed a crystal ash tray on the table and slid it purposefully towards him. 'It was soon after the war. Two young men fishing for trout, just over there.' He pointed towards a narrow inlet on the far side of the lake. 'One of them apparently fell in and somehow managed to get tangled up in the weed. Drowned, poor chap. An accident, they said, but his friend insisted that something had pulled him under.'

Donny drew hard on his cigarette. 'Yeah, OK, but it *could* have been an accident, couldn't it? I mean lakes can be dangerous places.'

'Quite so sir. Dangerous places indeed.' Bennington picked up a tray full of dishes and turned to leave as Maggie grabbed his arm.

'So, what about us girls?' she asked him playfully.

'Queen of diamonds and two aces.'

'Mrs Penfold is a very active spirit,' said Bennington. 'I feel sure she'll have made plans for each of you ladies.'

Rupert Hartley slowly clapped his hands. 'This talk of ghosts is all very entertaining, and I appreciate it's why we are all here but, with the greatest respect, I really don't think I can take it seriously.'

Lizzie cleared her throat. 'Have it your way,' she said quietly. 'But I've seen her.'

'Unfortunately nobody else has seen her darling,' Yvette sneered. 'Nobody at all, just you. And we only have your word for that.'

'Yes, why do you suppose that is?' Hartley wondered. 'Why haven't I seen this dead woman?'

'Perhaps it's because you're far too busy ogling the live ones,' she snapped back.

'And why not?' said Hartley, with an admiring glance towards Yvette. 'Let's face it, life is so very short.'

'Would you mind turning round?' Lizzie asked suddenly. 'With your back to me.'

Hartley emptied his glass and belched. 'I've always thought it rude to turn your back on someone, especially when you're talking to them,' he sighed.

'Don't argue,' she said abruptly. 'Just turn round.'

Hartley grudgingly turned away but glanced back across his shoulder as the tips of her fingers found the small of his back and pressed gently down towards his thighs. 'May I ask what you're doing?' he groaned, leaning forward, gripping the back of a chair.

Lizzie took a deep breath, hands held flat against his spine. 'I'm not sure,' she whispered. 'Something to do with damaged vertebrae; a riding accident?' She hesitated for a moment. 'Anyway, it's done.'

'What's done?' Hartley called out, still bent slightly forward.

'Whatever it was that needed doing,' she answered coolly. 'But you'd know more about that than me.'

Rupert Hartley straightened-up, thrust his hands deep

into his trouser pockets, and turned around. 'We'll have to see about that,' he said, looking past her into his own, private middle distance, avoiding direct eye contact.

She watched him stroll, leisurely, across the terrace and over to the fountain where he paused, head raised, staring up at the stone cherub on the top tier, dabbling his fingers nonchalantly in the cascading water below, apparently deep in thought. There was a brief moment of hesitation before, finally, he bent very slowly forward and cautiously reached for the caps of his brown, suede shoes. He managed to touch his toes half a dozen times, each with slightly more enthusiasm and vigour than the last then, with a more spirited step, he returned to the shade of the terrace.

'Surely not morning exercises darling?' Yvette Duncan called to him from the other side of the table. 'I'd imagined physical jerks were against your religion.'

'Oh, just a few morning knee bends. Nothing too serious or energetic,' he laughed. 'Limber up the old joints eh?'

Lizzie wiped the croissant crumbs from her lips, crumpled the napkin onto a plate, and leaned back against the pergola, eyes fixed on the back of Hartley's head, waiting for a reaction.

'Whatever it is you've done seems to have made a difference,' he said eventually, without turning round to face her. 'Faith healing; isn't that what they call it?'

'Not really,' she replied. 'Faith healing is when the person being healed has a little bit of faith. I, on the other hand, don't have much faith in anything and certainly wouldn't ask it of you.'

'Thank you anyway,' he said. 'But I need to think this one through.'

Lizzie threw a grape at his head. 'Didn't you just tell me it's rude to turn your back on someone when you're talking to them?' she said. 'So how come you haven't got the good manners to turn round and face me?'

He half turned towards her, shrugged his shoulders. 'Sorry,' he whispered. 'Truth is it's a bit of a surprise to be suddenly free of pain after ten years or more. I really don't know what to say.'

'Takes a pain to recognise one,' Yvette said dryly. 'Isn't this, after all, the same Lizzie Beckman who thinks that standing still, doing nothing, wearing even less, is worthy of public applause?'

'And why not sweetie?' Lizzie answered, nibbling at a strawberry, eyelashes fluttering wickedly. 'I do it to for charity and call it fund raising; you do it for a living and call it acting?'

The soft, ripe peach which narrowly missed Lizzie's face, splattered into a mushy pulp across the largest of the terrace windows, then slithered and dripped messily down the latticed panes to the tiled ledge below.

'Not for me thanks sweetie,' Lizzie said with a sarcastic sneer. 'I'll stick with the strawberries; so much more taste and they don't bruise as easily.'

Yvette fiddled uncomfortably with an emerald ring, adjusted it to exactly the right angle, and swaggered haughtily towards the terrace doors. She glared at Hartley across the table, eyes flashing impatiently, ready and waiting to be escorted away.

Hartley took the cue. 'I think it's probably time for us to say goodbye,' he announced with a commanding clap of his hands. 'We'll be off around lunchtime but I'd like to wish you all the very best of luck before we go.' He stepped away from the table and, with a fleeting glance at Lizzie, touched the ground in front of him with the flat of his hands and straightened up in one single, effortless movement. 'Nothing short of a miracle Lizzie,' he called out as he slipped his arm around Yvette's waist and turned to go. 'You're a star.'

Lizzie raised her glass. 'I'll drink to that,' she called after him. 'Stay cool Rupert.'

Bennington poured himself a glass of mineral water

and stood at the end of the terrace, legs astride, one hand behind his back, staring across the lawn while the TV crew packed up their equipment and trundled it back to the house, ready to leave. He checked his watch and turned to the others.

'And so their cards are on the table,' he announced with a wry grin. 'Yvette Duncan has played her ace, blinding Rupert Hartley's king with love and winning the trick in a perfect hand.'

Donny Jackson flicked the ash from his cigarette. 'And what's all that supposed to mean?'

'It means that three people have left Penfold Manor within twenty four hours of the start of the competition,' said Bennington. 'The first told us he was bored with the other guests and the other two say they want to be alone.'

'Right,' said Donny. 'We can safely say they weren't scared off by the so called ghost of Elizabeth Penfold then.'

Bennington raised an eye brow. 'On the contrary. I'd say the sub-conscious mind would invent all sorts of excuses for leaving when confronted with irrational but very real fears.'

Donny smiled uncertainly and stubbed his cigarette into the crystal ashtray. 'What about Lizzie? She reckons the Penfold woman appeared, large as life, in front of her, so why hasn't she come out in a nervous rash, packed her bags and buggered-off?'

'Because she's faced-up to her fears,' Bennington said at once. 'Lizzie's a young lady who needs no excuses.'

'But she's not holding a joker with its eyes poked out, is she?' Donny flicked the card across the table to Lizzie. 'Swap you for your ace of spades,' he murmured.

'Wha-ever,' Lizzie shrugged. 'Makes no difference to me.'

'It makes no difference to either of you,' Bennington agreed. 'You have each been given a card. Handing it to somebody else changes possession but not ownership. It would still be your card.'

'Old Hartley timed it right then,' said Donny. 'Out of the game in a blaze of publicity and no side effects.'

Maggie Keen slid her chair back into the shade of the wisteria and fanned herself with her hat. 'Is it me, or is it getting warmer?' she huffed.

'Weather forecast said it was warming-up,' said Bennington. 'But it'll be cooler down by the lake.'

'Sounds like a good idea,' Maggie drawled. 'But don't imagine I shall be stripping down to a thong for the hidden cameras.'

Lizzie stepped backwards, on to the lawn, and gazed up at the four imposing gables which shaped the rear of the house; rusty red bricks framed in sturdy oak, set like mountain peaks against a blue and cloudless sky.

'Which bit's the east wing?' she asked casually.

Bennington narrowed his eyes against the sun. 'The back of the house enjoys a southerly aspect so you are facing north,' he said. 'And that, of course, places the east wing a little way over to your left.'

'Would it be OK for me to have a wander around?'

'Feel free,' said Bennington. 'But, as I think I mentioned yesterday, you might find it a trifle dusty as nobody goes there.'

'Apart from Elizabeth Penfold,' Lizzie added. 'Hasn't she been seen there from time to time?'

Bennington nodded. 'I believe there have been a number of sightings over the years,' he said, picking up a tray of empty Champagne glasses and quickly disappearing back into the house.

Maggie rang a finger across her brow and stared thoughtfully at Lizzie for a moment. 'Haven't you seen enough of Elizabeth Penfold for one day without going looking for her?' she asked. 'Assuming, of course, that what you think you've seen is, in fact, Elizabeth Penfold.'

'I'm not at all sure what I've seen,' said Lizzie. 'But I think it's time I found out.'

'Why don't we all find out?' said Donny, jumping to

his feet in a sudden wave of enthusiasm. 'Let's face it, there's not much else to do around here.'

'I hope you don't think I'm joining your ghost hunt,' Maggie declared flatly. 'It's far too hot.' She adjusted her sunglasses and very slowly stood up, white caftan floating about her ankles. 'What I really need is a good night's uninterrupted sleep in my big comfy bed at home, alone,' she said with an accusing glance at Donny. 'But there's a game to be won here so I suppose I'll have to settle for forty winks down by the lake.'

A helicopter clackered noisily into view, just above the trees at the end of the lawn, hovered for a moment, and then curved out around the lake towards the front of the house, sending ripples across the water and a pall of dry leaves and dust high into the air.

'Noisy bastards,' Donny yelled. 'Probably come to take the Right Honourable Rupert and his bride-to-be away from all this and off to some exotic venue for lunch with a tabloid newspaper.'

'You're probably right,' said Maggie. 'But it's an odd state of affairs when the guests get more publicity by leaving Penfold Manor than staying. Isn't the winner supposed to be the last one to leave, not the first to get married or just plain bored by it all?'

'Our entire TV audience will probably be bored to death by now,' Donny grunted. 'Think about it for a moment; a haunted house without a ghost. It's about as interesting as the Wimbledon finals without a tennis ball.'

'But I've seen her so why shouldn't the hidden cameras have picked her up too?' Lizzie said indignantly, then turned away and stepped back into the house, closing the terrace doors firmly behind her before he could answer. She stood, alone and quiet, in the cool of the garden room, the rich scent of lilies hanging heavy in the air, a placid trickle of water from a bronze dolphin into a fish pool in the far corner the only sound. Time, she decided, to take matters into her own hands.

A random selection of clothes from Lizzie's wardrobe were tossed carelessly across her bed, one on top of the other, in a small pile; the long, velvet dress with skimpy neckline, a flimsy georgette skirt with coordinating top, her mother's pashmina wrap, a pair of leather gloves and two three quarter sleeve T-shirts with something printed on the back. She hesitated for a moment to admire a satin skirt but then, shrugging off any short-lived feelings of guilt, threw it on the bed with the rest; a rag bag of different styles and fabrics and everything black.

With a pair of nail scissors, half a dozen safety pins, a little ingenuity and rather more patience than came naturally to someone of her restless temperament, Lizzie Beckman set to work creating an outfit befitting an elusive apparition with a penchant for black.

For this was couture for the dark, styled exclusively for the shadows, thrown together to replicate a fleeting figure of the night and most certainly not for the scrutiny of day. She stared at herself in the mirror, head suitably shrouded, mascara smeared thinly around the eyes, gloved hands half hidden in the folds of her skirt, and moved slowly back towards the window.

In the garden below, shaded by the high point of the brick wall, Molly Bennington wore a blue striped apron, a pair of secateurs in her hand, freshly cut white roses in a bucket at her feet. She leant forward, clipped the leafy fronds from a cluster of fern then slowly straightened-up, one hand pressed firmly into the small of her back. Somebody called to her from the house; a man's voice, slightly snappy, bad tempered. Mrs Bennington glanced up towards Lizzie's bedroom window, hesitated for only a second, then went back inside.

Lizzie quickly undressed, folded her new black creation neatly into a draw, and stood in front of the bathroom mirror, examining her face. A brand new line, short, straight and slightly right of centre, had appeared on her forehead, just above her nose. Now there were three of them; worry lines, Porky called them, the 'Mark of Sorrow'.

A long soak in a cool, scented bath helped to change the mood of the morning then, face on, hair teased, she dressed herself in white, pure and unblemished; canvas pumps, a lacy, layered skirt topped by a T-shirt, tight as a second skin, which made no attempt to hide a slim, size eight, sun-tanned midriff.

As far as Lizzie was concerned, police cars and ambulances made pretty much the same ear-piercing and totally unnecessary din, so the sudden sound of wailing sirens at the front of the house could have been either one of them, perhaps both. But the noise had faded into the distance by the time she reached the terrace.

The table, resplendent with two marble vases of white roses, had already been laid for lunch; just two place settings, one either end.

Lizzie stood uncertainly on the steps, looking out over to the lake and Maggie's hat, wrong way up on a red tartan blanket stretched out across a grassy bank below the willow, her book laying, open, a few feet away on the lawn, everything perfectly still and quiet. She felt suddenly alone and vulnerable, like a child, centre stage in a play without a script, performed for an invisible audience by an ever dwindling cast.

The silence was shattered by the clackety click of Maggie's heels across the mosaic floor of the garden room. She stepped out on to the terrace, stood for a moment in quiet contemplation, then took a deep breath as if she'd surfaced from the bottom of a deep pool.

'Donny's been taken to hospital; broken leg,' she said brusquely.

Lizzie frowned in disbelief. 'How on earth did he manage that?'

Maggie shook her head, eyes closed to heaven. 'They say he tripped,' she sighed. 'Fell down some service stairs.'

'From the beginning, please.' Lizzie pulled two chunky,

green wicker chairs together for them to sit and waited for Maggie to settle herself.
'Apparently Donny asked Mrs Bennington to take him over to the east wing. He thought that's where you'd gone.' Maggie hesitated, fingers gently massaging the side of her head as if she might be trying to make up her mind about something. 'I suppose he could quite simply have tripped on his jeans,' she said at last. 'All that ridiculous frayed denim hanging round his ankles.'
'Was Mrs Bennington with him? I mean, did she see him fall?'
Maggie shook her head. 'She says she was already on her way back to the main house. But she heard him cry out.'
'Poor old Donny,' said Lizzie, trying hard to suppress an involuntary giggle. 'But I'd say he most likely tripped on his pony tail.'
Maggie stared back, unsmiling. 'I really don't think a broken leg's a laughing matter, especially when he might have been pushed.'
'Pushed?' Lizzie squealed. 'Is that what he said?'
'Not exactly. He was obviously in a lot of pain by the time they got him into the ambulance, but he said something about seeing your bloody woman in black at the top of the stairs.'
'Correction. That's exactly what he said.' Mrs Bennington, stony faced and adamant, appeared suddenly with a basket of bread rolls and placed them on the table. 'And why not? I saw her myself only twenty minutes earlier….. up at your bedroom window,' she said, turning to Lizzie.
Lizzie tried to look surprised. 'Are you quite sure?' she asked, relaxing coolly back in her chair, hands clasped behind her head, eyes only half open. 'It seems unlikely as I was there myself at around that time and saw absolutely nothing.'
'Perhaps you should have looked in the mirror then?'

Mrs Bennington snapped. 'This was no spiritual apparition, it was you.'

Lizzie felt her face redden. 'But you said you'd seen the woman in black.'

'So I did.' Mrs Bennington resolutely tightened the strings of her apron and fixed Lizzie with an icy stare. 'Only this one had blue eyes, red lipstick, and a bit of telltale blonde hair showing under her shawl. Sound like anyone we know?'

'Mystery solved then,' Lizzie declared flatly. 'You must have seen me trying on some of the latest fashions from the Beckman organisation of London's Margaret Street; designed to turn men's heads and, it seems, busy-body old ladies' minds too.'

Molly Bennington stood perfectly still, hands clasped together in a matronly pose. 'I'd say they were designed to deceive; put together to create your own lady in black.'

'To be honest, I'd thought about it,' said Lizzie. 'But I most certainly didn't push Donny Jackson down the stairs.'

'Of course you didn't, darling.' Maggie reached for Lizzie's hand and gave it a comforting squeeze. 'Besides millions of viewers would have seen you on TV so they'd have you under lock and key by now.'

'But there's something else,' said Molly Bennington with a hint of menace in her voice. 'I found this at the bottom of the stairs.' She took a playing card from her apron pocket and handed it to Maggie then went back into the house, leaving the other woman staring blankly at the queen of diamonds and the inky puncture marks.

'Like the other two,' she said, swallowing hard. 'Unseeing eyes. Death; isn't that what Bennington told us?'

'Well he was wrong,' Lizzie insisted. 'Rupert fell head-over-heels in love and Donny tripped arse-over-tip down the stairs.'

'But a broken leg, or worse; it wouldn't do much for my forthcoming tour.'

'Then stay away from the service stairs in the east wing.'

Maggie managed a weak smile. 'I can't help thinking that boring little comic had the right idea,' she said wistfully. 'Out of here on day one and back to the real world. Didn't even stay the night, did he?'

'Then why not simply pack your bags and go?' Lizzie mumbled through a stifled yawn, trying to disguise her natural enthusiasm for the suggestion. 'What's to stop you getting the hell out of this awful place right now?'

'Just you Lizzie,' Maggie answered without hesitation. 'Better get used to the idea, darling. I intend be the last to leave Penfold Manor. And that's a promise.'

Chapter 5

The pearl buttons on a garish shirt, silver with gold polka dots, struggled to hold back the folds of pale, pudgy flesh which hung like blancmange from Arthur Wheatley's belly. But this was a paunch with personality and purpose, excess fat worth its weight in gold; one million pounds worth to be precise.

Toby Stone's young assistant brushed curly red hair from her face and handed-out copies of the insurance certificate to the waiting reporters.

It was all there, in black and white; Arthur 'Chubby' Wheatley, up-and-coming comedian, had insured his stomach for a cool million, more than half a century after glamorous film legend Betty Grable had done much the same thing for her famous Hollywood legs, to an international fanfare of publicity.

Chubby Wheatley, both hands grasping his ample bum, thrust his belly forward for the photographers.

'It took more than twenty thousand pints to create this beer belly,' he called out proudly. 'That's over three pints a day for twenty years. Can't have it disappearing on me now, can we?

The 'Million Pound Paunch' publicity stunt was going well and, while it wasn't quite in the same celebrity league as Betty Grable's gams, it looked like grabbing some well-earned column inches for the overweight comedian in the following day's tabloids.

But Toby Stone's mind was on other things. He dabbed his brow with a crisp white handkerchief, checked his watch and, brushing aside demands from a handful of photographers for pictures of the swollen belly, in the flesh, without a shirt, left his assistant to bring the press call to a close.

He settled back in the taxi and stared out at a sea of overweight shoppers; a waddling, wobbling mass of surplus lard which strained the seams of skin-tight clothes and stretched fabrics to their elasticated limits, like bulging sacks of prime potatoes. Here, parading before him, was obesity to challenge even Chubby Wheatley's claim to a heavyweight celebrity stomach. But this flab wasn't in the same class; this was everyday, eat-too-much, amateur fat in need of a magical PR gimmick – like a million pound insurance policy, costing less than the price of a dinner for two at San Lorenzo – to transform it into the famous flesh of celebrity news.

He closed his eyes to the stark reality of outsize Oxford Street and allowed his thoughts to wander off to a haunted house in Sussex where Lizzie Beckman was in need of some PR magic of her own.

A less than flattering picture of Rupert Hartley, cheek-to-cheek with Yvette Duncan, wide-eyed and glossy-lipped, had appeared in a tabloid newspaper under the sensationalised headline 'MP and Actress in Haunted House Sex Romp', and there were a few lines about Harry Hale's fake heart attack in the evening paper a day or so earlier. But Lizzie Beckman and her talk of ghostly visions had largely been ignored, apart from an ungenerous suggestion by a cynical newspaper hack that the appearance of the mysterious lady in black might owe more to the Champagne than the supernatural. And, anyway, ten million viewers, whose numbers were reported to be dwindling, had yet to see anything even remotely spooky on their TV screens so, perhaps, she was slightly more sozzled than psychic.

Toby Stone didn't like that; he didn't like it at all. Drink, drugs and rock 'n roll were strictly taboo to Lizzie Beckman's carefully crafted PR profile. Not so much as a quick puff on a filter tip was meant to come between Lizzie and the happy, wholesome, healthy image he'd created when he linked her name with a light-hearted Doing Nothing project to raise money for charity.

But sozzled was a dangerous and damaging description which could quickly tarnish the reputation and block the path to future wealth. For it's an elementary PR principle that the pursuit of fame for fame's sake, without rich rewards, is the business of fools. Fame & Fortune; a prize partnership, bound together like crime & punishment, comedy & laughter, dirt & disease; one the most likely consequence of the other. And fortune most willingly follows fame when the famous lend their names to the predatory world of commercialism. Product endorsement; the effortless route to riches..... but only if the celebrity image fits.

The taxi jerked to a halt outside the lingerie shop in Beauchamp Place, seven pounds fifty on the clock. Toby Stone took a ten pound note from his wallet, waved-away the change, and paused at the kerbside, the sudden smell of garlic from the Italian restaurant two doors along tempting him in the direction of a plate of spaghetti and a glass or two of wine.

The fleeting but still vivid picture of Chubby Wheatley's high-profile belly decided him against the idea and sent him quickly up stairs, two at a time, to his first floor office and a cup of non-fattening, black coffee.

An ordnance survey map, instantly downloaded from the internet, gave the geographical low-down on a small but highly specific area of west Sussex countryside and suggested that, all things being equal, Toby Stone's outline plans for a publicity coup at Penfold Manor had more than a fair chance of success. And, like Lizzie wearing Beckman fashions on reality TV, this was a perfect two-for-the-price-of-one PR deal.

The call to Pandik Personal Security, a relatively new client, was brief and to the point. Yes, it could be done and yes, PPS was prepared to do it... tonight, if that was the brief.

Toby Stone stretched out in the red leather chair and swivelled it around to face the window as the afternoon sun slipped behind the tiled roof tops opposite, sending Beauchamp Place into shadow. He permitted himself a wry grin, thinking about all the time and money spent dreaming up company names for fledgling businesses who instantly abbreviated them to just two or three meaningless initials.

Reasonable people, untouched by the alien world of corporate advertising and promotion, could be forgiven for thinking the letters PPS meant Post Postscript, blissfully unaware that they might also stand for something else; something totally different, like Pandik Personal Security, for example. But, for reasons which defy simple logic, the directors insisted on the company being known as PPS, reluctantly disclosing their full corporate title only when someone bothered to ask. Then, and only then, would a PPS executive explain that Pandik is the reverse of Kidnap, and wasn't Pandik Personal Security a great name for a company in the business of guarding against kidnap and other security risks?

Toby blamed it on the lazy, listless language of the USA with its NYPD, CIA and FBI, not to mention MGM, CNN and TNT. And why some of its presidents had allowed their names to be pruned back to LBJ, JFK or GW, was beyond him. But Great Britain deserved an ASBO from the CPS for allowing itself to become GB or, worse, the UK and signing-up to a trend in which political parties could be reduced to a meaningless BNP or the quaintly condensed Lib Dems.

A computer on the other side of the room beckoned, the initials IBM shimmering in silver on the front. Toby quickly checked his last PPS press statement, the one which offered ten tips to avoid tragedy in case of kidnap, and re-read the bit about remaining totally calm.

In less than five hours, two covert PPS operatives would enter the Penfold Manor estate from the southern boundary, make their way across open farmland towards the lake and then quickly cross the main gardens to the rear of the house where they would decide on which of two options would offer the best chance of success in an audacious plan to snatch Lizzie Beckman from the premises.

It would be a slick PR exercise to demonstrate Pandik's much vaunted hostage release capability. OK, their clients were usually major corporations with senior executives held by Cambodian bandits, and Lizzie wasn't strictly a hostage but, to all intents and purposes, she was confined to the grounds of Penfold Manor so it was the next best thing. And as Operation Bizzy Lizzy would be performed in the full gaze of national television, it had to be fast, efficient and highly professional. Above all, it needed a touch of drama to capture the media imagination.

Then, after the daring details had been released to the press, Lizzie would take centre stage to talk about the ghost of Penfold Manor, setting the record straight about whether the lady in black had been conjured-up by supernatural powers or a glass or two of Moet & Chandon. Toby Stone had already arranged an exclusive interview for Lizzie with the Daily Mail.

Shortly after nine, when a pale, misty moon disappeared behind gathering clouds, it started to rain; light drizzle at first, followed by heavier downpours with, what the weather forecasters called, intermittent gusting but which sounded like a force nine gale. It didn't stop until well after midnight when Lizzie Beckman was delivered, like a parcel from Harrods, to the front door of number 13 Oakley Street.

Two shadowy figures who'd been standing immediately behind her, one either side, silent and expressionless, stepped back into the shadows and then quickly roared-off on motor bikes into the chill, wet night, avoiding further recriminations from their outraged passenger.

Lizzie wasn't wearing shoes. Head bowed, hair dripping, hands clasped meekly in front of her, she stared down in silence at mud-caked feet as if to emphasise her sorry plight. A white, cotton dress, clinging to her body like random sheets of wet tissue, left little to the imagination; no bra, no pants.

Toby threw the door open wider. 'Sorry I wasn't able to warn you my sweet,' he said, reaching out to the sad, soaked figure on the doorstep. 'There really wasn't any other way.'

She pushed him resolutely aside with a sharp jab to the shoulder, looking past him down the hallway as she tore the dress from her body and threw it to the floor like a discarded dishcloth.

Toby managed to check an involuntary smile as she marched, naked but purposeful, to the bathroom, slammed the door behind her and slid the latch.

'Can I get you anything?' he called out. 'Hot chocolate, hot toddy, that sort of thing?'

He fancied he heard faint mutterings during the next half an hour; short, sharp outbursts, nothing distinct or recognisable but with a definite hint of hostility.

It was past one o'clock when Lizzie finally reappeared, swathed in towels and smelling of Toby's favourite cologne. 'Scotch,' she said tersely before flopping down on the cream leather couch. 'Make it a very large one, no ice, and make it now.'

'Anything to eat?'

'Scrambled eggs; three. One piece of brown toast.' She

looked into his eyes for the first time that evening, her mouth locked in a fake smile which didn't involve the rest of her face. 'Then, Toby my darling,' she whispered politely, 'you can go fuck yourself.'

Toby refused to rise to the bait. 'We'll discuss things when I've made you a stiff drink and something to eat,' he said, hoping to pacify her. 'I need to explain the revised PR strategy.'

'PR strategy?' Lizzie repeated, hurling a copy of Vogue magazine after him as he made towards the kitchen. 'You send two thugs to get me out of bed in the middle of the night, drag me across muddy fields wearing next to nothing, sit me on the back of an over-powered motorbike and race me across three counties in the worst weather we've had this year. Do you call that a PR strategy?'

'Black pepper on the eggs?' Toby called out, ignoring the jibe. 'Or would you prefer Worcester sauce?'

'Wha-ever.'

Three scrambled eggs, served in silence with Worcester sauce, were quietly eaten and no more was said until Lizzie had returned her plate to the kitchen and re-filled her glass on the way back.

Toby stood in front of the window, feet well apart, hands behind his back, staring out across the dimly lit street. 'Let me try to explain about this evening,' he said quietly and as calmly as he could manage.

'Why do you always do that?' Lizzie asked.

Toby turned to her with a puzzled frown.

'You stare out of the window,' she sneered. 'Whenever you are about to make some sort of smart-arse comment about me, you stare out of the window.'

'I hadn't noticed. Perhaps I do it because I don't want to see that impatient scowl on your face whenever I take the trouble to explain things.'

Lizzie slipped a cushion behind her head and stretched out on the couch. 'Well you just carry on and I'll lay here placidly with a patient smile on my face until you've quite finished,' she said, forcing the words through tightly clenched teeth.

'OK, here it is then.' Toby pushed her feet unceremoniously to one side and perched on the edge of the couch beside her. 'The haunted house thing wasn't working for you so I decided to call a halt. It wasn't an easy decision but it was the right one. End of story.'

Lizzie shook her head in disbelief. 'Correct me if I'm wrong,' she sighed, 'but wasn't the winner meant to be the last of six people to leave the house? And wasn't I one of only two people still there before you dragged me out of the place?'

Toby nodded. 'But it wasn't that simple.'

'Two minus one equals one,' Lizzie snapped back. 'And I could have been that last one. Sounds pretty simple to me.'

Toby rose slowly to his feet and turned towards the window.

'Oh, here we go,' Lizzie called out, her voice beginning to tremble with rage. 'Here comes the smart-arse comment.'

He stood perfectly still for a moment, considering his words carefully before he spoke. 'Did you really see her?' he asked. 'Elizabeth Penfold I mean.'

'As plain as I can see you, only she had the decency to look me in the eye.'

'I thought you were faking it, simply going along with the ghost story to upset the others, the way we discussed.'

'There was no need to fake anything. I saw her.'

'Unfortunately,' said Toby, pouring himself a large whisky, 'one or two hacks were saying you were probably pissed at the time.'

'Me...pissed?'

'Exactly Lizzie. And that's why I had to call a halt.' He emptied his glass and placed it on the side table, next to hers. 'We may not have won a reality TV show but at least we're back in control of the publicity machine.'

Lizzie glanced up at the clock on the bookshelf; one

twenty, or it might have been five past four. She wasn't sure; both hands looked pretty much the same from where she was laying and, apart from the fact that she couldn't be bothered to move her head, it was much too late in the day to worry about the time.

'And how is the good old publicity machine these days?' she asked disdainfully through a stifled yawn. 'So far it seems to have been about doing nothing and wearing nothing. And when I'm sent off to actually do something, I get dragged back here to do nothing again; which all seems to add up to a great big nothing.'

Toby wasn't in the mood for an argument. He stared at her in silence for a moment and decided he wasn't even prepared to enter into a mild-mannered discussion. In fact, all things being equal, he didn't want to talk at all; not a word.

'Bedtime,' he announced dryly. 'We'll discuss PR strategy in the morning, before the press conference.'

Lizzie raised herself lethargically on one elbow. 'And what press conference would that be then?' she groaned.

'Ten o'clock tomorrow morning. We're going to set the record straight about Penfold Manor.' He leaned forward, preparing to pick her up. 'But right now we're going to bed,' he said.

Lizzie remained perfectly still, unmoving and uncooperative, arms rigidly by her side, while he struggled to lift her from the couch.

'On second thoughts,' he sighed after his second unsuccessful attempt, 'you can find your own bloody way to bed.'

She felt herself sink back into the rich cream leather of the couch as he slowly straightened up and turned away, towards the door, a disgruntled look on his face.

'You give up easily,' she called after him as he left the room.

'Always,' he answered. 'I don't have time for games.'

Lizzie peered over the back of the couch but he'd

already reached the bedroom and closed the door, quietly, behind him, turning off the lights in the hallway as he passed. She tossed a cushion across the room at his photograph which stared down at her from a silver frame on one of the book shelves. The cushion fell lightly to the floor but the framed face was unmoved, the smile perhaps even more smug and self-assured than before; triumphant even.

'Bloody bastard.' The words seeped slowly into the silence of the room as she wriggled free of the couch and swung her feet, wearily, to the floor. 'Complete arsehole,' she muttered, on the way to the bathroom to swap an uncomfortably damp bath towel for Toby's black velvet dressing gown she'd seen hanging behind the door. But it wasn't, and she'd already consigned the bath towel to a large wicker basket in the corner of the room when she turned to face the figure silhouetted in the doorway.

'Enough games for one evening don't you think?' Toby whispered. 'Now if you'd like to place your arms around my neck and lend a hand, I'll have another bash at carrying you off to bed.'

Lizzie Beckman, wearing nothing more than a smug smile, had a self-assured look about her; triumphant even.

An angry alarm clock rang out impatiently at half past seven, bringing a few snatched hours of sleep to an abrupt halt and the morning sunshine sharply into focus from somewhere in the centre of a frenzied muddle of navy blue sheets.

Toby Stone's eyelids quivered grudgingly into life while he stretched a listless arm across the bed to a stray pillow. He plumped it up, placed it lazily behind his head in one easy movement and waited, unmoving, for the first, faint trickles of energy to filter through to the rest of his body. Beside him, eyes shut tight against the day, long, blonde hair fanned out across her pillow, Lizzie tugged at the tangle of bed clothes and snuggled herself into an even tighter ball.

The tips of his fingers gently traced the line of her shoulder, down the smooth, suntanned back and across the delicate contour of her belly to the curve of her waist.

'I'm still asleep,' she moaned. 'Wake me up tomorrow.'

Toby's hand found the cheek of her bottom and squeezed. 'It's already tomorrow and time we were out and about,' he said sitting bolt upright in the bed.

She turned wearily towards him, eyes slowly blinking into focus. 'But I've got nothing to wear. I lost my clothes in a haunted house.'

'That's not a problem with Kings Road just around the corner.' Toby quickly unravelled her from the sheets, draped her effortlessly over his shoulder and carried her, yawning and protesting, into the bathroom. 'I'll cook breakfast while you sort out your hair, then I'll get you something suitable to wear for a press conference,' he said, setting her down in front of the bathroom mirror like a rag doll.

The taxi which delivered the white Rock & Republic jeans with coordinating cotton top and white calf leather boots shortly after nine, waited outside the flat while Lizzie dressed, then set off in the direction of Sloane Street.

Lizzie wriggled irritably in the back of the cab. She was, of course, grateful to the girl who'd kindly sent round the fashionably white outfit from her up-market Chelsea shop; but wearing someone else's knickers just didn't feel right.

Unfortunately the shop didn't sell underwear, Toby explained for the third time, so it was very thoughtful of her to send some of her own. And besides the briefer style in panties ensured that you didn't see a knicker line through the jeans.

'That's only because the knicker line disappears up your bum,' Lizzie protested.

'But you wouldn't want coarse denim chaffing your

more delicate parts now, would you,' Toby said in his lofty I've-got-more-important things-on-my-mind voice, insisting it was time to forget about knickers and concentrate on the media briefing in less than an hour's time.

The taxi came to a halt in front of the hotel's revolving doors and Toby led the way to the first floor conference room where his assistant, mobile 'phone pressed firmly against her ear, did what she could to transform a very ordinary baize covered table into a make-shift reception desk close to the open doorway; press statements stacked in a neat pile to one side, in front of the telephone, a signing-in book placed strategically in the middle.

She gave Toby a hasty smile before zigzagging her way through the chairs, arranged in rows like a small theatre, towards a second baize covered table and two chairs at the far end of the room, overlooking Cadogan Square; the informal setting for a punchy media announcement, to be quickly followed by a series of questions and answers.

By ten, when coffee was served, the room was already bustling with reporters and photographers and Toby was able to delete the first of the morning's potential disasters from his mind. For it's an irrefutable fact that the media is a fickle and faithless hunter which stalks and devours only the strongest news of the day, avoiding weak, unappetising morsels of spin and totally rejecting regurgitated puff. But, this morning, Toby Stone's offering was very much on the menu and, it seemed, one of the chosen news dishes of the day.

He rattled a spoon in a coffee cup and a call for quiet rang out across the room. 'Thank you for coming,' he said, seating himself close to Lizzie Beckman at the far table, face-to-face with his media audience. 'I hope our press statement explains Lizzie's premature departure from Penfold Manor last evening but I'd like to add a few comments before we move on to questions and answers.'

Toby glanced down at his notes and cleared his throat. 'Lizzie Beckman is adamant that the ghostly figure she encountered at Penfold Manor was neither an illusion nor a figment of her imagination. And it was most certainly not, as someone has unkindly suggested, an hallucination inspired by Champagne.'

He paused briefly to check the sea of faces for reactions and placed a reassuring hand on Lizzie's shoulder. 'While she at no time felt threatened by the apparition she was, nevertheless, justifiably concerned that whatever it was seemed to have singled her out from the others.'

Lizzie felt, quite suddenly, hot and more than a little drowsy. Probably the sun on her back through the large plate glass window, she told herself, or maybe just the tension of the morning, after an energetic and sleepless night. She reached for the mineral water, hands damp with perspiration, and decided it was more likely to be the onset of pneumonia after a wet and windy motor bike ride in the rain.

Somebody's mobile phone jangled to life with a thin, metallic performance of the 1812 Overture, quickly answered by a newspaper reporter who managed a weak, apologetic wave before hurriedly leaving the room. Two other calls, in rapid succession, sent a TV crew and a news agency photographer in the same direction. Somebody said something about a bomb scare in Whitehall and the second potential disaster of the day reared its ugly head; a more important news story, and just such a story was apparently 'breaking' in the heart of London.

But Toby continued, undaunted. 'The last point I'd like to make,' he said importantly, 'is that it wasn't Lizzie Beckman's idea to leave Penfold Manor last evening. Indeed I know she'd have carried on regardless, which is why I called in the experts from Pandik to free her from the premises.'

There was a brief moment of silence before the first question was lobbed, like a grenade, from the opposite end of the room, and exploded in Toby Stone's lap. Had Lizzie Beckman pushed Donny Jackson down the service stairs at

Penfold Manor, the tall, thin gentleman from The Mirror wanted to know. 'And wasn't that the real reason for her hurried exit?'

A hostile reporter, the third potential disaster of the day, stared at Toby through horn-rimmed glasses. 'Absolutely not,' he snapped back. 'Lizzie was in her room at the time of the accident and the decision to bring her home was entirely mine.'

The man from The Mirror rose to his feet. 'But isn't it true that Mr Jackson saw a woman in black before he fell and wasn't Miss Beckman seen, dressed totally in black, at approximately the same time?'

Toby hadn't anticipated quite such an aggressive line of questioning. 'That's probably true,' he said, forcing a smile. 'But the two facts are clearly unconnected.' He glanced quickly around the room, looking for someone with a new question to change the subject, but the attack continued.

'Mr Jackson believes he was pushed,' the reporter insisted. 'And he has multiple fractures of the leg to prove it.'

'But he doesn't.' Lizzie's words, confident and commanding, brought a sudden silence to the room. 'There's nothing wrong with his leg,' she announced with supreme confidence, as if she'd been privy to Donny Jackson's medical records.

Toby's face froze. His heart missed several beats as he glanced sideways at the new and totally unique disaster sitting on his right – a client who appeared to have lost her mind.

'I think Lizzie means she's totally confident he'll make a swift recovery,' he suggested half-heartedly, by way of explanation.

But Lizzie was resolute. 'There's absolutely nothing wrong with his leg,' she repeated. 'The plaster can come off right away.'

A woman with tightly permed hair stepped forward

from somewhere near the front. 'Are you saying his leg wasn't fractured and the X-rays were wrong?' she asked, waving her microphone at arm's length across the table.

'I've no doubt the X-rays *were* right,' Lizzie answered. 'But that was then and this is now.'

'You mean the fractures have healed?'

'That's exactly what I mean.'

'Healed completely, in just a few days?'

'Not days, minutes,' Lizzie declared flatly. 'In the past few minutes, to be precise.'

And this was also the precise moment that the ultimate in PR disasters gate-crashed Toby Stone's press briefing; a decisive instant in time when a negative news angle barges in, uninvited, and throws the positive story out of the nearest window.

Lizzie posed and pouted, cameras flashed and Toby knew he'd lost control of his own press briefing. Like a wild animal released from a cage, Lizzie's words rampaged around the room with bared teeth, tearing Toby's carefully-worded press statement into tiny shreds, devouring the planned, intended story in a single bite.

But when someone says something senseless and silly, there's no shame in trying to spin it back into perfect sense; governments do it all the time in a world where unpleasant facts are never allowed to tarnish the countless tales of political fiction which masquerade as progress.

The TV lights dimmed in an instant, microphones were switched off, and photographers replaced the lens covers on their cameras as the media audience began to slowly filter out of the room and on to the hotel landing.

'Perhaps we should wait to see the latest X-rays of the leg before we jump to any conclusions about Lizzie's comments,' Toby suggested to a hard core of reporters and photographers whose mobile 'phones were already buzzing with the words and pictures of the day.

One or two of them nodded, others smiled and shook their heads but most seemed happy with the story they'd already got and ignored him completely. Someone asked if he seriously believed multiple fractures could have healed in a couple of days.

Toby didn't bother to answer; he knew how it looked to the jaundiced eye of a newspaper reporter. Wannabe celebrity in reality TV show pushes fellow contestant down stairs. Fellow contestant breaks his leg in the fall. Wannabe denies everything. Says she didn't push him down the stairs then claims the leg was good as new in two days.

'Dizzy Lizzie's Bone of Contention'. Toby could already see the headlines. Something had to be done.

He waited until the last of the stragglers had gone before making the call to Donny Jackson's agent who was happy to pass on a message but refused to divulge client telephone numbers. He'd arrange for his client to call back but wasn't sure when that might be.

Toby slumped back in the chair and watched, in silence, while Lizzie brushed her eye lashes in front of a large gilt framed mirror.

'How do you think it went?' she asked casually. 'Everyone seemed happy with the pictures.'

'It was, as we say in the PR world, a complete bloody disaster.'

Lizzie turned around slowly, apparently unconcerned and faintly disinterested. 'Disaster?' she repeated. 'In what possible way was it a disaster?'

'In a crackpot-comment-about-broken-bones sort of a way.'

Lizzie shrugged her shoulders defiantly. 'I only told them what happened, that's all.'

'And what was that then?' Toby snorted.

Her face went pale. 'Donny's leg was mended,' she insisted. 'Healed if you like.' She turned back towards the mirror and set to work with a lip brush.

'How the hell do you know that?

Lizzie hesitated for a moment, looking slightly

flustered. 'I felt it; like a surge of energy running through me and then the heat, lots of heat.'

'Silly, silly girl,' Toby snapped. 'I warned you before. Only one celebrity healer's made the headlines in the past two thousand years. They crucified him and they'll crucify you too.'

'But it's not up to me; it just happens.' She seemed suddenly vulnerable and unsure, her words clipped and brittle, more of an apology than an explanation.

Toby felt a faint ripple of remorse and very slightly guilty. 'It'll be OK,' he reassured her at once. 'But we need a new X-ray to prove you were right.'

Her handbag snapped shut like a sprung trap. 'I already know I'm right,' she said, making towards the door. 'Catch you later.'

Toby rubbed his eyes wearily. 'I'll be at the flat around six.'

'Not tonight,' she called out, without bothering to look back. 'I've got important stuff to sort out with Porky.'

It was well into the afternoon when Donny Jackson finally called Toby's mobile 'phone. The conversation was brief and to the point. Yes, he was aware that Toby was Lizzie Beckman's publicist. No, he wouldn't agree to another X-ray of his injured leg. Why? Because he'd just had one – arranged and paid for by the BBC. And, yes, it showed that both the tibia and fibula fractures had inexplicably healed. But it was none of Lizzie Beckman's damned business.

'Tell her to keep her nose out of it,' he ranted. 'The condition of my leg owes more to doctors, nurses and medical care than Lizzie Beckman's bullshit.'

Toby listened in silence until he'd finished then, quietly and calmly, repeated what Lizzie had told the reporters. 'She simply said your leg had healed,' he explained. 'Nothing more.'

But Donny Jackson was not easily placated. 'BBC TV tells a different story,' he insisted. 'They say she talked about taking just a few lousy minutes to fix my leg.'

'You'll have to make your own mind up about that,' Toby replied, trying to bring the conversation to a close. 'Fact is your bones seem to have mended in record time, so perhaps you should be pleased rather than angry.'

'Screw you,' Donny Jackson yelled before the 'phone went dead.

'And screw you too,' Toby whispered to a silent, empty room. 'In fact, screw the whole bloody lot of you.'

Chapter 6

The front door of the Bayswater flat opened wide before Barry Gammon could slide his key into the lock. Lizzie Beckman, wearing one of his favourite blue striped Turnbull & Asser shirts and a big smile, but very little else, stepped smartly forward and kissed him on both cheeks before disappearing back into the kitchen from where an appetising smell of fried onions permeated the hallway.

'Steak au Poive,' she called out. 'Your favourite, but without the shallots I'm afraid.'

Porky had barely loosened his tie and slipped off his jacket when she returned with a glass of Glenfiddich, just a dash of soda, and no ice.

'Hope it's not too strong,' she cooed, then quickly waved him into the lounge. 'You know I'm not very good at fixing drinks.'

She tripped girlishly ahead of him, pumped-up the cushion on the couch, and gestured for him to sit beside her, in front of the TV.

Porky was bewildered. He carefully placed his drink on a side table and took her hand affectionately. 'What's going on?' he asked in a hushed voice. 'And where in God's name have you been?'

'But you must have seen my note?' she said, swinging her legs onto his lap. 'I've been appearing in a reality TV show.'

Porky frowned. 'Disappearing from it too, by all accounts.'

She reached for the remote. 'That was Toby's idea,' she shrugged. 'I had no say in the matter. They just turned-up and took me away.'

Porky looked deep into her eyes. 'And is that where you've been, with Toby?'

Lizzie shook her head. 'It wasn't like that.' She pointed the remote at the TV screen and began flicking through the channels. 'We explained it all to the press this morning.'

'Oh, well that's OK then,' Porky answered with a tight smile and a touch of sarcasm. 'Just so long as the press knows what's happening, everything's fine. No need to concern yourself about me.'

Lizzie slapped the remote into his hand. 'See if you can find the six o'clock news,' she sighed. 'I've got to check on something in the kitchen.'

But Porky wasn't in the mood for taking orders and slowly squeezed the 'off' button with an impassioned, relentless determination until all signs of life had finally faded from the screen. Then he relaxed his grip, reached for his drink and settled back in blissful but short-lived, silence.

'What's happened to the TV?' Lizzie called out. 'I can't hear anything in here.'

'That's because I've throttled the damn thing,' Porky answered.

Lizzie's poked her head around the door, the rest of her still seemingly committed to the kitchen, her eyes fixed on the blank TV screen. 'Six o'clock news…..It's on now.'

Porky glanced casually at his watch. 'Yes, I suppose it would be, it being ten minutes past six.'

'But I could be on it,' Lizzie protested, grabbing hold of

the remote and clicking the TV back into life. She flopped down and sprawled out across the couch.

'You're not wearing knickers,' said Porky with a sideways glance at the ungainly figure beside him.

She didn't bother to answer but, instead, raised a finger to her mouth and shushed for quiet as she turned-up the volume for the early evening news.

'And later in the programme,' said the announcer... 'Miracle cure?... We take a look at the broken bones which mended in a matter of moments.' They showed a fleeting picture of a leg in a plaster cast and then moved quickly on to the main news of the day.

'That's it,' Lizzie screamed excitedly as she rearranged herself into a comfortable ball, arms folded tightly across her breasts, feet tucked under. 'Donny's leg. They're going to show it.'

'Donny's leg?' Porky repeated. 'What's it got to do with you?'

Lizzie flashed a spark of mild irritation. 'You'll see, you'll see,' she said. 'In a moment.'

'Have you taken-up nursing?' Porky asked uncertainly.

'No, I've taken-up healing,' she said, eyes still focussed on the television. 'I make people better.'

Porky swallowed the remains of his whisky and handed her the empty glass. 'I'd feel a lot better with another one of those,' he said. 'A very large one.'

She took the glass and placed it on the table beside her. 'I said I'm a healer, not a magician. I don't do water into wine or conjure-up double Scotches from thin air.'

'You could always try the Glenfiddich bottle,' he shrugged. 'That always seems to work.' He bent forward, untied the laces of his best black brogue shoes and gently eased them off then settled back, legs stretched out in front of him.

The telephone warbled inconveniently for attention from the other side of the room at the same moment as the television reporter appeared on the TV screen, microphone in hand, face suitably solemn. She was standing outside a London hospital.

'It was just a few days ago that DJ and TV presenter Donny Jackson was admitted to this hospital with multiple fractures of the left leg...,' she announced in the flat, lifeless mono-tones to which many television reporters seem to aspire.

'But today,' she went on, pointing to the building behind her, 'there's been talk of a miracle recovery, right here at...'

The words faded into the background as Porky answered the telephone.

'It's Toby Stone,' said the voice. 'Is Lizzie there?'

Porky cleared his throat. 'Why?' he asked abruptly.

'Could you give her a message?'

'I suppose so.'

'Tell her to switch on the TV... BBC news... on now.'

'She's already watching it.'

'Perhaps you'd ask her to call my mobile.'

'Perhaps,' Porky said, managing to make the word sound like an insult, before he slammed down the 'phone. He paused for a moment, surprised at his own impudence, unsure of his feelings, then turned back towards the television in time for a close-up of Lizzie.

'There's absolutely nothing wrong with his leg,' she was confidently explaining to a group of reporters. 'The plaster can come off right away.'

But the slim, vulnerable figure in a man's shirt, curled-up self-consciously on the couch, seemed surprisingly detached from the slightly arrogant, posturing woman on the TV screen. Lizzie stared blankly at her alter ego, unmoved, expressionless, until the news item finally drew to a close with a liberal sprinkling of words like miracle, magical and unexplained.

'Who was that on the 'phone?' Lizzie asked.

'It was your Svengali,' said Porky. 'But, more importantly, who was that woman on TV pretending to be Lizzie Beckman?'

'That was the *real* Lizzie Beckman. It's me over here, the one with no knickers, who's the fake.'

Porky wandered slowly across the room to the couch and stood immediately in front of her, hands in pockets, legs wide apart, obscuring the television. 'Do you think you might have a bash at translating that into English for me?' he said quietly. 'I want to be sure I understand what's happening here.'

She raised her head slowly, carefully avoiding eye contact, searching for the right words but failing miserably. 'I'm not sure I understand it all myself,' she answered at last. 'Everything's in a bit of a bugger's muddle right now.'

'Perhaps we can sort it out,' said Porky, turning down the volume on the television. 'Let's begin with you and me and the way you took off to some haunted house or another without even telling me.'

Lizzie looked directly at him, for the first time, with unsmiling blue eyes. 'I left a note. It explained everything.'

'But why couldn't we discuss it first, like a normal couple?'

'Because we're not a normal couple,' Lizzie sighed. 'In your mathematical mind, everything's a simple equation; you + me = us + x years together.'

'That sounds pretty normal to me.'

Lizzie reached out for his hand. 'It *is* perfectly normal for you but not for me. I want something else.'

'I don't think you've got the vaguest idea what you want?' Porky whispered. 'But I'm fairly sure it's not me.'

'That's not true,' she said, fiddling nervously with the gold signet ring he'd given her the day after they first met. 'The trouble is I want so many things and I really don't know where to start.'

'The beginning's usually a good place to start,' said Porky.

'Oh yes, the beginning.' Lizzie leaned forward, rested her chin on lightly clenched fists, remembering a small girl in a pink, net ballet tutu, blonde hair in a pony tail, a smidgen of rouge on the cheeks, sparkly blue eye shadow, waiting anxiously in the wings at the British legion hall for the opening bars from Mrs Clutterbuck's upright piano. And then six girls, dancing together in a well-tutored line across dazzling footlights, the absolute centre of attention, followed by the precious, magic moment of praise and approval; the heady, intoxicating sound of applause.

But little ballerinas sometimes grow impatient and may quickly tire of tedious tuition and the demands of practise and commitment when fake fame offers the easier option; applause without pain, acclaim without ability, stardom without substance and an ever-open door to the wannabe world of cheap, counterfeit celebrity.

Lizzie resisted and opted, instead, for drama school, secure in the knowledge that acting amounts to little more than dressing-up and pretending to be somebody else; simply a matter of learning a few lines off by heart. So it was with shock and dismay that she discovered her thespian limitations and the sorry fact that, with the rising of the curtain, most of her stage characters, including one particularly inspired attempt at Joan of Arc, quickly mutated into the brash, over-confident teenager with a doubtful north London accent that was Miss Lizzie Beckman.

And her twice-weekly music teacher noted, early on in what was to be a short and unhappy relationship, that she had rather more fingers and thumbs than normally required by a concert pianist. But her piano problems had more to do with someone else's daft idea to provide eighty eight keys in only two colours; fifty two large ones in white, thirty six smaller in black, and each looking exactly like all the others. A touch of gold and silver here and there might have helped.

'I've had a go at so many things and made a mess of most of them,' Lizzie admitted wistfully. 'But they all boiled-down to the same thing…..a chance to be famous. It's all I've ever wanted.' She rubbed her eyes and slowly straightened-up. 'Daft thing is that I've got closer to fame by doing absolutely nothing than all the other things put together. But then even I couldn't make a mess of doing nothing.'

Porky looked around him, head high, chest puffed out, hands clasped behind his back, and sucked his teeth importantly. 'That's fabricated fame, nothing more than notoriety,' he announced to the wall on the opposite side of the room. 'A cheap gimmick,' he went on without pausing for breath, 'put together with smoke and mirrors by the likes of Toby Stone. It's not real, it's not credible and it's definitely not you.'

'And that's exactly what I've been telling you,' Lizzie said at once. 'I'm much more the person you saw on TV just now; a woman with a genuine talent, a power, not a young girl with no knickers and a gimmick.'

Porky shifted uncomfortably, looking slightly bewildered. 'Actually, Lizzie, you've told me nothing, not a flaming thing. Just take this broken leg business for instance; I know nothing whatsoever about it.'

She nodded apologetically. 'And you're quite right, of course,' she said. 'It was the week before you went to New York. I'm afraid I had an accident.'

Porky's eyes narrowed. 'An accident?' he repeated slowly, trying not to sound too anxious. 'What kind of an accident?'

'Oh, it was nothing; nothing at all,' she said, waving aside his concern with flick of the hand. 'I had this sort of dream; someone called Michael told me I'd got a power and to use it wisely. Then, before I knew it, I was sorting out people's aches and pains as if I'd been doing it all my life. Like Donny Jackson leg.'

'And a bit like my uncle Lionel's stomach,' Porky added.

Lizzie waited in wide-eyed anticipation for him to continue but, apart from his annoying habit of snapping his fingers when he tried to remember precise details, Porky didn't make a sound.

'So what about your uncle Lionel's stomach?' she asked, trying not to sound too impatient but hoping to move things along a bit.

Porky seemed uncertain, as if it had been a particularly complicated affair. 'I think it was an ulcer,' he said eventually. 'Yes, that's exactly what it was; an ulcer.'

'And what happened to his ulcer?'

Porky thought for a moment. 'As I recall, some bloke he'd met in a pub laid his hands on uncle Lionel's stomach and he was right as nine pence in no time at all. Just like that.'

Lizzie's eyes lit up. 'That's it. That's how it works,' she said excitedly.

'But it's not. Not always,' said Porky. 'Aunt Ruthie, uncle Lionel's wife, died of cancer not long after, so it didn't work for her. And then there was Maureen at the post office....'

'Anyway...' Lizzie slammed the word into the conversation like a sledge hammer before he could go on with Maureen's story. 'As I was saying......I seem to be able to help people just by thinking about them.'

Porky flopped down on the couch beside her. 'And that's really quite incredible,' he said, placing his hand gently on her knee. 'Truly fantastic.'

She lowered her eyes, nodding thoughtfully. 'Does sound a bit fantastic I suppose. But I can't take the credit for it.'

'Don't see why not. You make it happen, don't you?'

Lizzie shook her head. 'I'm a channel for healing energy but I don't do much. In fact, all things considered, I spend most of my time doing nothing these days.'

'Then you can do something for me,' Porky said at once, running his hand playfully across her thigh. 'Say you'll marry me.' He slid his other hand across her shoulder to the nape of her neck and drew her towards him, kissing her lightly on the cheek.

She pulled away but turned back to face him with an

uneasy smile. 'What are you like Barry Gammon?'

'Same as always.' He reached across for a small dish of peanuts and placed it on the couch between them. 'Like a chartered accountant trying to make one and one make two.' He threw a nut into the air, caught it in his mouth, and did it again, twice.

'Am I meant to be impressed by that?' she giggled.

Porky raised his finger for quiet. 'You haven't seen anything yet.' He placed three carefully selected peanuts in the palm of his hand. 'I'm going for the triple.'

She watched, silent, attentive and suitably still, as three peanuts were thrown up at the ceiling and two quickly fell to the floor in front of the couch. The solitary nut which landed in Porky's open mouth disappeared in an instant, eliminating proof of even partial success.

'It takes total dedication, years of practise and a lot of courage to achieve a triple,' Porky explained solemnly. 'Only a handful of people in the entire world have ever done it, and one of them choked to death in the attempt.'

'Probably had a peanut allergy?'

Porky looked puzzled. 'No, I meant the peanut went down the wrong way,' he said. 'An allergic reaction wouldn't be that quick and would probably require an ingestion of more than three peanuts to be fatal.'

Lizzie shook her head, let out a huge sigh. 'I was only joking.'

'And so was I,' said Porky. 'The chap I was telling you about didn't really choke at all; I made it up.'

'Well that's alright then,' she said, rising slowly to her feet and stretching her arms high above her head.

'Actually, as it happened, it wasn't alright. The peanut fell in his eye and blinded him.'

Lizzie stopped short, arms still in the air, shirt tail barely fringing the cheeks of her bottom. 'You're not developing a sense of humour, are you Barry Gammon?' she grinned.

He stared at her, unblinking, hands clasped together tidily in his lap. 'Very much doubt it,' he said. 'I've already got a highly-developed sense of sombre. And while we're on the subject, your bum's showing.'

She lowered her arms and tucked the shirt tail between her legs. 'That's not very gentlemanly of you,' she said, settling back on to the couch beside him.

Porky popped a peanut into his mouth. 'You're not developing a sense of modesty are you?'

"I'm afraid I don't do modesty. It's the same as shy and people who want to be celebrities are not supposed to be shy.

'Can they do honesty?' Porky asked, sounding more serious. 'Have you, for example, slept with him... Toby Stone, I mean?'

She hesitated for a second, carefully rearranged herself on the couch, and stared back with arrogant eyes. 'Confessions are for devout Catholics and small children. And I'm neither.'

I didn't ask for a confession, but a bit of honesty would be nice.'

'OK then, here's your hard-earned bit of honesty. Yes.'

The word seemed to fill the room like a poisonous gas. And then came the cold silence.

Porky stared at her in disbelief. 'Is that it?'

'Yes,' she whispered. 'Surely it's quite enough?'

He shook his head. 'Not sure. I suppose I half expected you to say something to make it all seem OK.'

'Like we only did it once, we were tired, and it meant nothing to either of us?'

'Something like that,' Porky sighed, reaching for his empty glass as he rose to his feet. 'Oh, I forgot to mention ... Svengali wanted you to call him back... on his mobile.'

Lizzie watched him cross the room to the kitchen. 'I'm sorry,' she called out after him. 'Really I am. I didn't mean to hurt you.'

He turned at the door, raised his empty glass. 'Whaever,' he said with a shake of the head. 'That *is* the monosyllabic equivalent of frankly-my-dear-I-don't-give-a-damn, isn't it?"

She was cross-legged on the floor with the 'phone wedged between her ear and shoulder when he returned with a glass of whisky; full to the brim, with no room for the usual dash of soda. There was a programme on TV about dealing with problem kids; some sort of professional nanny showing exasperated parents how to regain control of the family home. Porky straddled the arm of the couch, both feet firmly on the floor, and turned-up the volume.

Lizzie turned towards the sudden noise. 'Could you turn that down?' she called out, pointing to the TV. 'I can't hear myself speak.'

'You should take a look at this. It's all about over-indulged, bad mannered, inconsiderate children learning how to behave.'

'Sorry, I'll have to call you back,' she whispered into the 'phone. 'Porky's playing silly buggers.'

Porky rested an elbow on the back of the couch and waited for her to hang-up before he spoke. 'Correct me if I'm wrong but I got the distinct impression you'd set things up for a romantic evening when I arrived home. Scotch waiting at the door, steak au poive on the menu and, unless I misread the signals, sex very much on the agenda.'

She rolled her eyes, sighed wearily. 'What's the point you're trying to make?'

'I wondered why you bothered when you're already sleeping with Svengali?'

'Once,' she screamed. 'I slept with him once.'

'Oh well that's OK then. Just the once doesn't count.'

Lizzie rose awkwardly from the floor. 'I shouldn't have told you, should I?' she said, massaging her legs back to life. 'Your fault for asking.'

'Do you know what,' said Porky, 'I thought it might turn out to be my fault. How insensitive of me to discover you're screwing your PR.'

Lizzie made towards the kitchen. 'I'm very much afraid the steak's going to be a bit overdone. Do you fancy wine or will you stick with Scotch?'

'I don't bloody believe you.' Porky picked up his half empty glass, finished it, and slammed it down on the table beside him. 'How can you possibly think about steak at a time like this?'

'No problem,' she called from the kitchen. 'Forget the steak.'

Lizzie Beckman swept back into the room, whisky bottle in one hand, a can of soda in the other, and quickly placed them on the table next to the couch. She stood perfectly still for a moment then unbuttoned the blue striped shirt and let it slip slowly to the floor.

'Steak's off,' she said softly. 'We'll just have to settle for the Scotch and the sex.' She looked directly into his eyes. 'Two out of three's not bad though, eh?'

Porky wasn't at all sure that the fierce rush of emotion which surged, suddenly and completely, through his body had anything whatsoever to do with love and affection. At best it felt like unbridled lust but, from somewhere in the dark recesses of his mind, he recognised the selfish, animal power of personal gratification; the base, dominating sexuality of retribution and revenge.

'Can we forget about Toby Stone?' she murmured, wrapping her arm around his and pulling closer. 'I won't do it again......promise.'

Barry Gammon nodded but said nothing, acutely aware that he was crossing the narrow boundary between love and hate; a short, uncharted but decisive journey, without conscience or remorse, from which he might never return. He assured himself it was a temporary frame of mind and that his feelings would probably return to normal in the morning. But even as he took her in his arms he realised it wasn't the truth. Everything had changed.

CHAPTER 7

More than five years after he'd crumpled his very last cigarette into an ash tray in a frenzy of self-righteousness, Toby Stone still occasionally fancied a fag. It didn't happen often and he always managed to resist, but today was different.

An unopened packet of twenty Stuyvesant, picked-up with the morning papers, beckoned from the other side of the desk, enticing him back to the dwindling ranks of social pariahs who'd not yet kicked the habit; wretched outcasts who huddled in small groups outside shops and offices for their five minute fix of toxic fumes.

And cigarettes can kill; didn't it say as much in the big, black letters on the side of every packet? A health warning, they called it, but Toby only saw a challenge, a gauntlet flung at his feet. Dare you, it said. Bet you haven't got the guts to take a puff.

But, as reluctant smokers will be only too aware, while the first suffocating gasps may send the head into a sickly spin which blurs the brain, a deep inhalation will numb the troubled mind and tranquilize the stressed-out soul.

And Toby Stone was under stress, for it is written

[somewhere in the haphazard handbook of PR] that he who's dawn may see him flogging a dead horse, may ride a wild stallion by sunset. A slightly contrived but manageable story about Lizzie Beckman doing nothing had been superseded by the more volatile news about her powers of healing. The story had appeared in all but one of the morning papers, casting Lizzie as both hoaxer and healer in reports of Donny Jackson's remarkable recovery. But it was the constant stream of demands for radio and TV interviews that followed which clogged up the telephone lines at Toby Stone Associates.

Toby leaned back in the red leather chair, stretching the coiled telephone wire to its limits, and drew hard on a pivotal first cigarette. 'Let me get this straight,' he said to someone called Kylie from a TV news programme. 'You'd like my client to diagnose the medical problems of half a dozen people and then try to heal each of them in turn. Is that right?'

Kylie was fairly sure that's what her producer had in mind.

'And how serious would the various conditions be?' Toby asked. 'Are we talking minor ailments or terminal diseases?'

Kylie hesitated. 'Bear with me,' she said, for the fourth time. 'I'll have to check.' And she did, but nobody could say. It was still only an outline idea and they hadn't decided who would take part. 'We'll be doing it in our studios though,' Kylie volunteered, 'so they won't be all that ill or they'd be in intensive care or somewhere, wouldn't they?'

Lizzie, celestial in white, turned-up at ten; the dress diaphanous, flimsy and flirty but with an angelic, spiritual quality; the style straight out of the twenties yet tinged with a hint of saintliness. And the make-up, pale and delicate as porcelain. She stood for a moment in the doorway, head back, hands flat to her thighs, fingers spread.

'Will I do?' she breathed through pouting lips.

Toby flicked the ash from his cigarette and smiled. 'It's roughly what I had in mind,' he said. 'Angel without wings; Vestal virgin on a gap year.'

He glanced anxiously at the growing list of press interviews which now filled an entire page in his day book, starting almost at once and running through to early evening; mainly radio, some on the 'phone, others in the studios, and then three important television spots.

'They've issued a challenge.' Toby's voice was ice cool. 'Would you be able to diagnose the conditions of half a dozen poorly people?'

Lizzie shrugged. 'Dunno. I'm not a flaming doctor.'

Toby raised the cigarette to his lips and stared at her, unblinking. He inhaled deeply, blew smoke across the desk, coughed. 'I'll take that as a no then shall I?'

She stepped slowly towards the desk. 'I'll tell you this much, you don't have to be a Harley Street specialist to understand that smoking's not going to do your lungs any good.'

'Can you do it or not?' he repeated wearily. 'I need to get back to the TV people.'

'You asked me about my talents and ambitions when we first met,' she said, settling herself in the chair opposite him. 'Well, I can tell when people need my help. Their physical problem draws me, like a magnet, to the exact spot on their body and I put it right. But, in honesty, I don't have the first idea what's actually wrong with them.'

Toby lit a new cigarette from the first, crushed the stub into a brass ash tray. 'You'll be the death of me,' he said through a haze of smoke. 'I just hope you'll give me a healing hand when I need it.'

He picked up the telephone for the first of the morning's radio interviews, rose quickly to his feet, one hand over the mouth piece, and leaned across the desk towards her. 'Now remember,' he whispered, 'give them modesty and humility but leave them with a taste for miracles.'

Lizzie took the phone, pressed it apprehensively to her ear, and waited for the music to fade and the questions to begin.

'A golden oldie there from The Rolling Stones,' said a chirpy young man with a strong Liverpool accent. 'But now, from a Honky Tonk Woman to a young lady who seems to have amazed quite a lot of people with her powers of healing. On the line from London is Lizzie Beckman who, according to this morning's papers, can instantly mend a broken leg just by thinking about it. Good morning Lizzie.'

'Good morning.'

'Is it true then? Can you fix a fracture in a flash?'

'That's what happened yesterday, yes.'

'So how's it done? I mean a broken leg can takes months to mend. What's the secret?'

'I'm not sure. It just happens.'

'Could it have been a mistake? Perhaps it wasn't broken in the first place.'

'The doctors seemed pretty certain Donny's leg was broken.'

'That's right. I should have mentioned it was my old mate Donny Jackson's leg we're talking about here. But you fixed it for him even though you were nowhere near at the time?'

'I'm just a channel for healing. The power comes from somewhere else.'

'Are we talking God here Lizzie? A line to the big man, perhaps?'

'I'm saying it's a power, but I don't know where it comes from.'

'Wherever it comes from, it seems to have worked for Donny. But is that the end of it, or will you carry on doing this sort of stuff?'

'I'm happy to carry on but it's not up to me. As I said, I'm only a channel, not the power itself.'

'Well, whatever it is you're doing Lizzie, I'm sure we

all wish you the best of luck. Thanks for coming on the show today.'

Lizzie wasn't sure if anyone heard her thank the presenter but it seemed unlikely. He was already urging listeners to call-in with their own stories about unexplained happenings. It was as if she wasn't there. And then, suddenly, a new voice, a woman, who thanked Lizzie for her time before the line went dead.

Toby grinned. 'How'd it go?'

'Short,' said Lizzie. 'Very short. They didn't give me a chance.'

'It's always like that. There's never enough time to explain and they never seem to ask the right questions.'

But, nearly three hours and eight radio interviews later, two of which treated the whole thing as a joke while another claimed it was a hoax, Lizzie thought she might be starting to get the hang of it. The trick, it seemed, was to completely ignore the questions and say exactly what you wanted before they could interrupt.

The car, kindly sent by the TV studios, turned up soon after two and made straight for the nearest traffic jam at Hyde Park Corner, en route to Grays Inn Road.

'Perhaps it would be best to go through the park,' Toby hesitatingly suggested to the back of a plump, bald head. 'Turn left here, then up Park Lane?'

The driver half turned towards him, shook his head slowly but resolutely from side to side. 'Problems in Grosvenor Square,' he said unemotionally. 'Demonstration or something at the US embassy. Gridlock in Mayfair.'

'OK then.' Toby leaned forward. 'Do a right here, into The Mall, down The Strand, up Fleet Street, left at ………..'

'No chance,' the driver interrupted before Toby could finish the sentence. 'Chaos round Trafalgar Square. Piccadilly's our best bet.'

'Then we'll be late,' Toby said emphatically.

The fleshy head nodded in agreement but said nothing more for the rest of the journey.

Lizzie stepped from the car over to the huge glass doors and waited, feeling suddenly alone and vulnerable, while Toby seemed to be discussing arrangements for the return journey.

He took her hand, gave it a comforting squeeze. 'Are you OK?' he whispered. 'No second thoughts?'

'Everything's cool,' she said, with a confident swagger into the reception area. 'No probs.'

A sullen, thin-lipped girl, casual in a red track suit, black hair in a pony tail, accompanied them up to studios on the third floor where a battery of lights had been focussed on a long, narrow platform, covered in a shiny, silver metallic fabric and set against the far wall.

'Perhaps you'd like to sit over there.' She pointed to a black, swivel chair which looked as if it might be more at home behind an executive desk. 'Margot will be along in a minute,' she assured her, then turned and left without further explanation.

Toby frowned. 'Margot bloody Mason?'

Lizzie looked blank, shrugged her shoulders. 'Friend of yours?'

He shook his head. 'Tall, thin woman with a personality by-pass. Sometimes does that late night news programme.'

Lizzie shrugged again, shook her head. 'Never watch it.'

He reached for a cigarette, glanced up at the No Smoking sign, and quickly slipped the packet back into his pocket with a nervous chuckle.

Margot Mason, wearing narrow, frameless spectacles and an impatient smile, appeared through a door on the opposite side of the studio. She paused for a moment then ushered-in six other people, each of them wearing a red number across their chest. They quickly lined-up on the platform, in numerical order; one to six, left to right.

'I guess you'd be Lizzie Beckman,' she called across the studio. 'Nearly ready for you.'

Toby Stone flashed Lizzie a reassuring smile and backed quietly away, for it's an unwritten rule that PRs may be heard but not seen, especially in TV studios. Like the manager of a prize fighter, he took a ringside seat in the control room and waited for the start of round one.

It began with a brief chat about Lizzie's time at Penfold Manor and the incident with Donny Jackson's leg but then quickly moved on to the six people waiting on the platform; four women, two men, hands clasped self-consciously in front of them.

Lizzie was instantly drawn to the long, willowy limbs and Mediterranean glow of a young girl, late teens, with short, black spiky hair, and round, eager eyes which stared back at her like a startled deer.

'I'd like to approach number four,' Lizzie said as she rose, slowly, to her feet and stepped towards the platform.

Number four managed a weak smile, clasped her fingers together uneasily as Lizzie approached.

'Please try to relax,' Lizzie whispered. She reached out for her hands and gripping them tightly.

For a moment they both stood perfectly still. Then, without warning, the girl became more tense and started to pull away, her body shaking, the big round eyes tightly closed. 'It's hot, burning hot,' she cried out. 'I'm on fire.' Her breathing, laboured and irregular, began gradually to slow until it was little more than a whimper. And then silence and a sudden calm which wafted across the studio like a warm breeze.

Lizzie sank to her knees, weak and depleted. She slowly released her grip and at once recognised the now familiar sensation of emptiness, as if life itself had ebbed away leaving an abandoned shell, without power or purpose.

Margot Mason took off her glasses and moved closer; pensive and puzzled, hands together in a prayer-like pose, the head tilted quizzically to one side. 'Are you able to tell us what's been happening?' she asked.

Lizzie shook her head. 'No, not really. Perhaps you'd be able to tell me?'

'Let's see now,' Margot said, flipping quickly through the notes on her clipboard. 'I can tell you that number four has an acute arthritic condition, affecting her joints and mobility.' She paused, eyes narrowed, blinking impatiently. 'Do you think you may have helped her?' she asked.

'I hope so,' Lizzie answered. 'Why not ask number four?'

But number four had already flung slender, suntanned arms around Lizzie's neck and answered the question. 'I feel fantastic,' she cried. 'No knives in the joints. No searing pain. It's all gone.'

'And what of our other five participants?' said Margot, stepping up on to the platform. 'What can you do to help them?'

Lizzie shrugged and returned to her seat. 'Nothing. They don't need my help.'

Margot turned solemnly towards the camera. 'Are you saying there's nothing wrong with them?'

'I'm saying only that they don't need my help.'

Margot's expression softened into a well-practised but less than genuine smile. 'Lizzie Beckman, you're to be congratulated. Numbers one, two, three, five and six were each pronounced fighting fit before the show. Nothing wrong with them, so well done.'

The camera followed number four across to Lizzie's executive chair for the final interview while the others filed slowly out of the studio.

'How can I ever thank you?' she said. 'It was a miracle.'

But Lizzie wasn't listening, her eyes closed in quiet contemplation, finger tips gently massaging her brow. 'I'm so sorry Margot,' she said, rising giddily to her feet. 'I'm afraid I've completely missed something.'

Margot Mason smiled expectantly. 'What's that darling?'

'Your headaches,' said Lizzie. 'You really should take them more seriously.'

'Migraine darling,' she laughed, fiddling with the top of her pen. 'Nothing serious; I've got tablets.'

An uneasy silence fell on the studio as everyone seemed to stop whatever they were doing at roughly the same time. Suddenly and unaccountably, Margot Mason was the focus of attention, everyone's attention, and she knew it.

'What?' she called out, as if she might have just made an unintentional gaffe or the front of her blouse was suddenly undone. 'What is it?'

Lizzie smiled and offered her hand as she moved closer, but then gently withdrew it as the other woman fixed her with an icy stare and turned away.

'Can we get this interview started?' Margot shouted. She clapped her hands bossily. 'I want the two girls standing close together, face to face, for the next bit.'

'The 'two girls' have names,' Lizzie said indignantly. 'Mine's Lizzie Beckman, in case you've lost your notes.'

Margot glanced up to the control room and Toby Stone's jaded smile. 'Your publicity man mentioned it eleven times in a two page press statement,' she sighed. 'How could I possibly forget it?'

But all things are possible and she did; not so much forget it as totally ignore it. Lizzie's name was mentioned only once throughout the interview when she was introduced as a so-called healer.

It wasn't that Toby was upset with the way things had gone. It went well and, all things considered, the TV spot amounted to fifteen minutes of fantastic publicity the following day. What had begun to concern him were the legal implications of someone meddling with other people's ailments. An expensive Inns of Court barrister pondered the possibility that someone who had been medically diagnosed with arthritis might be less than happy if, after apparently being healed by Lizzie Beckman,

129

they found they were still medically arthritic or, worse, that the condition had somehow deteriorated? Could Lizzie be culpable, he wondered; a woman with no formal medical qualifications who publicly claimed to cure physical ailments? The answer, he decided, was very possibly yes. At the very least, there was a very big question mark over the likelihood of costly awards for compensation.

And what if Donny Jackson's leg, having apparently been miraculously healed, without authority or permission incidentally, suddenly cracked-up again? Could he sue Lizzie Beckman for negligence or perhaps even common assault? More question marks.

OK, litigation was highly unlikely, he concluded. But it was possible and Lizzie, and anyone else involved in the promotion and exploitation of her unregistered and unrecognised therapy, could be financially ruined. A custodial sentence could not be completely ruled out.

Toby wasn't a man to panic in the face of adversity but he could already sense the dull thud of a hammer on six inch galvanised nails, visualise the agonising sting as they pierced fleshy palms, skewered them to rough hewn, splintered wood, and tore the skin from the back of manicured hands. He'd been financially crucified before.

Lizzie spooned the froth from her coffee and stared blankly across the table, watching Toby's lips move, but not really listening to the sound they were making.

'Like it or not,' he mumbled through a mouth full of chocolate gateaux, 'we live in a litigious society. And we seem to be setting ourselves up for a major claim from some compo-crazy arsehole looking for easy money.'

She looked around the crowded café and decided it was neither the time nor the place for an argument. 'Can we talk about this some other time,' she asked quietly. 'I'm not really in the mood right now.'

Toby shuffled his chair closer to the table. 'Look, I'm not suggesting you to stop the healing thing, only that we find a way to protect ourselves.'

'Like an insurance policy?'

'Not exactly. I was thinking in terms of a slightly more newsworthy approach to the problem.'

Lizzie frowned. 'Meaning?'

'Let's just say I've had a recent attack of brilliance,' he said with a satisfied smile. 'Hit me last night, like a bolt from the blue.'

She looked into his eyes and recognised the unmistakable twinkle, the glint of boyish excitement that hinted at a recent trip to Topsy-Turvy Land where mundane reality is routinely stood on its head for the benefit of press publicity consultants.

'OK. I'm listening,' she said slowly and deliberately. 'What's the big idea?'

Toby winked and reached for his wallet. 'I'll explain in the cab,' he said.

And it was, of course, the simplest of concepts; the hallmark of all great PR promotions. The trick, it is said, is to take an idea – any idea – to its logical conclusion and then drag it a few faltering steps further, to a magical point beyond the predictable, where things are unexpected and surprising and where the improbable can become a reality.

Toby settled-back in the taxi and closed his eyes to the audacity of the sign opposite which thanked him for not smoking when the thought hadn't even entered his mind. But the smug look on his face spoke of other things.

'Tell me this,' he said with a suddenly reflective, philosophical tone to his voice. 'In what state would you say you leave someone who has been cured of a specific ailment?'

Lizzie momentarily stopped rummaging through her handbag and turned to him with a screwed-up look. 'What d'you mean, state?'

'I mean what, in your opinion, has happened to them?'

'They've been healed. They've got better, stopped being ill, that's what's happened to them.'

Toby leaned across, took her hand in his. 'So, in what way would they have they changed?'

'Get to the point.' She quickly pulled her had free and resumed the search for her lipstick. 'It's your big idea, not mine.'

'They'd be healthier than before,' Toby said, shielding his eyes from a sudden burst of sunshine which seemed to add a spiritual reverence to his words. 'And that means your services should reasonably be available on the NHS.'

Lizzie sighed. 'Me, on the NHS? I don't wear white rubber gloves and a face mask and I don't do operations.'

'But,' he persisted, 'when mainstream medicine can do no more, your healing powers offer what might be the one and only hope for thousands of people.'

She looked puzzled and slightly annoyed. 'Thousands?' she repeated as the taxi turned into Beauchamp Place and headed towards Toby Stone's offices. 'I'd be dead myself inside a week.'

'You're not the only healer on the planet,' he said, searching his pockets for loose change. 'They'll all be trying to cash-in on your publicity before you can say Florence Nightingale so we've got to beat them to it; seize control right away.'

'And just how do we seize control?'

Toby seemed flushed with pride. 'By championing the cause of spiritual healing on the NHS,' he said. 'You'll be the girl who gets healers state registered.'

'But even I know that's never going to happen.'

'It happened for osteopaths and physiotherapists so why not spiritual healers?'

'I'm sorry but nine-to-five healing is not the sort of celebrity career I had in mind.'

But Toby wasn't listening. He was already halfway out of the cab, confident in the real-world logic that, as the NHS itself so clearly demonstrated, what's supposedly on offer isn't always what's finally delivered. And, anyway, the plan was to select only a couple of the most newsworthy ailments each week. They'd do it on a Sunday, the slowest news day of the week, offering the best chance of press coverage in the national press.

Toby Stone settled himself at his desk, lit a large Bolivar cigar, his first in more than five years, and blew extravagant smoke rings at the office ceiling.

CHAPTER 8

Conscience came to Lizzie Beckman like toothache; unwanted, unexpected and with a persistent, nagging pain that demanded attention and warned of further agonies to come. It was delivered by the Royal Mail soon after nine on a sunny Tuesday morning; a sack full of letters sent from all over the country.

But when you boil it right down, there are probably only two reasons why anybody bothers to write a letter….. and the second is that the writer *wants* something. The piles of letters which turned-up on Lizzie Beckman's door mat during the next few days had definitely been penned for the second reason.

They asked her to cure them, heal them, make them better, stop their pain, take their run-down, worn-out bodies and fix 'em up, good as new. But, most of all, they asked for hope and they wanted it now.

Lizzie hadn't bargained for the sudden onset of conscience, a new and demanding force which insisted that perhaps the needs of others might, sometimes at least, take priority over her own. She resented the whole idea; it was incongruous, it jarred. But a few well-chosen words from

Toby Stone finally persuaded her to set aside Sunday mornings for two or three healing sessions, with the intention of grabbing the newspaper headlines on Monday.

And so to Britain's National Health Service and, its lofty guardians, the Department of Health.

There seemed to be rather too many zeros in the official reference number they'd given Toby's e-mail; five of them and all at the beginning. Response Ref DE00000169983, they called it, but it began on a positive note. *Alternative treatments, such as spiritual healing, are clearly attractive to a number of people and so, in principle, could feature in a range of services offered by local NHS organisations,* it declared promisingly.

It then went on to talk about Primary Care Trusts and the fact that it was open to GPs to provide access to specific therapies but started to go downhill from there. *It should be remembered, however, that clinical responsibility for individual health conditions rests with the GP, who must, therefore, be able to clinically justify any treatment to which they may refer patients.*

It ended with a veiled warning that......*the GP cannot be made to refer you.*

So the buck was swiftly passed down the chain from the Department of Health to individual doctors in their local surgeries, cleverly side-stepping a full-out assault on the Department itself and making it difficult to move things forward on a national basis.

But Toby wasn't about to leave a great idea on the shelf to gather dust, like a superior wine, for it is also written [somewhere else in the haphazard PR handbook] that if at first you don't succeed, make damn sure you get the glory for trying. The intent is always more important than the result; call it Toby Stone's Polar principle.

It's one of the proud pages of British history; Scott of the Antarctic. But spare a thought for Roald Amundsen, who planted the Norwegian flag in the South Polar snow weeks before Captain Robert Scott and his team finally showed-up.

So, Amundsen of the Antarctic? Never heard of him.

And what of our Enery? Never quite won a world heavyweight championship fight in his life but a nation fondly remembers Sir Henry Cooper as one of our boxing greats. And quite right too.

It's the courage and resolve, the effort and intent, which grab the imagination and steal the spotlight, whatever the outcome.

The Polar Principle is the backbone of politics. Take a problem, any problem, and set up an enquiry to make recommendations into resolving the problem concerned. Then, to a fanfare of publicity, present a report on the findings of the enquiry; call it the what's-a-name report, prefixing it with the surname of the person leading the enquiry, bask in the glory of a problem solved, and regularly quote from said report over the next twelve months. At this point the original problem can be forgotten until somebody raises it again, when it is prudent to appoint a special committee to re-examine the findings of the what's-a-name report and the whole charade begins again. And, by the way, what's-a-name will take the blame for any inconsistencies in his report and the fact that the problem has never been resolved. But the government of the day, having absolved itself of any blame, will have demonstrated concern and intent. It's all that matters.

And Toby made quite sure that concern and intent were spread thick, like over-ripe Camembert, across Lizzie Beckman's campaign. 'Spiritual Healing on the NHS?' the Daily Mail headline screamed, although more by way of a question than a fact. But then newspaper headlines are frequently no more than simple questions. 'PM to Resign?'……..probably not but, in the absence of any hard facts to back up the story, a question mark makes it sound as if it might be true.

So Lizzie's call for spiritual healing on the NHS would develop in one of two ways; either the Department of

Health would give the idea their blessing or, as seemed more likely, they'd roll out the red tape, create a bit of a tangle and, after a polite interval and a thorough review of the proposal, reject it without explanation.

And so what? 'Great idea gets thumbs-up' or 'Great idea gets turned-down'; the media coverage would be pretty much the same whichever way the story went. It would, as they say, run and run.

But, to bring a story to life, you need a picture. Worth a thousand words, they are, it says somewhere in the PR handbook, which is why Toby Stone had spent the following day looking for doves; one hundred of them to be precise, and they had to be pure white.

He found them in Brighton; the purest white racing pigeons, capable of flying further and faster than doves but which, to the untrained eye, looked exactly the same. It would take an expert bird fancier to spot the difference, the breeders assured him.

They were delivered, in wicker baskets, two days later; not quite the hundred he'd expected, but close enough, piled up on the pavement outside the Department of Health, just across the road from Downing Street.

Further down Whitehall, in Parliament Square, Big Ben struck eleven, scrambling a squadron of local pigeons to the elegant rooftops in a frenzy of feathers and flapping wings. In a moment, half a dozen photographers, who'd huddled together near the front door of Richmond House, opulent home of the NHS, shuffled slowly towards the darkened windows of a white stretch limousine which had just purred to a halt at the kerbside.

Lizzie Beckman stepped from the car in a white satin trouser suit, threw her head back to the morning sunlight, and smiled with the serenity of a Renaissance canvas. A plump, grey pigeon strutted importantly across the pavement in front of her and cameras flashed in unison. But this wasn't the picture they'd all come for.

The man in charge of the four bird handlers said it was

called a 'release'; all the birds into the air at roughly the same time, before they all headed back home to Brighton.

But Toby was more concerned about keeping twenty or so birds back to hover, like angels, around Lizzie's head, leaving the rest of the bunch in the background to soar symbolically towards God in a pale blue heaven.

The Secretary of State for Health had been advised of the photo-call and was invited to attend but politely declined due to diary pressure. It was the standard response, a letter you'd receive from any government department. Toby had a pile of them; all pretty much the same, each no more than three uninspired sentences, and always peppered with phoney good wishes, insincere apologies and the usual regrets.

But if the health minister wasn't going to show up, the photographers wanted Lizzie reaching for the heavens; arms spread wide in an expression of spiritual joy, eyes wide, and a swirl of doves about her long, blonde hair.

The man from The Independent took off his jacket and slowly stretched himself out close to the kerb, Looking like a hit and run victim, head resting uncomfortably on his camera bag. He fixed Lizzie in his lens, sun behind her in an ethereal haze, and waited for the first wave of birds to fill the frame.

Two other photographers crouched beside him, cameras focussed up into Lizzie's face, while the rest seemed happy to remain standing, apart from The Daily Star photographer who took up a slightly precarious position, balanced on top of a small, metal step ladder, for a downward shot. And then they were ready.

'On my count,' Toby called out. 'Backwards from five.' He glanced across to the bird handlers, nodded, then turned quickly to Lizzie who'd unbuttoned her jacket, ready for action.

She smiled, reached out, fingers rigid with expectation, and hoped to heaven her face was doing 'spiritual joy', the way they'd asked, and not 'silly bitch', the way it felt.

And it's an ornithological fact that doves don't do hovering; certainly not hovering like angels, around your head, anyway. What they do quite well is flapping and floundering, and poking feathers in your eye. But, with a highly impressive cloud of pure white doves soaring to the heavens in the background, even 'silly bitch' will do.

It wasn't the sort of photograph you could set up twice. Once the birds took to the skies, they were gone, gone for good, back to Brighton.

Half a dozen photographers packed their bags and took a leisurely stroll up Whitehall for a midday photo-call in Trafalgar Square; something to do with the Mayor's plans to introduce a levy on taxi fares. It was already being called the Taxi Tax and looked like raising the cost of hiring a London cab by ten per cent or more.

'What's the picture?' Toby called after them.

'Couple of birds, big knockers,' someone answered. The others laughed.

Toby looked puzzled. 'So what's the angle?'

One of them turned around, hands cupped at his chest. 'Eye appeal,' he said with a silly grin. 'The taxi tax is apparently going towards improving the sights. Geddit?'

Toby got it; another girlie picture to compete for space with Lizzie and the doves. Big tits for the tabloids, white doves for the rest.

But even the most carefully fabricated, well orchestrated PR story can sometimes be infiltrated by real news; the simple, spontaneous stuff that just sort of happens, and usually when you least expect it.

And it happened in Trafalgar Square, where the Mayor's latest PR production was well underway.

He stepped, slowly and deliberately, up to a wooden platform which straddled the edge of one of the fountains, and took up a presidential pose to deliver what some had already dubbed the Sermon on the Fount. Above him a banner announced 'A New Look for London' thanks, he explained to a small crowd, to expected revenues from the new levy on cab fares.

And then came the pictures.

Two buxom girls sparkled in pearly buttons; skimpy waistcoats and bum-hugging shorts, topped by Pearly King caps, set at a jaunty, costermonger angle. They sidled sexily into position, one each side of the hero of the day, and pressed pearly heads affectionately to his mayoral chest.

It was at this crucial point in the proceedings that the spontaneous stuff turned up, unannounced; a lone, feathered flyer from the local Whitehall squadron, banned ironically from the square by none other than the Mayor himself. He slowly circled the fountain, twice, maintaining altitude and speed above the chosen target, then swooped low to deliver his contribution with the relentless precision of an Excorcet missile.

The mayor struggled bravely with a constipated smile and wiped the purple parcel from his brow. Cameras flashed.

'Some say it's lucky,' he joked unconvincingly.

'Others say it's bird shit,' a voice screamed out from somewhere on the other side of the fountain. 'Load of crap,' someone else joined in. 'And there's pigeon poo on yer ed as well.'

Heavenly doves and pooping pigeons both fluttered colourfully across the pages of the evening papers, while even bigger spaces were given over to the 'Battle of the Birds' in the following morning's national press. But it was the undignified 'One-in-the-Eye' video footage of an embarrassed Mayor which qualified for the funny bit at the very end of the TV news and flushed any remaining credibility for a Taxi Tax straight down the toilet, at least for the time being.

Arguments for and against spiritual healing on the NHS, some more heated than others, began almost at once as self-important feature writers aired their views and kept Lizzie Beckman's face in the news for the rest of the week, instantly raising her celebrity rating from somewhere on the lower D lists up to around middle C; perhaps even higher, bordering on the B list.

And let it not be said that Barry Gammon didn't rise to the occasion. On the thirtieth of the month, a Friday, he duly acknowledged her newly elevated status with an invitation to a romantic Champagne flight over London. More of a spin than a flight, to be precise, and only 135 metres off the ground at the highest point of the unique thirty minute journey; Porky had checked the finer details of the on-line deal before he handed over his £299.

'This is the fourth tallest structure in London,' he whispered as the two of them were fast-tracked past queues of tourists to board the quaintly named Cupid's Capsule. 'It's equivalent in height to sixty four red telephone boxes piled on top of each other.'

Lizzie tried her best to look impressed. 'Imagine,' she said. 'All those telephone boxes in a huge pile.'

Their personal capsule host wore drab green and grey but smiled cheerfully with vivid blue, twinkling eyes. 'Welcome to the London Eye,' she said, quickly and efficiently filling two flute Champagne glasses with Laurent-Perrier before informing her VIP guests that the Eye could carry eight hundred passengers with each revolution. 'That's equivalent to eleven red double-decker buses,' she said.

'My goodness,' Lizzie gasped. 'So many red telephone boxes and double-decker buses. I wondered where they'd all gone.'

Porky took her hand, led her tactfully across the capsule and gently clinked their glasses together. 'To you Lizzie,' he said. 'A rising star in the heavens.'

She smiled, sipped her Champagne, looking out at London. 'Have we started to move yet?' she asked, visibly bored.

"At just over half a mile an hour," said Porky. "It allows people to get on and off without having to stop the thing.' He glanced across to their host who was now standing perfectly still on the other side of the capsule, and seemed set to remain there. 'You're coming with us then, are you?'

She nodded, head discreetly bowed, and carefully refilled their glasses. Then, with the natural ease of a seasoned waitress, she backed quietly away, almost unnoticed.

Lizzie turned to Porky, eyed him slowly up and down. 'How clever of you to arrange all this,' she said. 'So romantic here, just the three of us.'

Porky shrugged-off the jibe and pointed westwards, towards the late afternoon sun. 'You can see for more than sixty miles from the top of the wheel; as far as Windsor Castle, on a clear day.'

'Fascinating,' Lizzie sighed. 'Do you suppose the Queen might be able to see us too?'

'It's possible,' he said, checking the notes he'd made that morning. 'Would you believe that each of these thirty two capsules weighs ten tonnes. That's bloody big; about the same weight as a million one pound coins.'

Lizzie rolled her eyes. 'Absolutely amazing.'

Across the Thames, towards Parliament, the rush hour traffic had clogged up The Embankment. Porky glanced down river to St Paul's and its magnificent dome, silhouetted against the London skyline. 'It really is amazing up here, isn't it?'

There was a noticeable pause before Lizzie answered. 'If you could manage to give it a rest with all the boring facts and figures for just a moment,' she breathed, 'the answer's yes.'

He looked at her blankly, the beginnings of a frown creasing his forehead. 'Sorry, the answer to what?'

'The monthly question,' she whispered. 'This month's answer; it's going to be yes. OK?'

Porky emptied his glass with one large gulp, hesitated for a second, and then burped loudly. 'So sorry,' he chuckled excitedly. 'Took me by surprise, that's all.'

She tilted her head coyly, finger pressed to her lips in a well-practised pretence at modesty. 'But you still have to ask me the question, kind sir, even if I've already given you the answer,' she said softly. 'It wouldn't be a proper proposal of marriage otherwise; now would it?'

A flush of delight sent Porky's heart beat into overdrive and left his mind spinning with confusion; a heady mixture of euphoria and blind panic. He heard himself call out, ask her to marry him. He said it two or three times in quick succession. 'Will you marry me Lizzie?'

'Yes.' She said it quietly, calmly, and only once. But he felt the word permeate magically through the capsule and fill it, like the fragrant aroma of an expensive perfume.

She gently touched his cheek. 'I'd love to marry you darling Porky,' she said dolefully. 'But could you be a sweet and give me just a teensy bit more time? Perhaps in a year; no more than two?'

'Why not now?'

'I want to be a star not just a celebrity, and that takes time.'

Porky straightened up to his full height and breathed deeply, searching for the right words. 'And how, exactly, would our marriage prevent you being a star?'

'It's the fans. They like their celebrity heroes to be free, available, and unattached, not married to chartered accou....' The word snapped abruptly in two, like a dry twig.

'Chartered accounts,' Porky said in a brittle voice. 'People like me?'

'I didn't mean it like that.'

'But how else could you have meant it? And, anyway, what do you know about fans and their innermost fancies?'

'Believe it or not, I get fan mail. In fact I get quite a lot of it actually.'

'People asking for spiritual healing? That's not fan mail.'

She moved closer, fixed him with burning eyes. 'Well some of them want other things too my love; and we're not talking signed photographs here.'

He forced a defiant smile, lips trembling, acutely aware of the spontaneous sympathy and understanding which had silently, and unexpectedly, embraced him from the other side of the capsule. Two vivid blue eyes, filled with compassion.

'Please don't take any notice of us. We're like this all the time; par for the course,' he said in a voice which denied every word of it.

The next ten minutes passed slowly and in complete silence, at a speed of just over half a mile an hour until, at last, the wheel had finally turned full circle and they stepped down from Cupid's Capsule to the bustling South Bank of the Thames.

Porky stopped, buttoned his jacket, ran an embarrassed finger around the inside of his shirt collar. He looked back, waved half heartedly to his host. 'Sorry……. didn't catch your name,' he called out, 'but thanks anyway for your time.'

'It's Daisy. My name's Daisy,' she said.

'Daisy….right.' He hesitated briefly. 'I guess today was Cupid's day off then Daisy?'

She smiled, slowly shook her head. 'He's a twenty four, seven kind of a bloke. Never takes a day off.'

Porky nodded. 'Hope you're right.'

'So do I,' she said. 'Really I do.' But Porky was too far away to hear.

CHAPTER 9

Notting Hill Gate; a short walk from Bayswater, one stop on the Central Line. But, for a discerning few, it might as well be another planet.

It's not just that the Victorian terraces happen to be in the laid back Royal Borough of Kensington and Chelsea rather than the slightly stuffy and sometimes shabby City of Westminster, or the fact that movie buffs wouldn't dare mention Bayswater's eight-screen Odeon [situated somewhere on the second floor of Whiteleys shopping centre, apparently] in the same breath as the Electric Cinema in Portobello Road or Notting Hill's famous Gate, with its top notch foreign films. And, as anyone who lives there will tell you, it's got nothing whatsoever to do with the annual carnival.

No, a move from Bayswater to Notting Hill would be an escape from cultural wastelands, close to Paddington Station, to an oasis of style and chic not too far from Kensington Palace. And that says it all really.

It's the promised land of the A-listers; the place where the most reverent of the beautiful people have already unpacked their Louis Vuitton, hung up the Dolce &

Gabbana, cracked open the Cristal and settled down, for a short while at least, to watch property prices soar ever upwards to the heavens.

Notting Hill tugged at Lizzie Beckman's ego like gravity on a ripe apple; had done since she saw the Hugh Grant, Julia Roberts movie. It dragged her out of Barry Gammon's first floor Bayswater flat, pulled her along Queensway, yanked her down Westbourne Grove, across Kensington Park Road, and set her neatly down at the far end of Elgin Crescent.

An early twenty first birthday present, Samuel Beckman called it; a light and airy garden flat where a talented young daughter could enjoy the financial independence of a sound leasehold investment. And a snip at less than three hundred thousand pounds, especially when the tax benefits of a company purchase were taken into account.

But it wasn't until she'd shut the door behind her, stared blankly at the stains on somebody else's worn-out carpets, listened to the resonating silence of large, empty rooms, that she first sensed the solitary detachment and isolation which are both the pain and pleasure of single living. No twiddled TV channels, clattering cups in kitchens, tuneless songs from steamy bathrooms. No irritating fingers tapping tables, idle chatter when you're trying to read. No outbursts, arguments, rows and disagreements. No squabbles, tantrums, doors slammed in childish rage. No angry silences to follow. Nothing.

Porky surprised her. She'd expected him to put up a fight, try to change her mind, ask her to reconsider; that sort of thing. Truth is he said very little, kissed her fondly on the cheek and wished her every happiness in her new home.

But then he asked for his door key back; that's what really hurt. He leaned impassively against the open front door, hand outstretched, palm upwards, and waited while she rummaged through her handbag. She felt like a thief, caught red-handed with stolen goods.

'Look, couldn't this wait?' she sighed indignantly. 'I'll drop it round to you some other time.'

Porky shook his head. 'Better we sort things out now, don't you think? I've got a life going on as well as you.'

She eventually found his rotten key, slapped it grudgingly into his hand, laughed suddenly. 'And there was I thinking you'd be upset.'

An ambulance screamed urgently by, blue light flashing, then quickly faded into the distance; gone. A sudden silence.

He smiled, gently touched her hand and turned away almost at once. 'Goodbye Lizzie,' he whispered with no apparent sign of regret. 'I wish you the very best of luck.' The door snapped shut behind her.

OK, it wasn't quite how she'd planned it, seen it in her mind's eye, but she told herself it was probably for the best. A clean cut finish; none of that trial separation nonsense, see how we feel in a month or so's time sort of twaddle. For once Porky was right.

Over and done with, an end to it. A new beginning in Notting Hill Gate.

The couple in the flat upstairs recognised her at once; the girl with the healing hands. They'd seen her on television; name on the tips of their tongues.

It happened quite often; perfect strangers who knew the face but couldn't quite get the name. In the space of a week she'd been Lilly, Jilly and Billy, Patsy, Polly and Jeanie, with a range of surnames, alphabetically, from Beckwith through to Walkman. There was also a fairly close Lizzie Newman.

Lizzie kept a tally and promised herself she'd seriously consider a name change if enough people could agree who they'd like her to be. It might save a lot of time although she couldn't really see herself as a Lilly or Patsy; always thought of herself more as a Sophia or Francesca. Natasha, perhaps, or Jasmine at a push.

But the voice which called to her from the business

side of a stall in the Potobello Road antique market seemed fairly sure who she was.

'It's Lizzie Beckman, isn't it?'

Lizzie peered through the canvas awning. 'My goodness,' she said with a gasp of amazement. 'You're a long way from home.'

'Ten minutes actually. Shepherds Bush; just up the road.'

Bennington, straight-backed as always, unusually casual in jeans and a sweater, suede patches on the elbows. He set a mug of coffee down on a make-shift counter, ran the flat of his hand across neatly parted silver grey hair.

'But your job…….. Penfold Manor?'

He shook his head, grinned. 'Just a walk-on part. Short run, out of town theatre, so to speak.'

She laughed excitedly, clapped her hands together like a child. 'You're an actor?'

'Bit parts only, I'm afraid.'

'But an actor, just the same. I had no idea; none of us did.'

He moved closer, kissed her cheek. 'That was the general idea sweetheart,' he whispered.

'And Molly, your wife?'

'Absolutely not.' He took her hand, patted it gently. 'We must get together for a drink one evening and I'll tell you all about it.'

'That would be lovely,' said Lizzie. 'Come over to my place; just round the corner. Tonight, tomorrow night, whenever you fancy?'

'If you don't mind dirty denims and the smell of a market stall I could pop over later, on my way home. Say six o'clock?'

Lizzie smiled. 'Six it is.' She handed him a scribbled note of her address, hesitated. 'I've just realised, I don't know your first name.'

'Or my second,' he said at once. 'It's Diamond, as in gem. Simon Diamond; actor, antique trader, poet, occasional cleaner and amateur photographer.'

'See you later then Simon,' she said. 'Ground floor flat; name on the bell.'

Thunder rumbled overhead, the afternoon sun vanished behind thickening cloud and the air grew heavy with the threat of rain. Lizzie headed for home by way of the wine shop; three bottles of Spanish Rioja at discount prices and a chilled Chablis, in two plastic bags.

Fat drops of rain splitter-splattered across the pavement, slowly at first but then in torrents as the heavens opened over Notting Hill and gutters rushed with the sudden deluge.

Lizzie's pale blue cotton dress clung, lank and lifeless, like a wet tea towel; the line of her knickers finely embossed in the saturated fabric, boobs pert, proud and close to escape. She stopped, stared at her reflection in the shop window, brushed straggling blonde hair from her eyes, and decided that a carefully contrived celebrity image was all too easily washed away in a heavy downpour. Shorter, more manageable hair, seemed like an option worthy of consideration.

The rain stopped almost in an instant, like a tap turned off at the kitchen sink, and a hazy sun began to flicker back to life in a brighter sky. But that's when Lizzie began to steam. By the time she'd closed her front door and peeled the soggy cotton dress from clammy limbs, there was a faint but altogether visible mist hanging in the hallway and, with it, the nauseous smell of damp. A generous dousing of Escada, sprayed unstintingly from an obscenely large bottle, filled the flat with flowers and spices; not one of her favourite perfumes, she never wore it, but a definite improvement on the doubtful odour of warm, wet clothes and a practical use for one of Porky's redundant birthday presents.

In a little over an hour she emerged from the bedroom, modest but mildly exotic in Chinese silk; a flame red mandarin top with matching trousers, kung fu slippers in silk brocade, her hair twisted tight into a chignon with red

ribbon, and an undeniably Oriental touch to her make-up.
Simon Diamond turned up at six, bearing gifts; two Victorian wine glasses, ruby red with clear, slender stems.
'Worth a few bob as a set of six,' he confided with all the authority of someone who knows about such things. 'Don't suppose the other four survived the last century and a half though.'
Lizzie held them up to the light. 'Just beautiful,' she said. 'And exactly the right shade for Rioja.'
'Shouldn't it be Chinese rice wine in that outfit?' He made a square with fingers and thumbs, looked through it like a camera lens. 'Suits you. Perhaps I could photograph you sometime?'
She winked, relaxed back into the couch, sipped her wine. 'I bet you say that to all the girls.'
'Not usually to the girls sweetheart.' He smothered a nervous laugh, pulled a handkerchief from his pocket and gently dabbed the sides of his mouth.
Lizzie stared at him, silent, just for a moment. 'But you can't possibly be gay,' she whispered, eyes wide in amazement. 'Not you.'
'And why not me?' His eye brows arched indignantly. 'Some of Hollywood's most manly stars were probably gay. Burt Lancaster, Rock Hudson…….'
She shrugged indifferently. 'You're far too… well... normal.'
'Look sweetheart, you don't have to wear hooped skirts and a bustle to be gay. Besides I'm a veteran gay, from another time when the word meant carefree not queer.'
Lizzie straightened-up, tried to look more serious. 'Do you have a partner Simon?'
'Sadly no; not at the moment. But I'm working on it.'
'And there was I thinking Molly Bennington was your wife.'
'Edna someone or other,' he said, scratching the side of his head. 'Strange woman. Used to be a trapeze artist, something like that.'

Lizzie swung her legs on to the couch, crossed them effortlessly in a lotus position. 'So tell me about Penfold Manor.'

'Just a private house really; available for conferences, private parties, film location work, gay orgies.'

'And reality TV shows.'

He hunched himself forward, hands neatly arranged on his lap. 'Not one of the greatest moments in Penfold's history. Bit of a bloody disaster in fact.'

'Disaster?' Lizzie frowned. She refilled their glasses, slid the savoury biscuits across the couch towards him. 'In what way a disaster?'

'Just about every way. Let's face it, three of our so-called celebrities walked out before they'd had time to unpack, another one got knocked down the stairs by our leading lady, and you were spirited away in the dead of night by a couple of refugees from a James Bond movie.'

Lizzie looked bewildered, placed her glass down slowly and carefully on the table beside her. 'Sorry but you've lost me,' she said. 'What leading lady are we talking about here?'

'The star of the show, of course, Elizabeth Penfold.' He stared up at the ceiling, stroked his chin thoughtfully. 'Can't remember the name for the moment; not really what you'd call an actress; does mainly TV commercials…….that one with the tea bags.'

'Actress or not, she certainly looked the part. Scared the life out of me.'

'Scared the life out of Donny Jackson too.' Simon Diamond stood up, stretched his arms wearily, drained the last of the wine from his glass. 'The stupid woman was told to frighten him off, get him out of the east wing, not shove him down the stairs. Could have killed him.'

Lizzie wriggled to her feet, stabbed the cork screw into a second bottle of Rioja. 'I hope you don't think you'll be allowed to leave before I've heard the whole story,' she said with a mischievous grin. 'And I mean all of it.'

'Not a great deal to tell.' He gazed into his empty wine glass, smiled to himself. 'All a bit of a joke really; not very well organised.'

She perched herself tidily on the edge of the couch, patted the cushion beside her. 'So there isn't a ghost at Penfold Manor; not a real one.'

'Who knows? But I can tell you that no sane TV producer would rely on a ghost to materialise for the cameras.'

'So they hired one.'

Simon nodded. 'That's about the size of it.'

'So why didn't the others see her too? Why just me?'

'It's elementary spook psychology, the essence of a good ghost story.' He placed his hand on hers, gave it a comforting squeeze. 'If everyone saw ghosts all over the place they wouldn't be frightening, would they? But phantom spirits are much more cunning; they appear only occasionally, to a chosen few receptive souls who then put the fear of God into the rest of us.'

'And I was nominated.'

'You were supposed to set the others thinking; help the imaginations to run riot; scare the pants of them.'

Lizzie forced a cosmetic smile. 'I think it's true to say that Yvette Duncan's pants were already off at that point.'

'But, let's face it, her whirlwind romance with the MP attracted a lot of publicity.' Simon hesitated, looked at her with serious eyes. 'Nothing like the coverage for your plans to heal the world, of course,' he said quietly. 'That certainly placed you in the public eye.'

'It'll all be forgotten in a few weeks,' Lizzie sighed. 'Seems to me that fame is a bit like wine; you taste it, enjoy it, and then it's gone, although the effects sometimes linger.' She clinked their glasses together. 'The trick is to open a new bottle before your glass is empty.'

'That's a very deep, dark thought for such a young head.'

'You mean airhead.'

Simon slapped her knee. 'You're far too young for such cynicism,' he said. "And, anyway, that's not what I meant." He reached for the Rioja, gently tapped the cork part-way back into the bottle. 'If fame is like wine then what you see before you is lasting fame; cut off in its prime, unfinished, but fondly remembered and, most importantly, leaving us wanting more.'

Lizzie grinned. 'What are you saying?'

'Just that stars very often become legends simply by popping their clogs prematurely, unfulfilled, and with the best still to come.' He counted them off on his fingers; James Dean, John Kennedy, Marilyn Monroe, John Lennon, Elvis Presley, Buddy Holly......

'Jesus Christ,' Lizzie said, before he could finish. 'He was only thirty three.'

Simon Diamond shrugged his shoulders. 'Actually thirty three's quite old for a legend these days.'

But Lizzie Beckman's Rioja wasn't to be the stuff of legends. The cork was pulled once more from the bottle and any prospects of lasting fame and immortality quaffed within the hour. Fondly remembered? Perhaps. But unfinished? Not a drop of it.

'Would you say we've had too much to drink Simon?' The words tripped awkwardly across numb lips. She smiled giddily. 'Nearly three bottles of fame can make your head spin if you're not careful.'

Simon yawned, legs stretched out lazily in front of him. 'It's the heart not the head that spins when you get to my age,' he said. 'And then the hang-overs in the morning.' His head lolled towards her. 'Don't suppose you have those sort of problems, not at your age.'

'Can't say I do, no.'

He fixed her with heavy eyes. 'And if you did, you could heal yourself in a flash.'

Lizzie thought for a moment, ran the tip of her finger around the rim of the wine glass. 'Don't think it works like that,' she said. 'The healing power's for other people, not me.'

'A bit bloody unfair, don't you think?'

'Not really. I'm lucky enough to be fit and healthy so what's to heal?'

Simon dragged himself up from the couch, patted his belly. 'I'll have a copy of your fitness video then, when you get around to doing one,' he said. 'But right now I must be off to Shepherds Bush......love you and leave you.'

'Fitness video?' She looked slightly surprised, stared at him thoughtfully. 'That's not a bad idea.'

'It's a damn good idea. Anyone who isn't actually clinically obese seems to have a fitness video these days.' He walked, head erect, back straight, to the front door, kissed her fondly on both cheeks and stepped out into a balmy London evening with a careless wave.

She waited at the window until he'd turned the corner, towards the cab rank, before making the call to Toby Stone. 'D'you know what,' she said. 'I've just had an absolutely brilliant idea.'

Chapter 10

Daisy Henshaw was pregnant; four and a half weeks gone and totally ecstatic. What's more, it was a boy; she just knew it. Benjamin, a Liberal Democrat, born under the sign of Aries and destined for a dazzling career in law. Ben was going to be a judge.

Barry Gammon was in love but less than elated. For a start the whole thing was a clinical impossibility unless Daisy hadn't been totally honest with him. Men with infertility problems don't beget Lib Dem judges, and that's a scientific fact.

But Daisy was adamant; there was nobody else involved. Barry was Ben's father. And another thing; no self respecting father-to-be should allow people to call him Porky, so that would have to stop.

A weekend of doubt and uncertainty dragged by and it was late on Monday afternoon when Barry Gammon submitted his seminal fluids to medical scrutiny for the second time in his life.

They kept him waiting for more than an hour with only the fading covers of last year's wrinkled magazines for company. But from the hospital window he could see across Westminster Bridge to the top of the London Eye, the giant wheel which had picked him up, spun him around and then, calmly but quite deliberately, flung him headlong into the path of Daisy Henshaw. In the great scheme of things it was unavoidable, a cosmic certainty, adoration on impact.

It was getting on for five o'clock when someone in a crisp, white jacket handed him an envelope, the words Test Results printed, red, across the top. And that's when Barry Gammon, male, age twenty eight, reference number PST 4424, discovered he complied with World Health Organisation definitions of normal in the dad-to-be department. Twenty million sperm per millilitre of semen [somebody must have counted] more than enough to beget a Lib Dem judge and a couple of QCs besides.

An astonishing reversal of his previous infertility; nothing short of a miracle, they said.

Lizzie Beckman smiled at him with plump, high-gloss lips from the back of a bus near Victoria. He caught sight of her again at the top end of Park Lane; blonde hair noticeably shorter, spikey even, and with a subtle tinge of strawberry. By the time he'd rounded Marble Arch and turned into the Edgware Road, Barry Gammon had spotted her at least half a dozen times; knew the advertisement off by heart; word perfect.

'Fit for Nothing'; the words formed a sort of halo in gold letters above Lizzie's head. And below, concertinaed between her outstretched hands, the details; a free Lizzie Beckman fitness video with every garment from the Well-Fit Fashion range. There were some token sketches along the bottom; skimpy dresses, sexy underwear, and a signed pledge that each was an original design by Lizzie Beckman.

A couple of questions began to take shape in Barry Gammon's mind. Had Lizzie quietly put the life back into his loins with a quick prayer or two, when he wasn't looking, or was this miracle cure one of the inevitable side-effects of sex with a healer? There was, of course, another explanation; it could have happened naturally, all by itself, so to speak, with no help from anyone. People made unexpected recoveries all the time; he'd read about it. Definitely more logical than the crazy notion of some kind of spiritual sperm transplant which, apart from not going down well with Daisy Henshaw, would acknowledge Lizzie Beckman's hand in the creation of his first born. And that simply wasn't on.

But even as he contemplated the new and unexpected potency of his private parts, from the comfort of a Bayswater flat, Lizzie pondered her own future, a mile or so away, on the other side of the park where Toby Stone was putting the final touches to a masterpiece of the unexpected.

Putting it bluntly, Lizzie Beckman was on the market, up for sale, and the red line on Beckman Fashions' sales graph showed that young girls wanted to buy her, a little bit at a time; a dress, a top, some crazy jeans, and all with her new Well Fit label. Lizzie Beckman was a brand to be packaged and presented, labelled and priced, like Coca Cola, McDonalds, or Rolls Royce – but without the multi-million pound marketing budget.

So a give-away fitness video with every Well Fit purchase and a poster campaign on the backs of buses, plus a few well-placed, low-cost television advertisements, was about as good as it would get, for the moment at least. Samuel Beckman was resolute; the money simply wasn't available for Toby's ambitious advertising campaign. He shrugged forlornly, a disappointed man, eyes tightly closed to reason, head shaking miserably from side with the mere idea of such extravagance. The inevitable F-word followed.

Free publicity, that's what was needed. He always made it sound so simple, conjured-up a make-believe world where grateful newspaper editors queued patiently in line while kind-hearted publicity agents like Toby Stone handed-out press statements to help fill blank, desolate and otherwise empty newspaper pages. But in the real world, where bad news always outweighs the good, it isn't like that. War, disaster, death and destruction have a long-standing monopoly on available newspaper space and, if there's not enough of that to go round, the government can always be relied upon to make-up the shortfall with its own special brand of criminal lunacy.

So nobody, apart from Samuel Beckman, would have expected Lizzie's modest contribution to the world of fitness and fashion to become the stuff of headlines; a brief mention or two on the women's pages, perhaps, and that would be it. But Toby had a plan to change all that; a plan which relied on military precision and, like all the best military operations, the finer details were available on a need-to-know basis only. Samuel Beckman was someone who didn't need to know.

'Me?' Lizzie shrieked. 'In one of those?' She hugged herself protectively, her face filled with horror. 'Are you completely mad?'

Toby grinned, slowly turned the pages of the brochure. 'Apparently they're completely safe. Nothing to worry about.'

She peered over his shoulder at the picture; a huge red balloon, black and white triangles in a random pattern across the top, a wicker basket hanging underneath, four people standing shoulder-to-shoulder in the middle like a bunch of cut-price flowers.

'They burst,' she said. 'Explode in mid air.'

'Not hot air balloons.'

'*All* balloons. It's what they do best… burst.'

'Well these don't.'

'So how do you steer a balloon anyway?' She slapped the page with the back of her hand. 'Seems to me they just drift about in the sky until they crash into something… and burst.'

'You won't need to steer,' Toby answered. 'We'll have an expert to handle that side of things.'

Lizzie half laughed, covered her ears. 'I don't believe

this.' She turned towards the open window and brilliant afternoon sunshine. 'Why would I want to flit about in a hot air balloon?'

'Balloons don't flit about,' said Toby. 'They float above'.

'Flit, float, burst; wha-ever. Why bother?'

'Because it's time for you to descend from heaven; float down to earth from the sky, rather than simply turn-up from nowhere.'

She shrugged. 'I thought celebrities usually turned-up in private jets or helicopters not hot air balloons.'

'But that would be totally the wrong image for you.' He paused, searched her face for signs that she understood, eventually decided that she didn't.

'Look,' he sighed, taking hold of her hand. 'We're trying to put a little bit of heaven into everything you do. When we talk about your healing powers, we'll slip in phrases like heaven-sent, blessed by god, the answer to a prayer; that sort of thing.' He reached across the desk for a clip board, reminded himself of his recent notes. 'We'll talk about the fitness video giving girls a heavenly body, the shape and form of a goddess. And then the fashion collection; it'll be absolutely divine, created for birds of paradise and perfect angels. Get the idea?'

Lizzie looked dumbfounded. 'Where, exactly, do you just slip-in all these clever little phrases?'

'Press statements, radio interviews, TV appearances, adverts, leaflet drops....'

'Leaflet drops?' She stabbed at the picture of a balloon with a well-manicured finger nail. 'Is this thing going to fly about littering the countryside with bits of paper?'

Toby didn't answer. Enough's enough. A line has to be drawn somewhere and this was it. PR consultants can't be expected to reveal the intricacies of creative publicity campaigns to cynical clients who, more often than not, are incapable of comprehending the finely-tuned logistics; especially clients who don't even pay fees. So Toby Stone didn't bother to explain everything, and certainly not the details of his outline plans for a dramatic crash-landing and Lizzie Beckman's subsequent, and highly mysterious, disappearance. That could all wait for another time.

Toby's vision of an angel-shaped balloon quickly faded when the estimate came through; well over thirty thousand pounds for the envelope alone – the bit that inflates. And then all the other paraphernalia; basket, burner, ropes and a lot more besides. Out of the question.

He settled for something a little less ambitious; a silvery white balloon with Lizzie's name in large gold letters across the centre. But life's a compromise and a sparkly gold sash around the basket announced that the balloon was proudly sponsored by Beckman Fashions of London. Toby had been adamant; there was no room for an address and telephone number.

Samuel Beckman added up the bills for the second time but arrived at the same total as before. For almost ten minutes he examined the figures, silent, apart from the faint murmur of resentment which rumbled and grumbled from somewhere in the back of his throat; a low, guttural growl which finally gave voice to his feelings. In 1968 he'd bought a house which didn't cost as much as this balloon. And his house didn't need a chauffeur either.

'A pilot, not a chauffeur,' Toby told him. 'Balloons, like helicopters and airplanes, can only be flown by licensed pilots.'

The conversation deteriorated from there but, after the inevitable see-sawing of the shoulders and shaking of the head, it was finally but reluctantly agreed that a balloon without a pilot wasn't a viable option and that one Stuart de Lacy should be duly appointed to the task.

Mr de Lacy parked a red Aston Martin DB6 on double yellow lines outside Toby Stone's office shortly before twenty past ten the following morning. He stood by the open door of the car, brushed unruly red hair from his eyes and, with a cursory glance around Beauchamp Place, fixed a card to the inside of the windscreen – Doctor on Visit, it said. A dazzling white T-shirt, flannels to match, more dentist than GP, were quickly adjusted, a leather brief case grabbed from the back of the car and Mr de Lacy was ready for the business of the day. He paused for a moment in front of the lingerie shop window, winked at the girl behind the counter, then slowly climbed the stairs to his ten thirty appointment, checking his mobile messages on the way.

The meeting was slightly stilted. First Toby Stone outlined his expectations while Stuart de Lacy looked down at the floor, nodding impatiently from time to time as if he'd probably heard it all before. Then de Lacy explained that it wasn't going to be anywhere near as simple as Toby seemed to think; turning up in a balloon at precisely the right time and in exactly the right place had more to do with the vagaries of the weather than the best laid plans of mice and PR men.

It would be possible to determine the general route of travel by studying the forecast wind direction at one thousand feet and varying the take-off site accordingly. But then there was the Coriolis effect. Toby's eyes began to glaze over while de Lacy explained how balloons tend to swing ten to fifteen degrees or so to the left as they descend; something to do with gravitational pull unless, of course, you happened to be in Australia, when the balloon would swing to the right.

Toby waved aside the details. 'This is fascinating stuff but not strictly my problem,' he said flatly. 'The question is can you deliver my client to a series of pre-arranged locations or not?'

De Lacy nodded thoughtfully but said nothing.

'Then I'll need your signature on a confidentiality agreement.' Toby leaned forward, slid a single sheet of A4 paper across the desk.

The other man frowned as he read through the details.

'Bit cloak and dagger isn't it?'

'Nothing sinister,' said Toby, handing him a felt tip pen. 'Standard agreement to ensure that the finer details of my promotional arrangements never leave this room.'

'And if they did?'

Toby smiled coldly. 'If they did it would very likely cost the offending party substantially more than that Aston Martin outside.'

De Lacy shrugged, placed the felt tip to one side and reached into his briefcase for a Mont Blanc pen. 'I prefer real ink,' he said.

'Don't have much time for it myself,' Toby snapped back. 'Takes too long to dry.'

'Ah yes, I supposed it does.' He waved the paper about lethargically between finger and thumb before handing it back. 'But you see balloonists must learn patience; it's an essential qualification for the job.'

'Wouldn't suit me then,' Toby said, stretching back in his swivel chair. 'My life's a series of deadlines.' He stopped short, stared hard at de Lacy for a moment before going on. 'My next deadline, by which, of course Stuart, I mean *your* next deadline, is in exactly two weeks from now. Let me tell you all about it.'

De Lacy shuffled his chair closer to the desk and took out a note book.

'No notes,' Toby said at once. 'Nothing is to be written down. In fact the rest of this meeting didn't happen.'

The other man smiled, shook his head. 'I thought I'd signed a confidentiality agreement not the Official Secrets Act.'

'One protects a notion, the other safeguards a nation,' said Toby. 'As far as I'm concerned, it amounts to the same thing.'

Two days later, with the sun high in a clear blue sky, Lizzie Beckman?s heart raced as the silvery white balloon descended into the corner of a Surrey field; slowly and just a little unsteadily but with comforting, reassuring words from Stuart de Lacy. Over to her right at the garlanded entrance to a large, oblong marquee, festooned with golden flags, Toby Stone lead the growing crowd in spontaneous applause while the basket skimmed, bounced and shuddered into an area of long grass and came, at last, to a shaky, uncomfortable halt.

Two hand maidens from heaven, radiant in gossamer silk, long blonde hair cascading across delicate white shoulders, slender feet naked to the fresh cut grass, drifted across to Lizzie's side, lending celestial hands to a somewhat less than graceful escape from the unwieldy, clumsy wicker cage.

And while angels escorted her to the middle of the field and the waiting rostrum, Lizzie Beckman glistened like a goddess in a golden cloak, thrown carelessly to the ground at the moment she reached the steps to reveal a diaphanous white sarong, draped seductively around her and tied about the waist with a golden sash; a large, round, gold brooch in the centre.

The applause faded, a new stillness spread through the crowd, and then silence, apart from a gentle breeze which whispered through the willows lining the nearby river bank.

Lizzie raised her arms high above her head, stretched her fingers to the sky, and breathed-in the warm summer air before she spoke. 'Do you feel it?' she called out. 'Can you taste it?' she yelled, even louder. 'If you listen carefully you'll even hear it,' she screamed.

She paused, searched the faces of her audience with eager eyes. 'I'm talking about a power; a magnificent power to renew, restore, repair, rejuvenate each and every one of us. It's with us here right now, all around us, touching us, healing us, making us whole. I know because it followed me here today. And it followed me here today for one reason and one reason only; this magnificent power wants to take you by the hand, heal your hurt, stop your pain, suck out the poison that weakens your body.'

Toby Stone felt a hand on his shoulder.

'She's good, isn't she? Very good indeed,' Stuart de Lacy whispered. 'Seems to have a natural way with words; which is odd because she didn't say a thing on the way here.'

'Actually her way with words doesn't extend to 'whatever' and she's scared stiff of hot air balloons,' said Toby. 'Reckons they burst.'

'So why should that worry her if she seriously believes there's some kind of magnificent power following her about?'

Toby shrugged. 'Pass. Better ask her yourself.'

'Do these people believe all that stuff?'

Toby shrugged again. 'I guess most of them would like to believe or they wouldn't be here, would they?' He glanced across to a group of photographers standing idly to one side of the main body of people. 'Then again, that lot don't really believe anything unless it makes a good picture.'

Lizzie wailed and waved her arms about until a dry throat and aching shoulders told her to stop. She stood perfectly still and waited, head tilted back, eyes closed to the midday sun.

A bare-foot angel placed a glass of water at her side and quickly disappeared back into the crowd. Some of the photographers began to sense something and edged forward, unsure but with a sudden urgency in their movements, cameras held at the ready, elbows bent and raised for combat.

Toby hastened towards the rostrum and turned to face the crowd, looking for reactions. His eyes at once fixed on an elderly man in a beige linen suit and a Panama hat who struggled with the limp and seemingly lifeless body of a young girl. Another, younger, man who'd been standing behind them, reached forward and helped carry her to the shade of the willows where they laid her down, using the older man's jacket as a pillow.

Half a dozen photographers quickly followed but, after some initial enthusiasm and the usual jostling for positions, merely looked-on and waited, undecided if the reclining figure was today's news or, as seemed more likely, just someone who'd fainted with the heat.

But the sudden scream which shattered the quiet of the afternoon left no doubt that this was news.

'I can see.' The crowd turned as one as the words reverberated through the willows and the young girl opened her eyes to a blitz of flashing lights. She turned instinctively away, hands to her face, the older man cradling her head in his arms, shielding her from the advancing army of photographers, pleading with them to leave her alone. But nobody was listening.

Toby moved quickly forward to hold them back. 'Give the girl some space for Christ's sake,' he called out. 'Let's find out what's happened here before you start clicking-off like bloody madmen.'

'Why d'you invite us if you don't want pictures?' one of them shouted back angrily. 'We'll go if you like.'

And it's true to say that when the story and picture potential are weak, this would be the point when the prudent PR might tactfully back-off. But this wasn't one of those occasions. This was shaping up well and Toby seized control.

She had a very ordinary name but Suzie Hobbs was no longer an ordinary young lady. Blinded when she was very young, her uncle explained to the reporters, the result of a childhood illness, but now looking at the world for the first time in more than twenty years.

Suzie Hobbs cried, laughed, screamed and then cried some more; tears of joy, tears of excitement, tears of disbelief and, above all, tears of supreme happiness. She smiled, wide-eyed, for the cameras, kissed and hugged the person who'd restored her sight in a single, magical moment and gazed in wonder at everything around her. Her uncle, who seemed suddenly pre-occupied, called the local hospital on his mobile 'phone. It was important, he announced somewhat pompously, to establish a medical explanation for what had just happened to his niece.

'Miracle should cover it,' Toby suggested.

The elderly gentleman adjusted the brim of his Panama, smoothed-down the front of his jacket and smiled politely. He ignored Toby's comment and, instead, offered some mumbled thanks before setting-off, with his niece on his arm, towards a green Morris Minor Traveller.

Lizzie waited until their car had reached the gate on the far side of the field and indicated left, towards Guildford, before she turned back towards the crowd which had started to disperse. The majority were making towards the marquee.

'Suzie what's-a-name wasn't the only one today,' she said softly. 'There were others.'

Toby stared at her, frowned. 'Wouldn't they have said something?'

She let out a deep sigh, gazed up into the willow branches, slowly shook her head. 'They might not even know; not yet anyway.'

He took her hand, gently squeezed. 'I think you may have overdone it today. You look absolutely shattered.'

Lizzie nodded. 'And I feel shattered, but that's probably got more to do with ballooning than healing.' She glanced across at two men who'd started to pack the balloon into a trailer. 'I guess balloons are a bit of a one-way journey,' she said. 'It rather looks as if we're going back by car.'

'That seems to be how it works,' said Toby, searching his pockets for his car keys. 'If the wind's blowing in the right direction to get you somewhere, you can reckon it'll be blowing the wrong way to take you back again.'

'But surely winds change direction?' she said wistfully staring up at a cluster of puffy, white clouds.

Toby gave her a blank look. 'From time to time, I suppose. But there's always a prevailing wind which, if I recall, is from the south west in this part of the world.'

'So you just sort of go with the flow and hope you end up where you planned,' she sighed. 'But, if you get it wrong, you come down to earth, pack everything up, go back to the beginning and start all over again.'

He placed a comforting arm around her shoulder, kissed her cheek. 'Now why do I get the feeling you're not talking about ballooning?'

'Oh, it's nothing. I just wonder sometimes, that's all.' She hesitated, looked into his eyes. 'I don't think I'll be able to do this for much longer; the healing I mean. It's mine for only a very short while.'

A voice, amplified through speakers at either end of the marquee, announced that the Lizzie Beckman Well Fit Fashion show was about to commence and that a Champagne lunch was being served.

'They'll always be the spin-offs,' Toby grinned as they started towards the marquee. 'And, besides, I've got plans for my little celebrity; big plans which don't require special powers of any kind.'

The last of the photographers, who'd spent more than an hour setting-up an uncooperative laptop to e-mail his pictures back to a news agency, left at half past two with a reassuring nod of the head.

'Nice one Tobe,' he called out. 'Should do well.'

Toby nodded, gave him a thumbs-up. 'Drive safely mate.'

'If I wrap myself round a tree I can always get Lizzie to straighten me out again eh?' He smiled, clicked his fingers. 'Bloody incredible, that girl.'

Lizzie giggled girlishly. 'Don't rely on it,' she said, blowing him a kiss. 'I can't raise the dead.'

Toby waited until the other man had left the marquee before he spoke. 'How do you know that?' he asked in a half whisper. 'Perhaps you should give it a try.'

'Are you serious?'

His face relaxed into a smile. 'Just joking.'

'Didn't sound like a joke.'

'Joke. Promise.' He raised his hands in mock surrender. 'But it's a nice idea, don't you think?'

Lizzie wasn't impressed. 'Even if I wanted to, I couldn't.'

'Of course not; impossible.' He handed her a glass of Champagne, took one himself, clinked them together. 'To life,' he said. 'The long and happy variety.'

She stared into his face, forced a tired, reluctant smile. 'L'Chayim,' she replied.

'Which means?'

'It means the same thing. To life, but in Hebrew.'

'L'Chayim, then, the even longer and happier variety.'

The journey back to London was long and tedious; Toby's fault entirely. He'd insisted on making dozens of 'phone calls before finally dumping his things haphazardly in the boot of the car and driving straight into the middle of the early evening rush hour and a seemingly never-ending traffic jam which stretched from the A3 in Surrey, up into the southern fringes of London and beyond.

Stuart de Lacy closed his eyes to the problem from the relative comfort of the back seat and spoke drowsily of other things.

'A question for you,' he murmured, barely moving his lips. 'Why didn't they ask for your autograph?'

Lizzie frowned, leaned forward, tapped Toby on the shoulder. 'He's got a point. People don't seem to ask for my autograph.'

'Autographs are a bit old hat these days,' Toby replied firmly. 'The kids prefer to take pictures on their mobile 'phones.'

De Lacy thought for a moment. 'But most of them today weren't kids. And, anyway, I didn't see anyone taking pictures.'

Toby stared at him through the rear view mirror. 'So what are you trying to say?'

'Nothing. Just wondered why no autographs.'

There was a brief but uncomfortable silence before Toby tuned the radio to the six o'clock news and unconfirmed reports that a blind girl's eyesight had been totally restored by a faith healer. Lizzie's name was mentioned two or three times.

'I wish they wouldn't say that,' she sighed. 'I've never asked anyone to have faith in me or anything else for that matter.'

'That may have something to do with it,' said de Lacy, eyes still firmly closed. 'They're too much in awe of what you do to dare ask for an autograph.'

Toby shrugged. 'It's possible.'

'I hadn't really thought about it,' Lizzie said. 'But Stuart's absolutely right; you can't be a proper celebrity if nobody wants your autograph.'

'Trust me,' said Toby. 'We've got fashion spreads in three top glossies this month alone, a two page feature on your time at the haunted house in Britain's biggest Sunday newspaper, and an hour-long TV programme about spiritual healing, with you as the main focus. They'll be queuing for your autograph by this time next week.'

Stuart de Lacy slowly opened his eyes and stared out of the window. 'I assume you've explained the Parliament Hill project to Lizzie?' he asked. 'I mean the key points of the plan.'

Toby shook his head. 'Not entirely; thought I'd leave the details to you. After all, you're the pilot.'

Lizzie folded her arms and settled back, eyes narrowed, glaring at the back of Toby's head. 'I think I'd rather hear the details from you,' she said sarcastically. 'After all, you're the PR man.'

Toby half turned towards her. 'Well, in a word, Lizzie, I think it's time for you to, shall we say, disappear; just for a short while.'

❖

There were four more descents from heaven in the silvery white balloon during the following week and a half; different fields, different places, different faces in the crowd. But, always, a handful of people were sent home feeling healthier and happier than they'd dared to imagine when they arrived.

And with the healing came the headlines; some with a hint of scepticism and others pure, undiluted, over-the-top sensationalism. Toby was happy with either one of the 'isms', provided they spelled his client's name correctly, and the pictures were suitably flattering.

The idea of a descent to Parliament Hill had a lot going for it. For a start it's the highest point in London, nearly four hundred and fifty feet above sea level. What's more, it's set in the rambling eight hundred acres of Hampstead Heath, so there's no shortage of space to land a hot air balloon.

And Toby hadn't missed the historic link with Boadicea who, according to legend, is buried in an ancient mound on the hill. He loved the imagery of it all; Boadicea meets Beckman, two powerful women coming together in a sacred place, so to speak.

But finally, and most importantly from a publicity perspective, Parliament Hill is only four miles from the centre of London, just a quick cab journey from the offices of the national press. It was the perfect setting for a well-orchestrated media drama.

Lizzie Beckman signed autographs and posed for pictures in her golden cloak before the balloon climbed gently into a September sky. But the truth is that her mysterious disappearance from the scene of the crash, twenty minutes later, owed more to elementary sleight of hand than supernatural forces. And, while undoubtedly dramatic, the speedy and somewhat erratic plunge towards a stretch of heath beyond a densely wooded area, followed by a well-choreographed tumble to the ground, far from prying eyes and the main body of the crowd, had little in common with the violent, heart stopping, potentially catastrophic events described by Stuart de Lacy in subsequent interviews with both the press and the police.

He talked about a sudden gust of wind which lasted only a moment but long enough for him to temporarily lose control. And then, for reasons which were still unclear, the burners had partially failed, sending the basket plummeting to the ground. He'd reached out for Lizzie immediately after the initial jolt but she was gone. And, no, he couldn't explain it.

Lizzie's cloak was found close by, indicating that she'd probably been thrown clear of the basket, maybe suffered a head injury and perhaps wandered off, disorientated, unseen. Possibly she'd collapsed somewhere further down the hill, in the long grass, maybe.

But there were others with more spiritual explanations; taken by God, they said, returned to heaven, where she belonged. Four women, unsmiling and intense, shapeless in purple robes, were adamant; Boadicea incarnate. She'd returned to her earthly resting place and would rise again with the turning of the seasons.

Stuart de Lacy helped pack away the balloon on to the trailer before cadging a lift to Waterloo Station. The fast train to Guildford arrived soon after four thirty, then a taxi to the village of Albury and a small, thatched cottage nestling at the foot of the downs with views up to Newlands Corner. He smiled wryly at Toby Stone's sardonic sense of humour, ran his hand across the bonnet of the red Aston Martin, parked in the narrow drive, and went inside.

The old lady in black, grey hair pinned neatly into a bun, attracted little or no attention as she walked slowly and unsteadily, aided by a walking stick, across Parliament Hill Fields towards Hampstead underground station where she took the Northern Line to Waterloo.

CHAPTER 11

The rattling drone of lawn mowers sent a pang of dread to the centre of Lizzie Beckman's stomach, reawakening memories of a bored seven year old and interminable weekends at aunt Shirley's. Stanmore wasn't exactly rural England and cousin Jane couldn't help being so completely uncool but Lizzie always felt as if she'd left the civilised world behind, at home in St Johns Wood, and been transported far from London to a provincial backwater where an alien sub-class prayed for rain to feed their lawns and then shaved them back to the roots at the first sign of growth. Uncle Harry's mower rattled away industriously most Saturday mornings; first in straight lines running from the back of the house to the fir trees at the end of the garden, and then diagonally. More often than not he did it twice, working well into the afternoon to ensure that any evidence of growth had been removed and the velvet lawn was exactly as it should be.

But Albury had rather more than its fair share of lawn mowers. They were all around; different rhythms pitched at slightly different decibels but each with the same relentless intensity and commitment.

Lizzie flicked quickly through the pages of a well-thumbed magazine, seemingly filled with pictures of ploughed fields, horses and women with pretentious names, tossed it back with the others, in a small pile, on the coffee table. Her eyes flicked around the room and settled, finally, on the inglenook fireplace; freshly-chopped logs arranged on wads of screwed-up newspaper, ready and waiting to burst into flames at the strike of a match.

'How long are we supposed to sit around here doing nothing,' she called out.

Beyond the open window Stuart de Lacy lay perfectly still and as devoid of thought as he could possibly manage, on a floral sun lounger which he'd strategically positioned at the far end of a kidney-shaped pool, away from the house and potential distractions.

'Sorry, you'll have to shout,' he answered. 'Can't hear you.'

Lizzie leaned out of the window. 'I asked how long this goes on.'

'Why don't you ask Toby? He's running the show, not me.' De Lacy half-heartedly raised his head. 'And could you please stop shouting?'

She slammed the window shut, checked her mobile 'phone for messages, before calling Toby's office. He was out; back later. They'd get him to return the call. At times like this, when the world ignored her, Lizzie Beckman usually headed for the shops but Albury wasn't that kind of place and, besides, she was under strict instructions to lie low until further notice.

Stuart de Lacy's 'phone vibrated on the table by his side and played Rule Britannia. 'De Lacy,' he answered cautiously. 'How may I help you?'

'It's me and I'm fed up,' said Lizzie. 'Can't we do something?'

'We can relax in the sun and enjoy the country air.'

The 'phone went dead and Lizzie appeared at the back door, wearing a white satin dressing gown, loosely tied about the waist. 'Perhaps we could go for a drive somewhere?'

'We'll have to check with Toby.' De Lacy stretched back, hands behind his head. 'But I doubt it.'

She sat down at the end of the lounger, lifted his feet and moved his legs to one side. 'Do you fancy me?' she asked casually.

He removed his sun glasses, quickly looked her up and down, paused for a second. 'Not especially,' he said. 'Does it matter?'

'No, not especially,' Lizzie repeated. She stood up, slipped-off the satin dressing gown, and dived effortlessly into the pool.

De Lacy replaced his sun glasses and settled back, eyes closed to the sun and her nakedness. 'There now,' he said quietly. 'You've found something to occupy yourself.'

'Why don't you join me?' she called out.

'Later, perhaps.'

He half opened one eye as she floated, face-up, across the pool, legs kicking gently, arms spread wide, the contours of her body glistening immodestly in the sun, and decided it might be time to puncture an inflated ego.

At the point when it was clear that her audience wasn't paying attention, Lizzie Beckman stepped gracefully from the pool to a narrow stretch of grass where, hands on hips, head back, a pouting smile on her lips, she slowly rotated her pelvis, first one way then the other. The lower body gyrations progressed, seamlessly, into a series of gentle arm exercises before she turned her back on the reclining figure on the other side of the pool and bent forward to touch her toes in a single, well-rehearsed, flowing movement. She did it three or four times, each with a conspicuous wiggle of the bottom, and culminating with her hands flat on the grass in front of her.

De Lacy peered over the top of his sunglasses, stroked his chin thoughtfully. 'Sorry to interrupt,' he said softly. 'I couldn't help noticing.'

Lizzie turned away, hands crossed coyly in front of her.

'You shouldn't have been looking,' she said, peeking back over her shoulder, eyes fluttering in a futile attempt at modesty.

'The L5, lumber vertebrae.' He hesitated, seemingly embarrassed, searching for the right words. 'It's not the end of the world, really it's not. They can work wonders these days.'

She stared back at him with surprise. 'I don't need anyone to work any wonders, thank you very much,' she announced indignantly before storming off into the house.

De Lacy hadn't quite counted to ten when she returned, wrapped in a bath towel and full of resentment.

'Anyway, what's not the end of the world?' she demanded, standing over him like a gladiator at the kill.

He opened his eyes, looked up at her, compliant. 'Nobody's perfect,' he whispered. 'It's only a minor spinal deformity.'

'Deformity? 'I don't have deformities....anywhere.'

He raised himself up, took her hand, squeezed. 'My apologies; wrong word. And you're quite right; it's not a deformity. Not yet anyway. What you have is merely an abnormality but it is rather pronounced and could, of course, deteriorate over time.'

'How long?'

'Two years. Three at a push.'

She sat down suddenly, an anxious look on her face. 'The truth now; what's going to happen to me?'

He ran his fingers down her spine, stopped at the curve of her bottom and pressed hard.

'That hurts,' she screamed.

'I was afraid of that,' he said solemnly. 'Stand up please.'

Lizzie's eyes widened with trepidation. 'What are you talking about? Tell me.'

De Lacy rose slowly to his feet and stepped back to look at her. 'Would you mind losing the towel; just for a moment? And please try to stand absolutely straight, legs slightly apart, head up.'

She breathed deeply through her nose, huffed impatiently, while he stood behind her, unspeaking, prodding the cheeks of her bottom. 'Well?' she asked impatiently. 'What's happening to me?'

'Slip this on,' he said, handing her the previously discarded satin dressing gown. 'With a little bit of training, we may be able to substantially delay the onset of real problems.'

'Please. What's wrong with me?' she asked meekly.

De Lacy took hold of her hands, kissed them each in turn and gave her a sympathetic hug before he spoke, quietly but firmly.

'I'm afraid, Lizzie, the bad news is that you seem to have developed a rather chronic case of pain-in-the-arse syndrome.'

He hadn't quite anticipated the right hook to the head but managed to duck before it made contact.

'And you're a complete shit so that makes us even.'

A timely telephone call sent her running into the house. She returned half an hour later dressed in denim jeans and a white cotton T-shirt, carrying a cup of coffee, two biscuits in the saucer.

'Did you make one for me?' de Lacy enquired casually.

'Certainly not.'

He shook his head, sighed. 'Classic pain-in-the-arse symptom,' he muttered under his breath.

There was a long silence before he spoke again. 'What did he have to say then?'

'What did *who* have to say then?'

'Toby, who else?'

'What makes you think it was Toby on the 'phone?'

He sighed a second time, this time louder. 'Because he's the only living bloody creature on the planet who knows we're here.'

She dunked a biscuit into her coffee. 'Apparently I'm getting a lot of publicity. Everyone seems concerned about what happened on Parliament Hill. But Toby says we have to stay in this awful place for at least another week.'

De Lacy nodded in silence.

'Are you getting paid for lounging around here?'

He nodded again, remained silent.

'How much?'

'Mind your own business.'

She emptied the dregs of her coffee into a flower bed. 'It *is* my business. My father's funding this little escapade.'

'Look,' he said, slapping his hand on the table with a thud. 'I can think of better ways of spending the next week than being locked-up here with you. But that's how it is; that's the deal.'

'I don't see why you need to be here at all,' she shrugged.

'To avoid awkward questions about the crash. To be completely unavailable to the media; at least for the time being.'

She sat on the edge of the pool, slipped off her shoes, dangled her feet in the water. 'I suppose we'll just have to put up with each other for a while then.'

'Looks that way,' he said flatly. 'But you'll be back in the limelight soon enough, when you make your dramatic reappearance.'

Lizzie stared at de Lacy's thick red hair which flopped defiantly across his brow, and wondered if her own, shorter hair style had been such a good idea.

'I used to have long, blonde hair,' she said.

'Always preferred shorter hair myself,' he answered, refusing to look up at her.

She turned away, concealing a smug smile, and focussed her attention on the high ground in the distance. 'Is that the famous Newlands Corner; the place where Agatha Christie went missing?'

De Lacy glanced across to the hill which dominated the skyline to the north of Albury. 'That's the place.'

'How long was she gone?'

'Not sure,' he said, with a non-committal shrug of the shoulders. 'Two weeks or so; maybe less.'

'Toby said the story was all over the papers for days.'

'Couldn't tell you. 1920's; before my time.'

'She told the press she'd had amnesia.' Lizzie turned to face him, raised her hand against the sun. 'Do you believe that Stuart?'

'I believe that as much as I believe you disappeared into thin air on Parliament Hill.' He took off his sun glasses, stared at her. 'And that, by the way, is the first time you've called me Stuart.'

She returned the smile. 'Play your cards right and I'll make you a cup of coffee too… Stuart.'

'How do you fancy nipping out for lunch instead?' he said. 'Somewhere with a sea view.'

'Are you serious?'

'Absolutely.' He hesitated for a moment. 'That's always assuming you don't mind wearing the official incognito celebrity outfit, dark designer glasses and a head scarf, and we're agreed that we don't mention any of this to Toby.'

'Deal,' she said excitedly. 'Where are we going?'

'The Isle of Wight.'

Lizzie's jaw dropped, remembering beach holidays at Shanklin.

'It's very beautiful at this time of year,' de Lacy said at once, before she could find the words to match her despondent expression.

She ran her finger around the rim of a glass fruit bowl, pinged it indifferently with her nail. 'I'd prefer Brighton,' she said. 'Why don't we go there?'

'Because my boat is on the River Medina, two miles upstream from Cowes and nowhere near Brighton.' Stuart de Lacy glanced at his watch. 'We could be there soon after three if we move ourselves.'

'Just in time to turn around and come straight back I suppose?'

De Lacy was already half-way up the stairs. 'I rather thought we could spend a few days on the boat,' he called out. 'Get a bit of sea air.'

Lizzie stared at her reflection in the hall mirror and

decided she looked tired; skin slightly pallid, eyes lacking the usual sparkle. 'Perhaps a bit of sea air might be a good idea,' she told herself.

By the time she'd packed some clothes into a bag and de Lacy had explained to Toby how the house 'phone was on the blink, and to call his mobile instead, Lizzie was beginning to warm to the idea of a few days by the sea.

Twenty minutes later, as the red Aston Martin joined the A3 near Milford for a straight run down to Portsmouth and the two thirty ferry to Fishbourne, Lizzie closed her eyes to the Surrey hills and allowed her thoughts to wander.

'Do you really think I need the head scarf and dark glasses?' she asked drowsily. 'Be totally honest now, how many people would recognise the face and be able to put a name to it?'

'None, probably,' said de Lacy. 'But it only needs one to mess things up, so the scarf and shades stay.'

She opened the car window to the warm afternoon breeze. 'I saw what's-his-name, the bloke who played the James Bond before last, in Sloane Square last Christmas. Nobody else seemed to notice him except me, and even I couldn't remember his name.'

'That's because he was out of context.'

Lizzie shrugged. 'Meaning what?'

'Meaning if he'd been at film premier, on the red carpet, surrounded by photographers and fans, you'd have made the link. But Sloane Square....'

'Actually that's a good point,' she said, stabbing his knee with her finger nail. 'I saw a familiar face on the beach in Spain a few years back. Took me ages before I could place her; turns out we went to the same ballet school.'

'Brosnan, by the way,' de Lacy chipped in. 'The Bond before last; Pierce Brosnan.'

She stared at him blankly. 'No, I think it was Tim somebody.'

De Lacy frowned. 'Timothy Dalton? He was the Bond

before Brosnan, immediately after Roger Moore.'

'Wha-ever. Fact is nobody noticed him in Sloane Square so why would anyone recognise me out here in the middle of nowhere?'

'You're almost certainly right,' he said, accelerating suddenly into the outside lane, over-taking a long line of other vehicles. 'But there's no point in taking chances.'

Lizzie closed her eyes tight, sank lower into the rich beige leather of the passenger seat, folded her arms tightly across her chest. 'I spy with my little eye something beginning with R.'

'Road.'

Her head rolled lazily from side to side across the back of the seat. 'Nope.'

'Radio.'

'Nope'.

'Reflection... as in the mirror.'

She punched his arm. 'You're not very good at this, are you?'

'OK, give up. What is it?'

'Radiator,' she announced proudly.

'But the radiator's under the bonnet. You can't see it from here.'

'I can see dozens of radiators, hundreds maybe, on the cars going the other way.'

'No you can't. At best you can see their radiator grills.'

'Same thing,' she insisted. 'You're just a bad loser.'

'You should have said RG if you meant radiator grill.'

She shrugged, gazed out of the window at Petersfield's shops. 'You could have said ring; we're both wearing one. Or you could have said red, like your car.'

'And I could have said ridiculous, like your radiator.'

The sound of Rule Britannia interrupted the banter. De Lacy reached for his mobile 'phone and spoke abruptly. 'Can't talk now; driving. Call you later.' He snapped the 'phone shut and slipped it back into his trouser pocket.

'Girlfriend?' Lizzie asked.

He shook his head. 'Can't afford them.'

'But you afford hot air balloons, Aston Martins and boats on the Isle of Wight?'

De Lacy shrugged. 'All a question of priorities,' he said quietly. 'Besides, you can trade-in an Aston Martin anytime you like and almost certainly get back more than you paid.'

'You sound like an accountant; all capital outlays, appreciating assets, returns on investments, and net profits after tax.'

'Not me,' he said ruefully. 'Life's a gamble in a slightly dodgy casino not a fixed-rate, five per cent, guarantee with the Halifax.'

Her eyes widened. 'That's exactly it,' she said, turning towards him. 'Go for the big prize every time.' She leaned across, grabbed his arm, kissed him warmly on the cheek.

De Lacy seemed a little surprised. 'It's not a deep-rooted philosophical ideology on the meaning of life,' he whispered. 'It's just the way I see things.'

'And it's just the way I see things too.' She squeezed his arm tightly and nestled closer.

The ferry docked at Fishbourne shortly after three, just ahead of the rain which followed them to the marina at Island Harbour and seemed set to hover over Stuart de Lacy's forty foot motor cruiser for the rest of the afternoon. By five o'clock, when the clouds finally moved-on and he returned with two bags of shopping, Lizzie had seen all there was to see from the narrow windows of the boat.

She helped him unpack at least enough food for a week, chose a particularly large, red apple, and settled back on the velvet cushions.

'I'd rather hoped we could creep into a dimly lit bistro this evening,' she said, polishing the apple on the leg of her jeans.

He looked down at the pale, elfin face, the mischievous

blue eyes daring him to disagree, the smug smile telling him he wouldn't. 'We'll eat out on one condition,' he answered firmly.

'Which is?'

A Georgio Armani carrier bag was pulled, like magic, from his holdall. 'The condition is that you wear these.' He tossed it nonchalantly across the table, fixed her with an uncompromising stare. 'Deal?'

She nodded, reached for the bag, opened it excitedly. 'That's not fair,' she goaned.

He smiled gently. 'Never judge the clothes by their carrier bag.'

A button-through, black dress; Crimplene with large, patch pockets. A black cardigan with a cameo brooch. The lace-up granny shoes and a grey wig, pinned neatly into a bun. She emptied them unceremoniously over the table, sighed.

'The walking stick's in the boot of the car but you might prefer to take my arm for support,' he said. 'Then again, you might prefer to eat here.'

Lizzie didn't answer. She stared despondently at the wretched pile on the table, relived the awful journey from Parliament Hill to Albury in her mind; the exaggerated pronunciation and raised voices at the ticket office, help for the hard-of-hearing; the rampaging insolence of ill-mannered school children on the train; the inevitable sense of vulnerability on empty, open platforms and in gloomy subways. And the worst of it; the unspoken, unwanted sympathy from a thoughtful, caring few.

She shrugged her shoulders, pushed everything back into the bag. 'I'm not wearing fancy dress again; that's final,' she announced dispassionately. 'I'm going as me, and to hell with everyone.'

There was a brief but stony silence between them, emphasised by the gentle ripple of water against the hull and the screech of gulls overhead. Stuart de Lacy spoke first.

'It's your funeral,' he said, then hesitated for a moment. 'But, if I'm completely honest, I very much doubt that anyone would recognise you in this part of the world anyway.'

'Not so much out of context then as completely unknown?'

He ran a hand briskly through his hair, stood up. 'Only one way to find out.'

The Lobster Pot was just ten minutes drive from the marina, nestling between a dress shop and a florist at the narrow end of a cobbled side street, just off the quay. A chalkboard menu, pride of place on an end wall, festooned with nets and shells, offered a wide selection of fresh fish at prices which filled the restaurant seven nights a week. And tonight was no exception; no more than a dozen square, wooden tables, each laid with red gingham, and each fully booked for the evening.

Stuart de Lacy took a twenty pound note from his wallet, pressed it discreetly into the hand of a portly gentleman with a beard, who showed them to a table in the far corner of the room.

'That was a bit of luck,' said Lizzie, pausing to glance quickly around the restaurant before sitting down.

'That was a bit of bribery,' he replied. 'And you can turn-off the neon sign now; the one that flashes the word Celebrity just above your head.' He raised an empty wine glass, caught the waiter's eye, mimed the word red.

'How would they know which red?' she asked.

'There's only two wines on offer here; one red and one……..' He stopped at once, apologised. 'Sorry, perhaps you'd prefer white.'

She shook her head. 'Red's fine.'

De Lacy read from the chalkboard behind her while she listened, quietly, attentively, eyes studying his mouth.

'You have beautiful teeth,' she said when he'd finished.

'Crowns; all of them.'

'Sounds painfully expensive.'

He laughed, rocked back on his chair, waited until the waitress had poured the wine. 'All good things are expensive...wouldn't be good otherwise, now would they?'

'Ballooning obviously pays well.' She fiddled thoughtfully with her ear-ring, hoping he'd put some kind of figure on his life-style.

'Nobody gets rich flying balloons,' he said. 'The real money's in crashing things.'

She looked puzzled, waited for him to explain.

'I'm a stunt man,' he grinned. 'I crash cars, boats, bikes, buses, planes....even balloons from time to time. And sometimes, not too often I'm pleased to say, I burst into flames or fall out of top floor windows.'

Lizzie was impressed and showed it. 'My god,' she squealed, her eyes sparkling with excitement, head shaking in utter disbelief. 'That is just so amazing; a stunt man.'

Three different types of bread rolls appeared on the table in a basket, somebody filled their glasses with Australian Shiraz, and fresh lobster salads were placed in front of them on large glass plates shaped like fishes.

Lizzie seemed oblivious, moved the candle to one side so she could look directly into his eyes, reached out, gently touched the tips of his fingers.

De Lacy raised his glass. 'Bon appetite.'

She nodded, clinked her glass against his. 'Tell me,' she said, 'what movies would I have seen you in?'

He waved the question away with a self-conscious smile. 'I'm not a movie star; not even a minor celebrity which, incidentally, would be my idea of hell. What you see before you is just someone who crashes about on behalf of the glitzy gang.'

'Well I think it's incredible,' she said, dunking a piece of roll into her wine.

He hadn't anticipated the sudden gush of adulation from the opposite side of the table and, flattered though he was, he quickly changed the subject.

'Let's talk about tomorrow,' he said enthusiastically.

'We'll get up around nine, have a quick bite of breakfast and take a trip up river to Cowes. How does that sound?'
'Sounds great.' She turned suddenly to face a small girl standing patiently at her right arm.
'My mum says could she have your autograph?' She pointed to a couple near the bar, placed a scrap of pink paper on the table. 'Could you write it to Joanna please? That's my mum's name; mine's Sandra Bailey and I'm ten.'
De Lacy frowned, cupped his face in his hands, sighed, but said nothing.
Lizzie stared at the ballpoint pen, undecided, faltering. She hesitated, glanced quickly across the table for advice, help, a lead but his expression said it all; nothing to do with me.
Instead he handed her his Mont Blanc pen, the cap already removed. 'At least do it in ink,' he said quietly. 'So much more civilised.'
The signature was bigger, bolder than usual; the message friendly and accommodating; 'To dear Joanna with my very best wishes. Good health'. Love Lizzie Beckman, it said. The O in the word love had two dots for eyes and a half-circle smile.
Sandra's mum waved her appreciation, poured the remains of a can of lager into a long, thin glass and, with lips stretched wide across slightly protruding teeth, mouthed a silent toast.
Lizzie nodded, smiled and quickly looked away. 'No harm done, I suppose,' she whispered, more as a question than a statement of fact.
'She's certainly not paparazzi,' said de Lacy. 'And, with a bit of luck, she won't be up-to-speed with your disappearance, so it's fingers crossed time.'
Grilled calamaris and a cod fillet, served with French fries and a salad, turned-up at the table at about the same time as the Bailey's paid their bill and left. There were more smiles and waves from Sandra and her mum while Mr Bailey fiddled with a mobile 'phone.

De Lacy rubbed his hands together impatiently. 'If it's all the same with you I think we should finish this and go,' he said, glancing towards the door. 'We don't need some over-ambitious Hampshire hack clicking off his Nikon at us and blowing the whole thing.'

She stabbed a slice of squid with her fork, fed it to him slowly. 'You're not meant to rush food like this,' she said. 'And, besides, who knows we're here, apart from Sandra's mum?'

'Sandra's dad; he could have taken a shot or two with his mobile.'

Her eyes snapped shut like a china doll, blocking out any suggestion that things weren't exactly as they should be, exactly the way she wanted them to be. And what she wanted more than anything that evening was a quiet, romantic, uninterrupted dinner with Stuart de Lacy.

'How many bedrooms on your boat?' she asked, changing the subject completely.

De Lacy emptied his wine glass with a single swig, banged it down on the table. 'Three, if you count the main cabin.'

'Plenty of room then?'

He nodded. 'It's a fair sized boat.'

She smiled at him across the rim of her glass, spoke in a well-practised whisper. 'So what are our sleeping arrangements?'

'Not as comfortable as a proper bed on dry land,' he said, neatly side-stepping the question. 'But most people get used to bouncing about on the tide after a few nights.'

The grin slowly evaporated from her face. 'Sounds awful.' She sighed, looked straight past him at nothing in particular.

De Lacy crumpled his napkin on the table, pushed it to one side. 'It'll be fine.' He closed his eyes reassuringly, shook his head. 'And it's September so there'll be no lobster problems.'

'Lobsters problems?'

'I just said, no problems. They're completely docile at this time of year.'

She shrugged, reached for her handbag, busied herself with her lipstick for only a moment before she spoke. 'How could lobsters possibly be a problem?' she asked uncertainly.

'I've just said, they're not.' He turned away, called for a bill, rummaged through his pockets for car keys.

'Why mention it then?'

'Sorry,' he said, gently touching her hand as he stood up. 'It was stupid and thoughtless of me to talk about lobster aggression.'

'Aggression?'

De Lacy raised a finger to his lips. 'Subject closed.' He helped her from her seat, placed a comforting arm around her waist and started towards the door.

Lizzie paused at the fish tank, glanced at the largest of half a dozen lobsters. 'Why the rubber bands on their claws?' she asked the waiter.

'So they don't attack each other madam,' he explained with a polite smile. 'Lobsters can be extremely aggressive.' He opened the door and stood back for them to pass. 'Hope to see you again,' he called out cheerfully.

Lizzie was unusually quiet on the way back to the boat while de Lacy ran through the arrangements for the following day. They'd have boiled eggs for breakfast at nine, two each, then out through the marina lock, up river towards Cowes and, left, around the north west of the island in the general direction of Freshwater Bay.

She managed a few modest smiles, nodded from time to time but said very little until they were back on board.

'Not worried about the autograph hunters are you?' he asked, handing her a brandy.

Lizzie shook her head, sipped the drink. 'I don't think I like the sea,' she whispered into her glass. 'It's a noisy, smelly, fishy sort of place; worse even than suburbia with all the lawn mowers and piles of rotting grass.'

'You'll feel differently in the morning, after a good night's sleep.'

She didn't answer, leant back and peered out through the porthole into the darkness. 'How does anyone sleep with all this bobbing up and down and that clacking noise?' she said eventually. 'You said yourself, it takes some getting used to.'

'You'll be nice and cosy in the forward cabin; the brandy will help you sleep.'

She turned to face him directly. 'The lobster thing; it was a joke, right?'

De Lacy poured himself another brandy, stared thoughtfully at the cabin door. 'The forward quarters are usually quite safe from attack,' he declared solemnly, avoiding eye contact. 'Higher in the water you see.'

'Are you seriously telling me that lobsters attack boats?'

He shook his head slowly, turned away. 'Not so much boats as the people on board; and who can honestly blame them?'

Her eyes narrowed. 'And just how do they do that?' she asked flatly.

'Ah. That's the incredible thing. They float just below the surface of the water; dozens of them. Then, moving as one, they rip into the hull with razor-sharp, pincer claws, attacking their unsuspecting victims like vampires in the night.'

There was no denying that the apple which hit him on the back of the head hurt, but de Lacy was already too close to collapsing with laughter to care.

'You bastard,' she screamed. 'I almost believed you.'

'A total fiction sweet Lizzie,' he said, becoming more serious. 'My apologies. Actually it's the king prawns you have to watch out for; all over a boat like scorpions if you're not careful.'

She shook her head, smiled politely at his pathetic impersonation of a king prawn, and waited for him to sit down. 'I think you may have drunk too much brandy,' she said when he'd finished.

'I've certainly drunk two brandies, but that's not quite the same as drinking too much brandy.' He poured himself another, plumped up a velvet cushion behind him and settled back with his glass. 'You may rest assured that I shall not fall over-board.'

They both stared at each other, silent for a moment, before Lizzie spoke.

'I've never made love on a boat.' She made a little gesture with her head as if she might be giving the idea some thought. 'Is there a sort of boating equivalent of the Mile High Club?'

He nodded importantly. 'Sex in a storm; the Force Nine Club.'

'I never know when to believe you,' she murmured. 'Are you ever serious?'

'Never; not intentionally anyway.'

'How about serious relationships?'

'I've seriously fancied quite a few women, if that's what you mean.' He paused, swirled his brandy around the glass. 'But it's not what you mean, is it? You want to know if I've ever been in love.'

She shrugged. 'Not particularly. Just curious.'

'The honest, serious answer is that I really don't know.'

'Then the answer's no.'

This time de Lacy shrugged. 'How can you be so sure?'

'Because you'd have known if you were in love. There'd have been no doubt about it whatsoever.'

He poured more brandy into her glass, smiled. 'That sounds to me like the voice of considerable experience.'

Lizzie stood up, finished her drink in a single gulp. 'I think you said the front cabin was mine; higher in the water, wasn't it?'

'I'm sorry, that was clumsy of me,' he said, reaching for her hand. 'It came out all wrong.'

'No apologies needed.' She picked up her handbag,

pulled away. 'The fact is I've *never* been in love, so what do I know about it?'

Stuart de Lacy rose slowly to his feet, thrust his hands into the back pockets of his jeans, stared down at his feet. 'I think you'll find everything you need in there,' he said quietly with a nod towards the forward cabin. 'Soap, towels, toothpaste, king prawn repellent.'

She leaned forward, kissed his cheek. 'Good night Stuart,' she whispered. 'Give me a shout if there's a force nine gale.'

Chapter 12

A red vinyl folder was beginning to irritate Daisy Henshaw rather more than usual. The fact that it had expanded to twice its original thickness in a matter of a few short weeks was provocation enough but its reverential position in the centre of the coffee table threatened her future happiness; irrefutable proof of potential disloyalty.

But Barry Gammon didn't see it that way. He wiped some excess glue from the page with his handkerchief and looked dejected. A collection of Lizzie Beckman's press cuttings, he protested, was proof of nothing more than a natural interest in an old friend and accusations of disloyalty were an affront to his integrity. An apology was in order.

Daisy was proud of her innate willingness to admit when she was wrong and, more importantly, her readiness to apologise. But she was adamant; she wasn't wrong and she wouldn't apologise.

'How would you feel if I kept a scrapbook about an old boyfriend?' she wanted to know.

Porky answered in his nit-picking voice. 'For a start it's a press cuttings folder, not a scrap book,' he argued. 'And, as far as I'm aware, none of your old boy friends has appeared in even a parish magazine so there would be no point.'

Daisy Henshaw gently rubbed her tummy and reminded herself that their unborn, Arian son might sense the hostility between them, feel her indignation.

'We really mustn't argue like this,' she said with a weak, faltering sigh. 'For Ben's sake.'

Porky nodded, covered her hand with his. 'Quite right. Arguments are bad for all three of us.'

'That's settled then,' she whispered. 'The scrap book goes.'

He smiled affectionately, kissed her cheek, breathed gently into her ear. 'It stays,' he said. 'And it's a press cuttings folder.'

Daisy was dimly aware that Porky might be more concerned about Lizzie Beckman's much-publicised disappearance than he was letting on. He hadn't been altogether happy with Toby Stone's haughty assurances that she'd probably turn-up sooner or later and not to worry, it was all under control; far too patronizing, smug in the extreme, tantamount to telling him to mind his own business.

But if Samuel Beckman, the father of all doting fathers, wasn't fussed about his daughter's whereabouts and, for reasons which remained unclear, he wasn't, Porky saw no reason to believe the whole thing was anything more than one of Toby Stone's silly stunts.

One or two of the national newspapers had started to see it that way too. Not that it seemed to matter; the volume of press cuttings in the red vinyl folder increased in direct proportion to the degree of speculation surrounding Lizzie Beckman's disappearance. And the more fanciful the theory, the bigger the space it occupied.

So Porky might have been expected to forget all about it. But if it was curiosity that killed the cat, Porky had enough of the stuff to wipe-out the entire lion population of the Serengeti. Chartered accountants prefer facts and figures, to rumours and speculation, and Lizzie's disappearance was still a matter of conjecture. It didn't quite add up, which is why he'd called her mobile 'phone every day since the balloon tipped her out somewhere on Parliament Hill. He'd half expected her to answer, tell him what had happened, where she was, what she was doing. But she didn't so he always left the same message; 'Give me a call when you can'.

Lizzie, who admitted to the occasional pang of guilt about Porky, seriously thought about calling back but decided it simply wasn't worth the risk. Porky was never one to keep a secret and, besides, they'd gone their separate ways, in opposite directions.

She adjusted the top of a white bikini, turned her head towards the sun, squinted through jet black Dolce & Gabbanas at the figure silhouetted in the cockpit behind her. 'What about another one of these?' she asked, waving an empty cocktail glass.

Stuart de Lacy dropped four large ice cubes into the cocktail shaker and rattled a third vodka martini to life. 'Coming up,' he called out. 'This one may be a bit dryer than the others; bit short on the martini.'

Lizzie screwed up her face, stared across the bay towards the jagged, chalky peaks of The Needles, a flotilla of tiny sailing boats weaving around the point, close to the lighthouse. 'They all seem to be darting around in circles,' she said dolefully. 'Like a load of ducks on a pond, searching for food.'

'That's what messing about in boats is all about,' de Lacy answered. 'Going nowhere for a few drinks on a sunny day.' He filled two glasses with the ice cold mixture. 'Shaken, not stirred,' he said, adding a twist of lime to each.

'What's the difference?'

'Shaking with ice makes the cocktail colder, breaks down the oil in the vermouth, and gives the drink that cloudy look when it's first poured.'

Lizzie sipped her drink, stared thoughtfully at the

glass. 'I thought 007 had his martinis stirred, not shaken?'
'I sincerely hope not.' De Lacy, in denim shorts, settled down beside her, head resting on a rolled-up towel. 'Stirred martinis are like warm Chablis or instant coffee,' he sneered. 'Strictly for the plebs.'
'I do believe you're a snob,' she whispered into her cocktail.
'If, by that, you mean I prefer things to be done the right way, then I admit it; I'm a snob.' He said it with conviction, raised his glass and drank a toast to everyone who bothers to do it right.
She sat up, twisted around, back towards him, took off her top. 'Would you mind?' she asked, pointing to the tube of sun cream.
De Lacy squeezed it out in an S across the top of her back. 'That felt like an S for Stuart,' she giggled. 'Am I right?'
'Almost.' He massaged the cream across her shoulders, down her back and into the curve of her waist. 'It was an S for snob,' he said when he'd finished. 'Welcome to the club.'
She half turned her head. 'Me? A snob?'
'Not a self-made snob like me,' he said loftily. 'You're a natural snob; born with an allergy to the fake, the inferior and the cheap and nasty. But, above all, you've been blessed with a natural instinct for the best.'
'You make me sound like a real toffee-nosed bitch,' she breathed. 'Can't you think of anything nice to say?'
He moved closer, put an arm around her waist, drew her gently towards him. 'Actually yes,' he said, nuzzling the nape of her neck. 'You have extremely proud, arrogant boobs with pert, haughty, and thoroughly immodest nipples; right couple of toffee-nosed snobs, the pair of them.'
Lizzie leaned back, silenced him with moist lips. 'Feels to me as if there might be a bit of a wind blowing up,' she murmured. 'Do you think, by any chance, we could be headed for a storm?'

De Lacy glanced up at a clear, azure sky, nodded. 'I'm very much afraid so.' He dipped a finger into his martini, raised it to the still of the afternoon, sighed pensively. 'Gale blowing from the south west, I'd say; force eight, perhaps even stronger; could hit us soon, very soon.'

She draped her arms around his neck, pulled him closer, felt the warmth of his chest. 'Better batten-down the hatches then, captain,' she whispered. 'It's too late to turn back now.'

Somewhere below deck, beyond the hearing of prospective members of the Force Nine Club, a mobile 'phone played Rule Britannia, its warbling vibrations lost forever in the rustle of a gentle breeze.

Toby Stone slammed-down the office 'phone, sprawled out angrily in his red leather chair, one foot on the desk, and double checked the number in his note book before redialling. He called half a dozen times, in quick succession, enquired about possible line faults in the Albury area then, finally and reluctantly, conceded the inexcusable; Lizzie Beckman had clearly ignored his explicit instructions and left the house.

The call to Lizzie's mobile was terse. 'Where the hell are you?' he said in a quiet but intimidating voice. 'Call me at once.'

Toby stared at his computer and the draft press statement, less than half written but with all the key facts crammed tightly into the first two paragraphs. Below a headline 'Lizzie Beckman's Lost Week', the story hinted at an abduction from the scene of the crash while studiously avoiding any mention of aliens or unseen forces.

Lizzie's incredible story would begin with her disappearance on Parliament Hill and end, happily, with her safe return and absolutely no memory of the week in between.

But while Toby hadn't yet fixed the point at which she'd miraculously turn-up, and still pondered two viable options, he'd settled on the date and the hour; three days' time, Sunday, sunrise.

At exactly five thirty, when Toby had resigned himself to the inconvenience of driving down to Albury, he made one last telephone call. It rang out only twice before Stuart de Lacy answered.

'Where've you been?' Toby demanded.

'Oh we're just fine thank you,' de Lacy answered.

'Kind of you to ask.'

'Enough of the sarcasm. Just tell me what's going on?'

'Nothing's going on; we've been right here.'

Toby's voice grew louder. 'Then why haven't you answered the 'phone all afternoon?'

'Been in the garden mostly.' De Lacy cringed, turned to Lizzie, fingers crossed. 'Obviously didn't hear it ring. Sorry.'

There was a noticeable pause before Toby Stone spoke again. 'So,' he said, 'it'll be OK for me to pop down this evening to give Lizzie a briefing.'

Stuart de Lacy screwed-up his face and said a very small prayer through tightly clenched teeth. 'What time shall we expect you?' he asked with all the confidence he could muster. 'Dinner's at eight.'

Toby hesitated, reassured by de Lacy's impromptu invitation and more than happy to avoid a rush-hour drive down to Surrey. 'Actually tomorrow might be better,' he said. 'Say about three'ish?'

'Whatever suits you best. See you tomorrow afternoon.'

Lizzie looked up with a mischievous grin . 'What are you like Stuart de Lacy?' she giggled. 'Such bare-faced lies.'

He shrugged, sat down, cross-legged on the deck, leaned back against the stanchions. 'Fundamental gamesmanship,' he explained, closing his eyes to the late afternoon sun. 'Always call their bluff before you throw in your hand.'

Lizzie's smile left her face and her expression darkened. She drew her knees close to her chest, cuddled them tight like a small child. 'When do we have to leave?' she asked.

'First thing tomorrow. Back in Albury before noon.'

She sighed wearily. 'Just in time for the afternoon lawn mowing shift I suppose.'

'We'll have to get underway shortly; back at the marina before dark, with a bit of luck,' he said. 'How do you fancy some battered cod and a bag of chips for dinner?'

'Sounds disgusting and very fattening.'

'Your decision; take-away from the chippie or the Chinese.'

'Chinese,' she said at once. 'Less batter.' She reached for her glass, drained it, waved it about vaguely. 'One for the road, captain, if you please.'

'Bar's closed,' he said, rising to his feet. 'Time to weigh anchor.'

Lizzie watched him step down into the cockpit. 'Should I be doing something?' she called out as the boat rumbled into life.

He shook his head. 'Just make sure you don't fall overboard.'

The engines quickly settled into their familiar, rhythmic throb, the slumbering power purring through the hull like a wild cat waiting to pounce, and Lizzie, stretched-out on deck in the last of the afternoon sun, a towel for a pillow, sunglasses straddling her head like a tiara.

In a moment the bow surged slowly forward, slicing a path through a calm, smooth, bottomless sea, before swinging out around the point, beyond wispy, cliff-top trees and tumbled rocks below, on towards the distant hubbub of Cowes.

Lizzie Beckman took a last, lingering look back at the bay and told herself that the unfamiliar emotions rampaging through her body had more to do with alcohol than affection. And, no, she was definitely not in love.

A less than melodious but spirited voice from the cockpit behind her sang a schoolboy shanty of dead men's chests and bottles of rum. She smiled at the 'yo ho hos' somewhere in the middle, felt the tingle of excitement which rippled across her shoulders, and closed her eyes to a perfect day.

A warm, comforting breeze from the west wrapped itself around her like a silk sheet. *'Fifteen men on a dead man's chest, Yo ho ho and a bottle of rum'*; the words evaporated into the distance as sweet, inescapable, inevitable sleep numbed the senses. And then silence.

But also dreams; the confused, disjointed eruptions of the psyche, mischievous fragments of reality; fears, phobias and inhibitions, bundled together in a tangle of inverted logic and random nonsense; truth and lies, fact and fantasy, blurred into a single whimsical madness.

It was Spring and she was back on the Serpentine, adrift in a row boat, and Michael, once more gazing into her eyes. The same blinding light, the reassuring smile. But this was different; this was an ending, a parting.

He gently touched her cheek. 'It's done Lizzie,' he whispered. 'The power has passed.'

The light faded with his words, lost in a muddled haze and, from nowhere, Toby Stone, urging her forward towards an advancing rabble of photographers, flashing cameras and coarse, bellowed commands. 'Over here Lizzie.' …..'This way Lizzie.'….. 'Smile Lizzie.'… 'Stick yer bum out Lizzie.'

Above the clamour, beyond the commotion, a silvery white balloon soared towards the clouds, and was quickly gone, leaving her with a jostling crowd, unsmiling faces, grasping hands tearing at her clothes, the sound of mocking laughter. She turned, tried to run, screamed.

Lizzie Beckman's eyes opened suddenly and very wide to a flotilla of small ships, silhouetted against a smouldering sunset away to the left. The breeze, now stronger, cooler, sent a shiver down her back.

'Won't be long now,' de Lacy called out. 'Better get some clothes on.'

She stood-up slowly, looked back at the shimmering horizon, an ever-changing line between the here and now and the rest of the world, and realised that, in a single afternoon, her own vision of the future had become blurred, her horizons shrouded in mist.

De Lacy shouted instructions from behind the wheel, pointed to a rope, neatly coiled at the bow of the boat. 'Grab the line,' he called out. 'Jump when I go astern.'

Lizzie took the end of the mooring line, nodded unconvincingly. 'Jump where?' she yelled, her expression locked in confusion.

'Over there; where else?' He nodded towards the jetty, set the engines in reverse and eased the boat into the mooring. 'And don't forget to take the line with you.'

She tried to ignore the yawning gap between the boat and the jetty, the swirling waters below, steadied herself on the wrong side of the stanchions and prepared to jump.

'Now would be good, if it's not too much trouble.' His voice was quiet, calm, but with a clear note of irritation. 'Unfortunately boats don't have brakes, you see my love.'

Lizzie closed her eyes to what appeared to be certain death, took a giant leap from the side of the boat and landed unscathed, on two feet, mooring line gripped firmly in her right hand. 'Now what?' she called out as the engines went silent.

'Just hold the front steady.' He grabbed the aft line, stepped effortlessly down to the jetty, and secured the rear of the boat to a wooden bollard. 'Now tie-up the front,' he said, pointing to a second bollard at her feet.

She stared at him in silence, made a timid attempt at securing the line, and stood back.

'That won't do,' de Lacy said at once. 'It has to be properly knotted.'

'I wasn't in the boy scouts,' she yelled, arms folded defiantly across her chest. 'Can't tie reef knots or rub two sticks together to start a forest fire.'

'Surely you learned to tie your shoe laces?'

She shrugged, turned away. 'Not really.'

De Lacy finished tying-up the front of the boat,

straightened-up, rubbed the small of his back wearily. 'So what's got up your nose Lizzie Beckman?'

'Oh nothing really,' she said quietly; almost an apology. 'Just a bit tired, that's all.'

'Tired?' He tilted his head to one side with a quizzical smile. 'But you've been sleeping for the past hour or so.'

'I've had some very exhausting dreams as well.' Lizzie looked suddenly fragile, uncharacteristically vulnerable and in need of protection. 'I was being chased by a bunch of mad photographers and this jeering crowd,' she whispered with a sudden tremor in her lips. 'But you just took-off in your balloon and left me. It was really frightening.'

De Lacy tried to say something funny, make a joke of it, but could see that she was genuinely upset. He drew her towards him with a reassuring smile, hugged her tight. 'Just a dream Lizzie. Nothing to get upset about.'

She shook her head, started to pull away. 'But that's the problem,' she sighed. 'It wasn't just a dream.'

He pressed a finger to her lips. 'Not now. We'll talk about it later, over a bag of take-away chips.'

'Take-away Chinese,' she said with a half-hearted smile. 'You said I could choose.'

'I'll do better than that.' He kissed her hand and led her towards the quay. 'The best sizzled seafood this side of the Solent and to hell with the expense.'

'What about me being recognised?'

'Recognised?' he squealed. 'Even I don't recognise you after an afternoon of sun, salt and sea breezes.'

Lizzie ran a hand through her hair. 'Do I look that bad?'

'Bloody terrible. Just as well love's blind eh?'

She looked up at him with questioning eyes. 'Love's a very big word for a professional bachelor.'

De Lacy squeezed her hand affectionately, but said nothing more.

The spicy tang of Chinese food permeated the car long

before it came to a halt on a patch of waste ground at the rear of the restaurant.

De Lacy hesitated for a moment then switched on the radio. Somebody was talking about street crime; the usual clichés about broken homes and disaffected youth; all the fault of society, nothing to do with individual responsibility.

'Say when,' he said, with a finger poised on one of the station pre-set buttons.

Lizzie looked bemused, gave a little shake of the head. 'Say when to what?'

'Our song. You say when, I then press the button, and whatever is playing at that precise moment will become our song for always and ever.'

'What's the programme?'

'Not sure. Does it matter?'

Lizzie shrugged. 'On the count of three then.'

De Lacy counted with her, down to one, pressed the button with due ceremony but found only the inharmonious crackling, buzzing, and high pitched whine of clashing radio stations. Somewhere in the background there was a foreign voice, a man, probably French, might have been Italian, barely audible.

And then the sound of Rule Britannia as de Lacy's mobile 'phone warbled into life with a wrong number.

'I'm afraid they're playing our song,' he said, pushing unruly red hair off a slightly sun-burned forehead.

She laughed gently. 'Not the most romantic song in all the world,' she said. 'And apart from Britannia ruling the waves and the rest of us never, never being slaves, I can't say I know the words either.'

"But there's an upside,' de Lacy said, giving her a peck on the cheek. 'Every September, Royal Albert Hall, last night of the Proms, a full orchestra will play our song and everyone will join in the chorus.'

They strolled slowly towards the restaurant, arms wrapped around each other, la, la, la'ing their special song, until they reached the ornate tiled entrance, a stone lion-dog either side, doorway to the delicate, tinkling of Chinese music.

'I suppose we should be thankful for small mercies,' Lizzie declared as she sat down at the table. 'You might have tuned-in to that awful jingle for car window replacement or the woman who yodels something about her little van.'

De Lacy looked puzzled. 'Don't think I know either of them.' He glanced quickly at the menu, laid it down again almost at once. 'How about crispy duck, then some sizzled chicken, honey king prawns, fish with black bean and mixed vegetables?'

She leaned forward, cupped her face in her hands, stared into his eyes. 'Sounds fine,' she said softly. 'Leave it to you.'

'Chopsticks?'

She nodded.

'Jasmine tea?'

She mouthed a silent 'please', gave him a coy smile.

De Lacy signalled to a waitress who quickly took their order, bowed politely and had already turned to leave when he called her back, said something in what sounded like Chinese and grinned. The woman stifled some involuntary giggles, whispered something in his ear and made off towards the bar; a colourful, bamboo pergola nestling in the corner of the restaurant.

Lizzie looked amazed. 'My goodness, was that Chinese?'

'Cantonese,' he murmured. 'Not strictly Chinese but OK if you're in south east China or Hong Kong. You'd need Mandarin for Beijing and the more influential parts of mainland China.'

'So why was the waitress giggling?'

'I asked for some fortune cookies; told her to bring only the good news variety as I was trying hard to impress you.'

'Who could fail to be impressed by an Englishman who speaks Chinese?'

'The waitress actually,' de Lacy grinned. 'Seems my translation into Cantonese wasn't quite word perfect. I apparently told her I was trying hard to seduce you.'

'Impress, seduce; it's all Chinese to me.' She stopped short, as if she'd forgotten something, the smile gradually fading from her face. 'In my dream you were leaving me.'

'You're probably as bad at translating dreams as I am with Cantonese,' he said cheerfully, trying to sound upbeat. 'Hard to tell if things are coming or going when you're asleep.'

Lizzie shook her head. 'My precious, fragile, little talent left me this afternoon; I'm sure of it. He didn't say much, just 'it's done'; that it had passed. No explanation; nothing.' She looked up with moist eyes. 'And then you left me too, without a word.'

De Lacy sat perfectly still, expressionless, unspeaking, while she told him about the Serpentine and Michael; how, to begin with, she hadn't really believed in his so-called healing power but gradually learned to accept it. And now, at the point when it had become an important part of her life, perhaps her only real talent she'd ever had, it was gone forever.

When she'd finished he poured the jasmine tea and spoke quietly in Cantonese; just a few soft, rounded words without consonants, which seemed to blend smoothly into one.

'What does it mean?' she asked.

'It's just a very small piece of advice; instead of worrying about not being known, make sure that you are worth knowing. That's not exactly what Confucius said, but it's close enough.'

Lizzie looked up slowly. 'And am I worth knowing?'

'Unquestionably,' said de Lacy firmly. 'Especially when you stop pretending to be someone else.'

She leaned forward, shoulders slightly hunched, eyes wide and questioning. 'And who, exactly, am I pretending to be?'

'How about Lizzie Nightingale, lady with the lip-gloss, healer from heaven?' De Lacy was at once contrite, quickly covered her clenched fist with his hand. 'Look, all I'm saying is that you don't need all this Michael mumbo jumbo. Just try to be the beautiful person you keep hidden away from the rest of the world.'

'But it wasn't pretend. I had a power; I cured people. You saw what happened to the blind girl.'

De Lacy hesitated, sighed. 'What I saw, what we all saw, was a girl who said she'd been blind and could now see.' He slowly shook his head. 'Just suppose, for a moment, that Toby Stone set it all up for the benefit of the press?'

She looked first surprised then dispirited, slowly nodded her head. 'Maybe,' she said softly. 'It's possible but I know what I felt, what I always feel. There's a surge of power through my body and then sudden weakness; I don't imagine it.'

'That's my point Lizzie; you believed in it, in yourself, and that's what matters. Don't allow somebody who exists only in your dreams to turn you on and off like a tap.'

'But I know the power's gone; I feel it.'

'Then it's gone because of what *you* feel, what *you've* decided, and nothing to do with a bloke called Michael or anyone else.'

She turned slightly away, touched the corner of her eye with the napkin. 'So, Doctor De Lacy, what do I do now?'

'Start thinking about who you really are, what you want, and stop worrying about being a celebrity.' He moved the tea pot to one side with the arrival of the crispy duck. 'Confucius said something else. Wherever you go, go with all your heart. You can achieve anything, anything Lizzie, but be honest with yourself, listen to your heart.'

She seemed suddenly preoccupied, took a pancake from the basket without really looking, rolled it up with plum sauce, strips of duck, cucumber and spring onion. 'Thanks for the advice,' she said. 'If I'm totally honest I don't quite know who I am or what I want right now. It's all a bit mixed-up.'

De Lacy slowly sipped his tea. 'Then why not stop playing one of Toby Stone's prefabricated PR characters and start being the real Lizzie Beckman? It'll be less confusing and considerable more honest for everyone concerned.'

She thought for a moment, studying a single red rose in the centre of the table. 'Suppose the real Lizzie Beckman is a rather dull, uninteresting character and the press totally ignores her?'

He laughed loudly. 'Oh come on now, you're just fishing for compliments. You, dull?'

'OK, perhaps not altogether dull, but without Toby Stone the press wouldn't be interested in me.'

'So what?'

'So I wouldn't be a celebrity.'

De Lacy threw up his hands. 'Is that all that matters to you?'

'I thought it was,' Lizzie said pensively. 'Now I'm not so sure.' She smiled suddenly, handed him the carefully rolled pancake. 'Sorry, I talk too much,' she whispered. 'The crispy duck's getting cold.'

'Small price to pay for making contact with the real Lizzie Beckman at last.' His mobile phone gave a muffled performance of Rule Britannia from inside his trouser pocket.

'Our song between courses,' she said quietly.

De Lacy glanced quickly at the screen. 'Courtesy of Toby Stone, I'm afraid.' He pressed the 'phone to his ear. 'Hi Toby.'

'I wonder if we could we make it a couple of hours earlier tomorrow?' he asked. 'Say one o'clock.'

'No problem. Look forward to it.' De Lacy slipped the 'phone back into his pocket, sighed. 'He'll be at Albury at one so we'll have to leave earlier than planned.'

She smiled indifferently. 'Why don't we go this

evening? At least we can sleep in a proper bed?'

'I suppose we could catch the nine thirty ferry,' he said, looking at his watch. 'But we'll have to forget the toffee bananas.'

Lizzie Beckman cringed. 'And thank god for that.'

The possibility that this might be one of their last nights together crossed De Lacy's mind as they disembarked from the ferry at Portsmouth a few hours later, but he didn't want to think about that.

Chapter 13

Britain's scruffiest man loitered conspicuously outside The Dorchester Hotel, content that everyone was doing their very best to sort out the unfortunate misunderstanding. Just behind him, centre piece to a paved terrace, a marble fountain surged and splashed while two elegant revolving doors pirouetted for a steady stream of Savile Row suits and swaggering chic, sanctioned by a doorman in a green top hat.

The morning traffic tooted and raged along Park Lane, light drizzle turned to heavy rain, and Britain's scruffiest man turned up the frayed collar of a ragged blouson jacket, wondering why he'd allowed his mother to enter him in the competition in the first place. But she had and there was no going back; his photograph had impressed the judges and he was now, officially, this year's 'Mr Scruff'.

At the point when he'd seriously considered catching the bus back to Kings Cross Station and a train home to Yorkshire, 'Mr Scruff' was escorted to a side entrance of the opulent building and quietly ushered inside.

Toby Stone, debonair but discreet in a black pin-striped suit, took a deep breath and shook his head apologetically.

'What can I say?' he gushed. 'I'm so very sorry.'

'Mr Scruff' looked bewildered, shook the wet from badly torn, paint-stained, denim jeans, and glanced around him in awe. 'What exactly have I got to do?' he asked anxiously. 'Nobody's told me.'

'Just follow me and relax.' Toby smiled, led him towards the lift and up to a junior suite on the eighth floor where the make-over team was waiting.

Edward, a short, plump man with a fashionably bald head, stood back and clasped his throat with a bejewelled hand. 'It's got to be much shorter,' he proclaimed after only a cursory glance at his new challenge. 'I'm not talking Robbie Williams, you understand, more Robert Redford when he was younger.'

'Mr Scruff' touched his hair nervously. 'It hasn't been cut for a while; I think it might have been last Christmas.'

Edward wasn't interested. 'Shampoo; quick as you like.'

A young girl with spidery eyes and orange hair took the chewing gum from her mouth, steered her assignment into the bathroom and quietly shut the door.

Edward's eyes rolled. 'I'd have brought hedge clippers if you'd told me it was the wild man of Borneo,' he said through pursed lips. 'How long have we got to perform this minor bloody miracle?'

Toby, who wasn't normally one to panic, was obviously concerned. He checked his watch, ran a worried finger around the inside of his shirt collar. 'Not nearly enough,' he said flatly. 'They wouldn't let him in to begin with so we lost half an hour.'

'And I can't say I blame them.' Edward wiped his hands on a small towel in disgust, took a sip of water. 'We'll all need a good scrub down with carbolic soap after this gig.'

Toby Stone's client peered above The Times newspaper from the comfort of a pink velvet chez lounge, apparently relaxed and unperturbed. 'Just so long as the clothes fit and the press mention our name, any infestations, blights, pestilence or plagues needn't concern us too much,' he declared.

Edward cringed. 'You won't want that suit back then?'

'It's part of the prize,' said Toby. 'The scruffiest man in Britain gets a make-over and receives the Hamilton Tailoring Changed-Man award, plus a completely new outfit of clothes.'

At exactly half past eleven, 'Mr Scruff' emerged, unrecognisable but immaculate, and took his place in The Dorchester's Park Suite alongside a life-size cut-out of his former slovenly self. Cameras flashed and the living proof that Hamilton Tailoring could make a Changed-Man out of even Britain's scruffiest prepared himself for a few, well-earned minutes of fame.

'Actually he's not bad looking,' Edward conceded after a third glass of Champagne. 'Robert Redford's eyes, don't you think?'

Toby Stone smiled, picked up his briefcase and headed for the car park, already half an hour late for his one o'clock appointment in Albury.?

The rain stopped, as if by magic, as he reached the top of the hill at Newlands Corner and began the sharp descent down the Shere Road into the village where the sweet, cidery smell of early autumn hung heavy in the damp air. He stopped the white Mercedes as the cottage came into view, carefully checked his notes, reassured himself that his new plan still made complete sense, and prepared himself for a potential argument.

Lizzie Beckman opened the door to a huge bouquet of yellow lilies and an apologetic smile.

'Sorry I'm a bit late,' Toby said at once. 'Problems with a press reception.'

She laughed gently, offered her cheek for a kiss, and showed him through to the garden where Stuart de Lacy, face down on a floral sun lounger, was reading a book.

'Bloody incredible,' said Toby, shielding his eyes from the sun. 'It obviously hasn't been raining here.'

De Lacy rolled on to his side, raised himself on an elbow. 'Not a drop for days. Why?'

'Just that it's been pouring down since mid-morning in London.'

'London,' de Lacy repeated with a passable attempt at a rustic, rural accent. 'We country folk don't never go up there these days sir. Full of thieves and vagabonds they do tell us.'

Toby Stone slipped off his jacket, draped it over the back of a wrought iron chair and sat down, briefcase on the garden table in front of him. 'Any chance of a coffee?' he called out, loosening his tie.

Lizzie slammed the kitchen window closed and busied herself with the flowers. She watched while he took some papers from his briefcase and laid them carefully on the table.

'What are you reading?' he asked de Lacy, without looking up.

'Book by Dirk Bogard; 'Voices in the Garden'.' He waved a paperback above his head for the other man to see.

'Can't say I know that one. What's it about?'

De Lacy sat up, swung his feet to the ground, leaned forward. 'I suppose you could say it's about celebrity deception; glittering people from the film world who find it difficult to separate fantasy and reality.'

Toby Stone raised his head, grinned. 'But surely they're completely inseparable? Isn't fantasy merely an oblique view of reality?'

De Lacy fixed him with questioning eyes. 'No difference then between fact and fiction? Is that what you're saying?'

'Not at all, but show me your reality and I'll show you my fantasy.'

De Lacy looked around. 'I see a thatched cottage in Albury,' he said after a moment's thought.

Toby turned around slowly, gazed up at the thatched roof. 'But I, on the other hand, see an enchanted cottage set in a magical valley.'

'Enchanted? What's enchanted about it?'

'The little known fact that wonderful things have magically happened to everybody who ever lived here.'

'Who says so?'

Toby Stone laughed loudly. 'Everyone; it's certain, guaranteed. Wonderful things happen to people all the time. If I bothered to contact three or four previous owners, asked them to list the most wonderful things in their life, I could very well argue that my enchanted cottage was the common link in their good fortune.'

'And do you seriously think they'd believe you?'

'Possibly not, but it's the sort of tummy-warming story that would help to sell a thatched cottage in Albury.' He paused, his face suddenly more serious. 'Perhaps something wonderful has happened even to you since you arrived at my enchanted cottage?'

'Actually yes,' de Lacy said without hesitation. 'I fell in love.'

Toby Stone smiled dispassionately, shuffled his chair closer to the table, rearranged the papers into two piles. 'I rest my case,' he murmured, as if he'd anticipated de Lacy's announcement. 'You were obviously bewitched, spellbound, beguiled by my enchanted cottage.'

De Lacy flopped back on the lounger, slowly shook his head. 'Exactly the same thing would have happened if we'd been in a camper van on Clapham Common.'

'Or, perhaps, even a motor cruiser at Cowes?'

The two men stared at each other in silence. Seconds passed before Toby Stone took an envelope from his inside pocket, laid it on the table.

'Pictures from a mobile 'phone?' de Lacy asked uneasily. 'Chap called Bailey?'

'Picture. Just the one,' said Toby, taking a print from the envelope. 'Mr Bailey was obviously inexperienced in these matters; seemed to think Lizzie's publicity agent would pay more for his grubby little picture than the press.' He paused. 'I didn't, of course. But even two hundred and fifty quid was more than I'd budgeted for blackmail.'

'Blackmail? Who's being blackmailed?' Lizzie placed a tray on the table, poured three cups of coffee, set down a plate of biscuits.

'He knows about the Isle of Wight,' de Lacy said wearily. 'Sandra's dad obviously took a shot with his mobile.'

'Bastard,' Lizzie sighed. 'Might have bloody well known.'

Toby's face hardened. 'Which begs the question why you took-off without telling me in the first place.'

She shrugged, tilted her head defiantly. 'No harm done.'

'No thanks to you.' He dunked a biscuit into his coffee, settled back in the chair, studying his notes.

'So what happens next?' she asked.

He looked up, obviously irritated, and spoke slowly and precisely. 'What happens next is you do exactly as I say, and nothing else.'

'Which is what… exactly?'

'You'll reappear where you vanished, on Parliament Hill; first thing tomorrow morning, same place, same clothes, but with no memory of the previous week; no idea where you've been, what you've been doing. It will be a complete and utter blank.' He paused, searched her face for a reaction. 'Do you understand Lizzie?' he said.

She nodded. 'But I can't just wander around aimlessly.'

'Nor will you. There are always at least half a dozen people walking their dogs on Sunday morning. All you have to do is make sure one of them sees you.' He stopped to sip his coffee, let out a deep sigh. 'Look, just fall to the ground, collapse or something,' he said dismissively.

Stuart de Lacy rose to his feet, a towel draped around his neck. 'They'll probably call an ambulance or the police.'

'Or both,' Toby added. 'Either way there'll be a medical check, you'll be pronounced fit and, while I issue a press statement about your safe return, you can run to your lover's waiting arms.'

Lizzie turned to de Lacy with a look of disbelief.

'It's OK,' he said quietly. 'Toby knows about us.'

Toby shook his head wryly and prepared to move on to the business of the day. 'We've been doing some market research,' he began in a suddenly resolute voice. 'I'm afraid the healing thing has to go; seems people can't relate to it. Fact is they don't really believe it. Anyway, it might be as well if your healing instinct vanished along with your memory of the missing week.'

Lizzie's laugh echoed around the garden. 'Not a problem,' she cried out. 'Consider it gone... forever if you like.'

He smiled weakly, surprised and a bit confused by her enthusiastic response, handed her a single sheet of paper. 'We will, of course, try to hang on to the existing heavenly imagery, keep the spiritual feel of things, for now at least, but the plan is to switch to a more fundamental promotional theme.'

Somewhere in the distance a lawn mower rattled into action, first off the mark in the afternoon marathon, with the promise of more to follow. Lizzie comforted herself with the thought of returning to London at the weekend, glanced casually at a hand written letter attached to Toby's notes.

'Oh my god,' she squealed suddenly. 'Who wrote this?'

'His name's unimportant,' said Toby, pushing a buff envelope across the table towards her. 'The point is we've received dozens like that since you disappeared.'

De Lacy peered over Lizzie's shoulder. 'This chap's obviously a bit of a fan. Are the others the same?'

'He's a bit more than a fan,' Lizzie interrupted. 'Says he's in love with me, adores me, wants to spend the rest of his life with me if I ever return.'

'The others are roughly along the same lines,' said Toby. 'Not so much fan mail as love letters.' He paused to make sure he had de Lacy's undivided attention before going on. 'One or two were, shall we say, a bit more graphic with the details.'

De Lacy placed both hands on Lizzie's shoulders, gently massaged the nape of her neck. 'Tell 'em they're too late. She's mine.'

Toby brushed his words aside with a casual flick of the wrist. 'Moving on,' he said importantly, spreading the other letters out on the table. 'You will notice they each have something in common.'

'They're all love letters,' Lizzie replied with a shrug. 'And, what's more, they're all addressed to me.'

'Not strictly true,' said Toby. 'They were all sent to you but addressed, care of me, at my office.'

'Same thing surely?'

Toby tossed an envelope across the table. 'You're still missing the point.'

'They were sent through the post rather than by e-mail or texting,' de Lacy interjected, hoping to bring the conversation to a close.

'Exactly that,' said Toby. 'The only way Jo Public can contact celebrities is via their manager or agent, and this bunch of ardent admirers has chosen snail-mail above e-mail because it's more private and personal.'

Lizzie flashed a spark of irritation. 'So you decided to open my private letters?'

'Oh get a life,' Toby huffed. 'Private letters are from people who know your private address. These are business letters, part of your job, which is why they landed on my desk and not you doormat.'

'Is there a point to all this?' de Lacy asked impatiently. 'You seem to be going around in circles.'

Toby Stone stood up, poured himself another coffee, stepped across to the edge of the pool. 'The point is that these letters set me thinking,' he said, staring blankly into the water. 'The obsession with vowel-free texting and grammarless e-mails has created a generation which can't write legibly by hand. And that, of course, is a promotional opportunity for a manufacturer of fountain pens.'

But Lizzie wasn't listening. She reached out for de Lacy's

hand, gave him a reassuring smile, mouthed the words 'I love you' at the exact moment Toby turned to face them.

'If you could manage to pay attention for a moment or two,' he said, rattling a spoon in his coffee cup, 'I'll explain how you're going to revive the lost art of handwriting.'

She looked up in surprise. 'Me? But my handwriting's terrible.'

'Your handwriting's unimportant. We're going to encourage the nation's eligible males to put pen to paper with a love letter to you.'

Stuart de Lacy didn't like the sound of it. He gazed uneasily at his feet, arms tightly folded across his chest. 'Why on earth would they want to do that?' he muttered, unconvinced.

Toby let out a roar of laughter. 'Oh, there are many, many reasons,' he said airily. 'Not least because they want to, like the chaps who wrote those letters on the table, but mainly for the cash prizes and the chance to see their names in print.'

'But what do I have to do?' Lizzie said, looking increasingly perplexed.

'You, my sweet, will decide which letters are to appear in a paperback called Love-Letters-to-Lizzie.'

Lizzie warmed to the idea almost at once. 'A book of love letters to me?' she said, her face softening into a gentle smile as she pondered the thought. 'I'd like that very much indeed.'

'It'll be more than just a book. Love-Letters-to-Lizzie will be an inspiration for everyone and anyone to write letters to their loved ones; up to a hundred prime examples of how to speak from the heart with pen and paper.'

De Lacy cringed. 'It'll turn Lizzie into a national floozy for every pervert with a pen.'

'On the contrary,' Toby answered, his voice slightly louder, more heated. 'Lizzie will be the focus of a national revival in the lost art of hand writing, the champion of the twenty first century love letter.'

Lizzie liked the sound of it. 'It's a wonderful idea,' she said with mounting enthusiasm. 'Letters to me but a guide for others to copy.'

Toby thrust his hands deep into his trouser pockets, threw his head back in quiet contemplation. 'I see the book launch as the biggest blind date in history, Lizzie; the writers of the best one hundred letters and you, the focus of their passion, together for the first time at a press luncheon. Great picture.'

'Who's paying for all this?' De Lacy asked.

'Who else but the makers of the world's top fountain pens,' he announced proudly. 'They've bought the idea, lock, stock and barrel.' Toby Stone reached for his briefcase, packed away his papers and prepared to leave. 'We'll launch the project middle of next week, a day or two after we reveal Lizzie's safe return.'

Lizzie walked with him to his car. 'Thanks for coming,' she said, as he settled himself behind the wheel of the white Mercedes. 'And congratulations on the book idea; it's sounds really great.'

'Actually it's more than great, it's fantastic. I only wish I could say the same about you and Stuart de Lacy.'

She shrugged, ran her fingers through her hair. 'But I love him,' she said almost apologetically. 'I love him very nearly as much as me.'

Toby Stone tooted his horn three times, waved his sun glasses out of the window as the car turned the corner and headed back to London.

Shouldn't have told him how I feel about Stuart, she told herself, realising she hadn't even admitted it to herself until that afternoon. A rolling crash of thunder rumbled across the Surrey hills and warned of rain; probably Toby's rain, on its way down from London, heaven sent to silence the lawn mowers. She rubbed her arms against a suddenly chill breeze and went back into the house.

De Lacy, a damp towel tucked around his middle, was hunched over a small writing bureau to the right of the inglenook when she entered the room. He rocked back on his chair. 'For you,' he said, waving a sheet of paper above his head. 'Hot of the press.'

She took it from his hand, flopped back on to the couch and read the words aloud.

MY LOVE
by
Stuart de Lacy
My love is like a new potato
waiting for my lips
I love her in so many ways
but best as deep-fried chips.

'I thought I'd better get my poem on paper before the nation's love letters start flooding in,' he said. 'As a matter of interest you can sing it to our song, too, with a few minor adjustments.'

She clutched his words to her breast with slender fingers, gazed theatrically at the ceiling. 'I shall treasure it always Stuart,' she giggled. 'I wonder how many girls can honestly say they've been compared to a new potato or deep-fried chips?'

De Lacy stood up, shook his head slowly. 'Not many, I can tell you. It's all red, red roses and summer's days from Burns, Shakespeare and that lot; not a single mention of French fries from any of the buggers.'

She looked down at the damp footprints which criss-crossed the terracotta tiles. 'I assume you had a quick dip before putting pen to paper?'

He nodded. 'After all that twaddle from Toby I needed to cool-off.'

'I assume you don't like the book idea then.'

'You assume wrong,' he sighed. 'I positively hate it.'

'Perverts with pens; isn't that what you called it?' She smiled, patted the cushion beside her. 'Sit down; let's talk about it.'

'Later, maybe. I'm going for a bath.'

'Need anyone to scrub your back?' she called out as he reached the stairs.

He hesitated for a second, one hand on the banister, slowly shook his head. 'This bloody book's bad news,' he said solemnly. 'I just hope you realise what you're doing.'

She turned towards the sound of thunder and the first silver droplets on the open window. 'Looks like Toby's rainstorm has finally arrived,' she whispered to an empty room.

Stuart de Lacy examined his naked body in a long bathroom mirror and discovered unwelcome flab in unexpected places. Close on a week of leisure and pleasure, hooky from the gym, and a surfeit of good food, seemed to have added up to six unwanted pounds to a previously well-toned torso. And it had to go.

He lay flat on the floor, raised a bathroom stool above his head with both hands, and slowly lowered it behind him, stretching shoulder and chest muscles in the beginnings of a make-shift workout.

Lizzie appeared at the bathroom door and tried her best not to laugh. 'Is this a private party or can anyone join in?' she asked chirpily, trying to lighten the mood.

De Lacy grunted, swung the bath stool forward to his thighs and then back behind his head in a steady, rhythmic motion. 'Got to lose some weight,' he huffed, sounding as if he might be breathing his last.

She stepped closer, spoke to the top of his head. 'I've decided not to do the book thing.'

De Lacy lowered the bath stool slowly to the floor, slid it back against the wall. 'Good,' he said looking up at her. 'Best thing.'

'Does that mean I can join the party?'

He reached for her hand, pulled her gently to her knees, unclipped the top of her bikini. 'Actually you're a bit over-dressed,' he murmured into her ear. 'It being a birthday party, birthday suits are the official dress code.'

Lizzie pulled away, startled. 'It's not really your birthday?' she squealed.

He nodded. 'Fraid so; thirty four and counting.'

'But you can't be. It would make you a Libran.'

'Well spotted.'

'That's impossible. Porky's a Libran and you're nothing like him.'

De Lacy shrugged 'I'm an early Libran; only just missed being a Virgo. And who, by the way, is Porky when he's at home?'

'Oh just someone I once knew.' She paused, a hint of sadness in her eyes. 'I'm sure I must have mentioned him before.'

He shook his head, ran his finger around her waist, pulled gently at her bikini bottom. 'OK if I unwrap my birthday present now?' he said, drawing her slowly towards him.

'Happy birthday,' she whispered. 'And, of course, many happy returns.'

❖

An open-topped Cadillac turned-up in Lizzie's dreams from time to time, had done since she was a small child; solid gold with red leather upholstery and white wall tyres, chauffeured by a man in a coordinating red and gold uniform who sped her away to a vast Italian piazza filled with crowds of screaming, cheering, adoring fans. A bell would ring out from a tower somewhere on the opposite side of the square at the precise moment she stepped from the car into a dazzling spotlight and a swirling carpet of rose petals. It was always the same, never varied. She knew it off by heart but tonight the dream was different.

Tonight a black London taxi took her to Trafalgar Square, ten pounds on the clock, dropped her off as Big Ben struck midnight and New Year's Eve revellers hugged and kissed in a frenzy of drink-fuelled passion. But she went unnoticed, ignored, and was quickly lost in the swelling crowd. A gold Cadillac appeared, just for a moment, on the opposite side of the square then vanished into The Mall, in the direction of the Palace.

She woke with a start to the rumble and grumble of thunder, torrential rain spilling from the roof gutters to the patio below, a window rattling on the landing, tall conifers, close to the house, swaying with the gusting winds, sending phantom shadows across the bedroom ceiling.

The bedside clock flipped silently from 02-59 to 03-00. A time for doubt and despair, isn't that what they always said? Mind and body at their most vulnerable, their lowest ebb. It was a medical fact, she'd read it somewhere, three in the morning was a potentially perilous hour, Sundays included.

Stuart de Lacy lay flat on his back, perfectly still, arms by his side, hands flat to the mattress, and took slow, strong, rhythmic breaths as if, even in deep sleep, he remained in complete control of his body, the act of rest, itself, a matter of dedicated practice and precision.

She wriggled closer, felt the warmth of his body, and reminded herself that what they had together was more important than a brief fling with fame. And anyway, there was no reason why she couldn't have them both, so what was the problem?

The house telephone rang shortly before sunrise. De Lacy answered it, grunted, dropped it back into place. 'Your five o'clock alarm call,' he mumbled into the duvet. 'Time for the mystical reappearance.'

'Suppose nobody takes any notice of me,' Lizzie yawned, staring up at the ceiling. 'I could be wandering around Parliament Hill for hours.'

He turned to face her. 'Unlikely,' he said. 'Somebody's bound to notice a diaphanous white sarong floating across the hill at seven in the morning, especially with a body like yours inside.'

The second call of the morning was from Toby Stone.

He wasn't happy. Why they were still in Albury with only two hours to go?

De Lacy was in no mood to argue. 'We'll be there at seven,' he said sharply and hung-up.

Burned toast and instant coffee wasn't the breakfast Lizzie had planned but the eggs had passed their sell-by date, the toaster had developed a mind of its own, and there was no time for the usual rigmarole with the percolator.

'Don't bother with make-up,' de Lacy called out from the hall. 'You need to look a bit pallid, ashen even, out of sequence with the world; you know the sort of thing.'

She took a last hurried look in the mirror, shrugged, unsure whether she was sufficiently out of sequence or not, and hastened down the stairs to the waiting car.

The wet Surrey streets dazzled in the early morning sun which promised a fine, warm day ahead, but Lizzie was already looking forward to the end of the charade and a quiet evening, alone with Stuart. Something simple for dinner, she'd decided; perhaps spaghetti with some kind of sauce from the delicatessen in Portobello Road.

'Where shall I meet you after all this nonsense?' she asked, suddenly aware that she had no idea where he lived.

De Lacy peered over the top of his sunglasses at the flimsy, white sarong. 'Surely you'll want to change into something a little less spiritually exotic before you do anything?'

'Hadn't really thought about. I seem to spend most of my time without clothes when we're together.' She turned to face him, rested her head on the back of the seat. 'So, Mr de Lacy, where exactly do you live? You've never said.'

He reached across to the glove compartment, handed her a black card with flamboyant gold lettering. 'It's all there,' he said. 'Name, rank and serial number.'

'Calculated Risks Ltd. Is that your company?'

'Not so much a company, as a philosophy.' He hesitated, sighed, wondering whether this was the right time to talk about what he did for a living. 'My job's about adding-up the pros and cons of a stunt and calculating the element of risk,' he said with obvious reticence. 'The trick is finding a way to reduce the risk or, better still, eliminate it altogether.'

Lizzie slipped the card into her sash. 'I didn't realise people actually lived in Baker Street, apart from Sherlock Holmes, of course.'

'Baker's Mews actually. Just around the corner; three small rooms above a garage.'

'Sounds very bijou, romantic even.'

De Lacy cleared his throat. 'The words you're looking for are small, pokey and cramped, but then I'm rarely there.'

'See you at Baker's Mews then,' she said excitedly.

A little over half an hour later, at exactly 7-00am, she stepped, bare foot, from the car near Gospel Oak and hurried towards a thicket on the fringes of Parliament Hill, launch pad for her return to reality.

A black Labrador appeared from nowhere, lolloped clumsily around her in a playful pass, swerved away towards a second, smaller, dog who rolled over in dereference a few times before they both bounded off to someone who called to them, unseen, from a point closer to the brow of the hill.

In the distance the muffled hum of traffic, the warning blast of a train speeding through a station, dogs barking defiantly somewhere beyond the trees, but nobody in sight. Toby's battalions of Sunday morning dog walkers seemed to have taken the day off.

Lizzie looked about her and decided the whole thing was absurd. Here she was, a grown woman, with cold, wet feet, wearing next to nothing, waiting for someone, anyone, to find her. This was definitely not the stuff of celebrity.

Just ahead of her a cluster of sparrows hobnobbed together around a discarded sandwich; two rooks, jet black in their legal robes, strutted importantly around them considering their options and then, in a sudden flurry of flapping, all of them gone, scattered to the trees. Lizzie turned anxiously towards the rustle of bushes and an elderly man in a beige anorak. He doffed a flat, tweed cap with tobacco stained fingers, fixed her with an obstinate stare, but made no immediate attempt to come closer.

'Would you be lost?' he asked her with a gentle, Irish lilt.

'No, not at all,' she said at once. 'I'm waiting for someone.' She cursed herself for the stupid remark, tried to regain composure.

He nodded, glanced around him, slowly scratched his chin. 'I can't see anyone. Maybe they'll be along in a while.'

'Definitely,' said Lizzie trying to hide her growing unease. 'He's a military man, always absolutely punctual.' She stared back at him with a look of disdain. 'And who might you be?'

'Oh, just a man of little consequence, unimportant and of no interest to anyone.' He glanced down at her feet, slowly shook his head. 'But what about yourself? No shoes on your feet and on a damp, cold morning as well.'

'We like to train with bare feet,' Lizzie replied with as much confidence as she could muster. 'Long distance, London Marathon, that sort of thing.' She swung her arms above her head, twisted her hips from side to side in a feeble pretence at limbering-up.

He lit a cigarette, flicked the spent match towards her, inhaled deeply. 'Very impressive,' he said quietly. 'But I bet I could outrun you, even with a cigarette in my hand and a lung full of smoke.'

Lizzie decided she'd heard enough, quickly tightened the gold sash around her waist and made a sudden dash for the open grassland further up the hill. 'I think I can see my friend,' she called out without looking back.

In the distance, a man with a walking stick; an Alsatian dog running ahead, two small boys in pursuit. Further down the hill, to her right, a couple of women talking together, a terrier cavorting by their side.

Lizzie stopped, turned to face her assailant, but he'd gone. She fancied she saw cigarette smoke rising from beyond the thicket as she slumped into the damp grass, exhausted, wondering if anyone had seen her.

But Toby was right; somebody bothered to call an ambulance for the frail, pallid, lone figure found wandering aimlessly on Parliament Hill.

CHAPTER 14

Sir Eugene of Betchworth snapped shut his visor, slowly raised his lance and steadied his horse for the first charge against the Black Knight who waited menacingly at the opposite end of the arena.

Flags flapped and cracked in the wind and a hush fell over the crowds of onlookers as heralds in red tunics and feathered hats lined-up on the edge of the field to trumpet the start of the tournament. Sir Eugene gripped his shield, double checked the position of the white marker, the spot where he was scheduled to fall to the ground, wounded, on the second pass.

Everything went exactly as planned and the subsequent sword fight began on cue; a blow to the hand, agonising yells, blood flowing freely from the wound, a dropped sword. Sir Eugene yielded to his opponent in a well-rehearsed sequence, and someone shouted "cut". But then the director wanted to do it all again, this time with a slightly longer progression for the sword fight; perhaps more blood.

Stuart de Lacy slumped down heavily on a canvass chair, took off his helmet, and called for a bottle of still water. The Black Knight found a seat beside him and listened while he explained the new choreography for a more violent, bloodier combat with the broad swords. In less than an hour they were ready for a second take.

There were four more exhausting, painful takes before the director was happy with the jousting scene and de Lacy could swap Sir Eugene's armour for a white T-shirt and jeans. After a glance at next day's shooting script, in which he was to fall, headlong, from the battlements of a Medieval castle into the moat below, he went home for a hot bath.

It had long been one of Stuart de Lacy's pet theories that the steady rise in the nation's blood pressure was entirely due to parking spaces or, more importantly, the lack of them. He could feel his pulse begin to race, body temperature rise, at the very moment he saw the white Mercedes parked across the entrance to the garage; his garage.

Three short, sharp blasts of the horn went unnoticed apart from a cautious wave from the elderly lady opposite who peered, unsmiling, from behind lace curtains. De Lacy crashed the Aston Martin's gears into reverse, screamed to the end of Baker's Mews and turned sharp right to a parking space in the next street, where he searched his pockets for pound coins, blood pressure at deadly levels, and rising.

It was beginning to feel as if a full-time chauffeur might be a cheaper option to twenty minutes on a parking meter, when the Mercedes cruised passed him, Toby Stone at the wheel.

De Lacy walked slowly back to the mews, up a single flight of stairs to the tiny flat above the garage and a modest but comfortable room, dominated by a great Afghan rug on shiny black floorboards, two fat leather sofas in front of a log-burning stove, a round oak table and six farmhouse chairs tucked away in the far corner, books in piles near the door to the kitchen. And Lizzie, kneeling on the floor, newspapers spread around.

She looked up, surprised, eyes smiling. 'I didn't hear your car,' she said at once.

'That's because it's round the corner on a parking meter.' De Lacy tossed a black canvass holdall across the room, stretched his arms out wearily. 'Some inconsiderate bastard of a publicity agent left his car in front of the garage.'

'Sorry. I should have told him to park somewhere else,' she said, looking genuinely apologetic. 'But he was only here for five minutes; dropped off the press coverage from yesterday.'

De Lacy glanced down at the papers, random pages highlighted with a red felt tip pen. 'And how was it? I didn't see anything in The Standard this afternoon.'

'That's because it was in all the nationals this morning.' She handed him a page from The Mirror. 'This one's probably the best.'

'Lizzie Beckman back – but from where?' It was a top of page headline above a story which hinted at a publicity stunt but then went on to talk about alien abductions, fact or fiction?

'If it's all the same with you, I'm going to have a bath,' de Lacy said, flipping his shoes off. 'It's been an absolute sod of a day and I need to soak away some of the stress and strain.' He pulled the white T-shirt over his head, loosened the belt on his jeans, hopped about on one leg, taking off his socks, and then stopped, suddenly. 'Oh Christ I forgot the bloody meter,' he screamed. 'It'll run out in a couple of minutes.'

Lizzie jumped quickly to her feet. 'Not a problem. I'll feed it; give you another half an hour or so.' She raked about in her handbag for change, found two pound coins and a fifty pee piece and started down the stairs. 'Where is it by the way?' she called back.

'Turn right out of here to the end of the mews. It's just round the corner.' He hesitated, thought for a moment. 'But why not take the keys, drive it back?'

Lizzie peered around the banister at the top of the stairs. 'Love to, if it's OK with you.'

'Just take it easy,' he said, tossing her a small leather wallet. 'Aston Martins have a mind of their own.'

The parking meter had clicked into excess by the time she reached the car but the peak-capped attendant was preoccupied, loitering close to a white van on the opposite side of the road.

Lizzie settled herself uncertainly at the wheel, shifted the seat forward, adjusted the seat belt, fiddled a while with the rear view mirror. She sank back into the soft leather and felt the latent power pulse through her body as the engine vibrated into life. A quick spin around the block, she assured herself, but set off, instead, towards Regents Park.

De Lacy had bathed, changed and poured a second lager by the time he heard the garage doors open. He watched through the open window as Lizzie reversed slowly, cautiously, into the narrow space below; no obvious damage to the car and everything sounding as it should. But it didn't take half an hour to drive a few hundred yards and although he wouldn't admit to being worried, he was certainly concerned and just a bit irritated.

'You'll never guess what happened to me,' Lizzie breathed excitedly as she flopped down beside him on the sofa and reached across to steal a sip of his lager.

De Lacy stared at her, unblinking. 'I'm not even going to try,' he said.

She grabbed his hand, pulled it to her lap. 'Please don't be angry but I couldn't resist taking your beautiful car for a spin, and one thing sort of led to another.'

'What, exactly, led to what?'

'Well, to begin with, I was stopped by a policeman on a motor bike; said I was doing over thirty in the park. I wasn't, of course.' She smiled, gave his hand a squeeze. 'Don't worry, I didn't get a ticket or anything like that.'

De Lacy reclaimed his lager from her hand, took a sip, closed his eyes.

'Don't you want to know what happened next?' she asked impatiently.

'I'm all ears. What happened next?'

'This policeman asked for my autograph, that's what.' She seemed unreasonably pleased, as if a policeman asking for her autograph might be some kind of special accolade.

But de Lacy wasn't impressed. 'Are you sure he wasn't asking you to sign for a speeding ticket?' he said.

She punched his arm. 'Can't you be serious for a moment?'

'Well, did you give him your autograph?'

'Of course. In fact I gave him two; one for his son. Apparently he's writing me a love letter.'

De Lacy, hesitated, searched her face for an explanation. He leaned forward, chin cupped in his hands. 'Now why would this policeman's son do that?' he asked.

Lizzie pushed a hand through her hair. 'It's just something on the website. Love-Letters-to-Lizzie; Toby's new project.'

'I wonder if I've got this right,' he said pinging his glass impatiently with a finger nail. 'Would that be the screwball letters from psychos project; the one you told me you *weren't* doing?'

'Oh come on now Stuart, nothing's been agreed.' She stood up, went over to the window, hugged herself protectively. 'Look, it's only an invitation on the web site.'

'But surely you told Toby you weren't doing this love letters nonsense?'

She shook her head. 'I thought I'd wait and see how it goes first. Let's face it, I can pull-out anytime; probably will.'

De Lacy was silent for a moment but then suddenly more animated. 'I'll fix you a drink. Lager do you, or something stronger? What do you fancy?'

Lizzie held out her arms to him. 'Please say you're not angry with me Stuart.'

'OK, I'm not angry.' He picked up the empty glass,

turned towards the kitchen. 'Now what can I get you to drink?'

'I'll call Toby tomorrow,' she said. 'Tell him I'm not doing the love letters thing; promise.'

'And what will you say when he asks why you've changed your mind?'

'I'll simply tell him you don't like the idea.'

De Lacy leaned against the kitchen door, folded his arms, slowly shook his head. 'That's not the issue,' he murmured. 'The idea's nothing short of brilliant but I'm not having spotty, pubescent teenagers writing steamy letters to my future wife.'

Lizzie laughed suddenly, as if she'd been caught off balance. 'Wife?' she said, somehow managing to make the word sound like a minor insult. 'You want to marry me?'

De Lacy shrugged his shoulders, raised his hands in silent submission. 'Look, I know marriage isn't very fashionable or cool these days but, all things considered, I quite like the idea.'

She thought for a moment, screwed-up her nose. 'Lizzie de Lacy.' She repeated it several times, nodded her head approvingly. 'It's got a certain aristocratic ring of quality about it,' she said, draping her arms loosely around his neck. 'But how come nobody told me I was getting married?'

'To be totally honest I only found out myself just over half an hour ago. It crossed my mind that you'd maybe crashed the car, had some kind of an accident, perhaps even killed yourself.' He threw his arms around her, grabbed the cheeks of her bottom, pulled her closer. 'I decided you need looking after; keep you out of trouble.'

'In that case I'll have a celebratory glass of Champagne,' she said. 'But shouldn't you be on your knees proposing or something?'

De Lacy raised a cynical eye brow. 'My alter ego, Sir Eugene of Betchworth, might possibly have bent a knee to plight his troth to a maiden fair. But that was way back in the middle ages.'

'And middle-aged Mr de Lacy,' said Lizzie, 'How would he do it?'

'Him? Oh, he'd be much more twenty first century about it; text it to your mobile, short message on your voice mail, that sort of thing.'

She took his hands from her bottom, pulled away. 'In that case I couldn't possibly marry you kind sir,' she said, looking him square in the face with a thin, uncertain smile. 'But I'll have a glass of Champagne anyway.'

Stuart de Lacy dropped to one knee, head bowed. He took her hands, kissed them gently, looked up into her eyes. 'Would you mind being a wee bit old fashioned and totally uncool?' he whispered. 'Will you marry me?'

She waited for him to laugh, turn the whole thing into a joke, jump to his feet, declare he'd been attacked by king prawns or rampant lobsters, corpse into his awful Norman Wisdom impersonation, or maybe just reach for another lager and pretend it hadn't happened. But he didn't.

'I do believe you're serious Mr de Lacy,' she declared hesitantly, still unsure whether or not he was joking.

He glanced across to the kitchen and a modest wine rack, tucked away neatly on top of the fridge. 'I'm afraid celebrations may suffer a brief delay,' he said. 'It appears we don't have any Champagne; not a drop.'

But Toby Stone had no such problems. He'd celebrated the arrival of the hundredth love letter to Lizzie that very afternoon; and they were still coming, thick and fast.

OK, a thousand pound prize for the best of them was certainly an incentive to put fountain pen to paper but Toby had noticed a surprising sincerity in many of the hand-scrawled offerings. And Stuart de Lacy would have taken umbrage at the liberal sprinkling of marriage offers to be found among a selection of less chivalrous proposals if Toby hadn't resisted the urge to show him.

A call to the nation's red-blooded males had gone out through the pages of regional daily newspapers a day or so earlier. It directed them to the Love-Letters-to-Lizzie website where, in a symphony of hearts and red roses, the essential details were spelt out in hand-scripted lettering, the logo of the pen manufacturer discreetly displayed at the top of each web page.

The letter from Barry Gammon was nothing like the others; more of a note from an old friend; nothing too heartfelt, no sexual innuendo, no risqué suggestions and only a hint of passion. But for Barry Gammon it was a letter in a bottle, tossed into a cyber sea, never to be read by anyone and, least of all, by Lizzie Beckman; a convenient and uncomplicated way to get things off his chest, wipe the slate clean, say goodbye to the past, without conscience, without regret and, most importantly, with not the slightest trace of disloyalty to Daisy Henshaw.

Toby Stone read it twice before he slipped it into the shredder, sandwiched between half a dozen other unsuitable missives, and set to work choosing fifty likely lads to attend the press photo-call; the official launch the Love-Letters-to-Lizzie project.

Media interest was running high with education correspondents showing particular interest in what appeared to be a worthwhile initiative to revive the lost art of letter writing. The tabloids saw it slightly differently with the emphasis on a ready-made source of 'Words to pull the Birds'. But it really didn't matter; the angles were endless and the result would almost certainly be international press coverage for the nation's self-styled sweetheart.

Toby Stone Associates had already applied for a licence to film and photograph in Piccadilly Circus; more specifically on the steps below the statue of Eros, Greek god of love, ancient Rome's very own Cupid, and the all-round symbol of sexual inspiration. The main press picture would have Lizzie Beckman at the top of the steps, next to the statue, with fifty adoring young suitors, each carrying a single red rose, carefully positioned on lower steps at her feet. Then, after the photographs, there'd be the interviews at a Champagne reception in the nearby Criterion Restaurant.

But even as he congratulated himself on a brilliant idea, perfectly planned with flawless precision and set for unquestionable success in a few days' time, Toby Stone was aware that everything was not quite as it should be. He recognised the familiar feeling at once, thought of it as a sort of second sense; a faint twinge of unease which rankled somewhere, almost imperceptibly, in the centre of the stomach. And he'd long since understood that it wasn't to be ignored.

It wasn't complicated. All you did was lay all the facts on the table, take a long, hard look, with eyes wide open, and face up to reality. And the stark reality was that Lizzie's relationship with Stuart de Lacy was a threat to the whole project. The nation's sweetheart, female focus for a thousand love letters, simply wasn't permitted to fall in love.

Toby spent a moment or two persuading himself that he wasn't being difficult or unreasonable. And, no, he wasn't trying to upset any apple carts, rock any boats, set cats among pigeons or a dozen and one other clichéd expressions which regularly masquerade as creative prose in the flimsy literature of the PR press statement. It was essential that Lizzie remained free, single and, to all intents and purposes, available. And that, in practical terms, meant Stuart de Lacy had to go.

But it would be an even-handed fair swap, replacing him with something of equal, if not greater emotional importance in Lizzie Beckman's volatile life. Toby Stone was fairly sure he knew just the thing; a fair exchange from the magical world of maybe.

The idea for a match-making TV programme, singles in search of soul mates, partnered together by a lyrical studio computer, wandered into Toby's mind one Sunday afternoon as the perfect follow-on to his unique vision of Lizzie as the queen of love letters. It was still no more than an idea, a possibility with potential, but in the magical world of Maybe, which Toby visited from time to time when everyday logic began to sound trite, this was a programme headed for the schedules, with Lizzie as the star host.

And the equation balanced perfectly; one de Lacy being roughly equal to the sum of the parts in a series of thirteen TV shows, plus increased public recognition and stardom. [$X = TV \times 13 - dL$].

At about six thirty the following evening Stuart de Lacy nodded his approval for the waiter to open a chilled bottle of cuvee rose brut, listed at a cool seventy pounds, and settled back into the art Deco splendour of the Savoy Hotel's Laurent Perrier bar. But this was a celebration, a red letter day, and he wasn't counting the cost. He pushed a small dish of olives across the table, took one for himself, raised his glass in a toast.

"To us,' he announced with a flourish.

Lizzie raised her glass to his, smiled. 'These Champagne coupes were modelled on some French queen or another's boobs.' She ran her finger down the narrow stem. 'Apparently it was the king's idea.'

De Lacy nodded. 'I'd heard something of the sort. Just as well they didn't know about breast enhancement in those days or we'd never be able to lift them.' He paused for a second, sipped his Champagne thoughtfully. 'You probably also know that the common or garden soup bowl took its shape from the cheeks of her buttocks.'

She peered at him across the rim of her glass, her brow wrinkled into a quizzical frown. 'Her buttocks?' she repeated. 'Are you sure?'

'Certain. What's more, the traditional silver punch

bowl is an exact replica of her belly when she was eight months' pregnant.'

Lizzie huffed. 'I suppose the legs on our table are hers too?'

He shook his head. 'No way. She had rather unshapely legs, which is why they invented the crinoline. And that, by the way, was the original inspiration for the lamp shade.'

Lizzie spluttered into her napkin, wiped her mouth. 'You're an inveterate liar,' she giggled. 'Do you ever tell the truth?'

'Not often but, when I do, my right ear lobe twitches.'

'But it's not twitching.'

'That's because it's not true.' He smiled one of his big gash smiles which instantly lit-up his face, like a sudden burst of sunlight on a dull day. 'I think it's true to say that at least fifty per cent of what anybody says is probably untrue.'

She clasped her hands together, leaned forward across the table. 'Do you promise to love me 'till I pop my clogs?'

'I promise to try,' he said, his face more solemn. 'But it's odds on that my clogs will be popped before yours, so I may not quite stay the course.' He quickly perked up, flashed the smile, poured the remains of the bottle into their glasses. 'Right now, however, I think we should eat. I'm bloody starving.'

They walked slowly along The Strand and up through Covent Garden to Stuart de Lacy's favourite trattoria. Luigi's, just around the corner from the Royal Opera House, a short walk for West End theatre goers, serves some of the best Italian food in London; has done for the best part of forty years. But it owes nothing to the new breed of slick, modernist, Italian restaurants and, in a changing world, has managed to cling to its traditional charm.

Signed photographs cover the walls, a permanent epitaph to some of the biggest stars in show business and a stark reminder that fame is merely a temporary blessing, yesterday's legends often no more than faded sepia prints, unrecognised in walnut frames.

Lizzie looked about her for a vacant space on the wall. 'Where will they put pictures of new celebs?' she asked casually.

'Actually it's not strictly about celebs,' de Lacy answered as tactfully as he could. 'This is more to do with star performers; actors, comedians, singers, dancers, musicians.'

She shrugged, glanced down at the menu. 'Well I've never seen most of them in my life so I don't know where stardom comes into it.'

De Lacy wasn't going there. 'I can recommend the scallops with black trenette pasta,' he said. 'The minestrone's usually good too.'

'I spoke to Toby this morning,' Lizzie said, still concentrating on the menu. 'You know, about the love letters thing.'

'Was he annoyed?'

'Not exactly,' she murmured, munching on a bread stick. 'We just talked it through; tried to make some sense of it.'

'But you told him you weren't going to do it?' De Lacy stopped short, closed his menu with a slap. 'You *did* tell him, didn't you?'

She sighed impatiently, shifted about on her chair. 'It wasn't quite like that.'

He stared at her, unblinking, waiting for her to continue.

'Toby explained it all to me. Private and public lives are completely separate, he says, nothing to do with each other.' She reached out for his hand as he tightened it into a fist and pulled it away. 'Please try to understand,' she pleaded. 'Toby says I can do this love letter sweetheart thing and still be with you; both at the same time. We can be married even, as long as nobody finds out.'

De Lacy's face hardened. 'Toby Stone's a devious

236

bastard,' he growled. 'And he's lying through his back teeth.'

She shook her head. 'But why would he do that?'

'Listen carefully Lizzie,' he said firmly. 'Your whole PR image is based on being available to the entire male population. But Toby knows the press would find out about us in no time and he's banking on us splitting-up if you go ahead with his little love letters escapade.'

'And would we?' asked Lizzie, slightly tearful. 'Could he split us up, just like that?'

De Lacy screwed his napkin into a ball, slapped it down on the table. 'I don't think I'm very hungry, after all,' he said. 'Perhaps we should both sleep on it, talk about it tomorrow.'

'But the launch is tomorrow,' she whispered. 'Eros, eleven o'clock. It's all arranged.'

He stood up slowly, shrugged. 'So, all done and dusted,' he said, then seemed to freeze for a moment. 'I'll call you a cab. You'll need a good night's sleep.'

A photograph of Olivier as Hamlet peered back at him near the door. 'I know just how you feel old mate,' he thought. 'Right now I'd settle for the "not-to-be" option.'

Mid morning traffic flowed surprisingly smoothly through Piccadilly Circus towards Coventry Street. Thanks for that went to the Mayor's Congestion Charge, according to the newspaper seller, perched on a box at the entrance to the underground station. 'Keeps day tripper drivers out of the West End,' he confided to Toby Stone's assistant as she handed over her fifty pence for an early edition of The Standard. 'Just as well too,' he went on, slapping a folded newspaper firmly into her hand. 'The Dilly was one bloody great traffic jam.' What's more, he'd ban cars altogether if he had his way; it would be "elfier aw rarnd."

There was a short paragraph on a plan to revive the

lost art of writing. No mention of the sponsor but that would probably come with later editions, after the photo-call.

Toby Stone stared, stern-faced, at his mobile 'phone. It was nearly eleven and Lizzie Beckman was about to be late. He redialled and left yet another message. Was it the fifth or sixth since he'd arrived an hour earlier? He wasn't sure and he wasn't happy.

Fifty eligible young men, each carrying a single red rose, waited like a brigade of bridegrooms at the altar; neatly arranged in a cascade of masculinity from the highest levels of the fountain down to the bottom step.

Photographers, about thirty in all, lined-up in two tiers on the pavement; some crouched down or kneeling, one or two on small step ladders and the rest standing shoulder to shoulder in a vertical scrum. A few had taken up positions on the opposite side of the road, zoom lenses pointed like cannons towards an unseen target.

'How long's she gonna be Tobe?' one called out.

Toby Stone flashed a reassuring smile, gave a thumbs up. 'Any minute now. Won't be long.'

'Well bugger me.' A photographer with the statue in his lens had made a discovery. 'Eros,' he yelled. 'Someone's nicked his bloody arrow.'

'Muppet,' someone yelled back. 'He never had one. Just a bow; no arrow. I thought everyone knew that.'

Toby didn't like the feel of things; they were getting restless, checking their watches. Photographers were always in too much of a hurry to be somewhere else.

At the lower end of Regent Street Lizzie Beckman stepped, unnoticed, from a taxi, paid the driver with a twenty pound note and told him to keep the change. She paused, briefly, to adjust the gold sash on the diaphanous, white sarong and swaggered importantly towards the crowd on the opposite side of the fountain.

'She's here,' someone shouted and the press pack became suddenly animated.

Toby Stone took her hand, smiled, kissed her cheek. 'And where the hell have you been?' he whispered into her ear.

'Making myself presentable,' she replied jauntily, and followed him, head high, to the top of the steps where she posed and pouted while two young men, carrying large satin hearts, positioned themselves at her feet, ready for the picture.

The lorry, which partially blocked nearby Jermyn Street, attracted little or no attention and no more than a fleeting glance from the parking meter attendant who'd already been assured by the driver that it would be gone in a matter of minutes. The back doors had already been opened and a ramp quickly lowered to the road when heads turned in unison towards the shrill blast of trumpets from first floor windows of the Trocadero building just around the corner. And then, quite suddenly and inexplicably, and only for a unique splinter of a second, Piccadilly Circus was strangely quiet.

It was a fleeting, eerie calm, shattered in a moment by the sound of iron on stone; the clatter of plunging hooves across the pavements of Piccadilly. A white charger on the steps of Eros and Sir Eugene of Betchworth, a knight in shining armour riding, fearless, bold, to rescue his very own damsel in distress.

A chorus of cameras clicked and the unmistakable sound of celebrity filled the air as Sir Eugene raised a gauntlet to the sky and swept a fair maiden off her feet.

Lizzie Beckman's carefully-crafted image of availability to the youth of a nation galloped away, off down the Haymarket towards Trafalgar Square, without so much as a backward glance. And in the distance, on cue at the far end of The Mall, where proper knighthoods are ceremonially bestowed on the great, the good, and rather too many who are less deserving of the nation's praise, the band of the Coldstream Guards played Rule Britannia.

But at the precise moment Lizzie disappeared from

view, a flash of lightening struck in Piccadilly; a big, bright, thunderous blaze of the stuff, bursting with extraordinary possibilities, unseen by mere mortals. It flared down Shaftesbury Avenue, rounded the corner towards Coventry Street, crashing to a magnificent halt near the steps of Eros. And somewhere in a parallel universe, where mundane reality is routinely abandoned to spectacular illusion, the whimsical planet PR trembled with anticipation.

Toby Stoned nudged his assistant. 'Do you know what?' he whispered, 'I think I've just had a bloody brilliant idea.'

THE END